"*Where did you come from?*" *she gasped.*

His smile touched a dozen different parts of her. "I materialized. It's a talent I have. I can also transform myself into a wolf or a bat. If you fight me," he warned with a chuckle, "I'll bite your neck." Squinting at her, he said, "Has a man ever told you, Dr. Schellenegger, that it's disconcerting to look straight across into a woman's eyes on the same level as your own? There's nothing wrong with it, though. Actually, it's quite nice. Actually, I like it."

That broke the spell, naturally, as he had meant it to. Brittany drew on her best armor and prepared for war.

"If I hadn't just happened to leave my wooden stake in my other purse, Lieutenant Curry," she said through a deadly smile, "I'd drive it into your heart."

Dear Reader,

Spellbinders! That's what we're striving for. The editors at Silhouette are determined to capture your imagination and win your heart with every single book we published. Each month, six Special Editions are chosen with *you* in mind.

Our authors are our inspiration. Writers such as Nora Roberts, Tracy Sinclair, Kathleen Eagle, Carole Halston and Linda Howard—to name but a few—are masters at creating endearing characters and heartrending love stories. Their characters are everyday people—just like you and me—whose lives have been touched by love, whose dreams and desires suddenly come true!

So find a cozy, quiet place to read, and create your own special moment with a Silhouette Special Edition.

Sincerely,

The Editors
SILHOUETTE BOOKS

LINDA SHAW
Fire
at Dawn

Silhouette Special Edition

Published by Silhouette Books New York

America's Publisher of Contemporary Romance

To Shelley Webb,
my daughter, whose helping hand is always there.

SILHOUETTE BOOKS
300 East 42nd St., New York, N.Y. 10017

ISBN: 0-373-09367-5

First Silhouette Books printing March 1987

America's Publisher of Contemporary Romance

Printed in the U.S.A.

Books by Linda Shaw

Silhouette Special Edition

December's Wine #19
All She Ever Wanted #43
After the Rain #67
Way of the Willow #97
A Thistle in the Spring #121
A Love Song and You #151
One Pale, Fawn Glove #224
Kisses Don't Count #276
Something About Summer #325
Fire at Dawn #367

Silhouette Intimate Moments

The Sweet Rush of April #78

LINDA SHAW

is the mother of three children and enjoys the life she shares with her husband in Keene, Texas. When Linda isn't writing romance novels, she's practicing or teaching the piano, violin or viola.

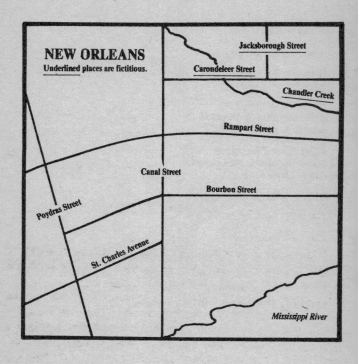

NEW ORLEANS
Underlined places are fictitious.

Jacksborough Street

Carondeleer Street

Chandler Creek

Rampart Street

Canal Street

Bourbon Street

Poydras Street

St. Charles Avenue

Mississippi River

Chapter One

The problem with sleep, to Brittany Schellenegger's way of thinking, was that there was never enough. Like gold. Or happiness. Or panty hose without runs.

Then there were the stories everyone liked to tell about Thomas Edison and his famous catnaps. Or Napoleon. Or the impressive list of movie greats who existed so brilliantly well on four hours' sleep a night. Besides—and Brittany invariably asked herself this on the bad days—hadn't Eleanor Roosevelt been an insomniac?

Except that she was neither a genius nor a famous film star. She wasn't even a great lady. She was only a tired, underpaid doctor and one of the world's all-time great workaholics. When the garbage can tipped over in the alley behind her apartment at three o'clock in the morning, she was sprawled facedown and fully dressed upon her bed while, blocks away, sirens were wailing deliriously up and down Canal Street.

Only her subconscious registered the police helicopter overhead. It was searching from the Mississippi River to the midcity ghetto, its light whipping up and down the streets and its rotorwash setting up a fierce chatter in the windowpanes. As it drifted away, she heard the garbage can's clatter down her driveway—a weary bump and grind like that of some timeworn stripteaser taking her final strut off the stage and leaving feathers and spangles and worn-out tinsel behind.

"Dammit!" hissed a voice outside her bedroom window.

"Oh, man—"

"Shh!"

Moaning, Brittany tossed upon her bed.

Outside, the garbage can came to a stop against a utility pole. But the lid, continuing to play out one last drunken arabesque, bounced off the curb, careened tipsily on its rim and wobbled out into the dirty street. There, in the intersection of Carondeleer and Jacksborough, it finally *wa-wa-wanged* itself to death.

Brittany's dream evolved into a full-blown nightmare. The fantasy wasn't one of cute tripping monsters and the gentle Star Trekish phantoms one smiles about over breakfast toast. It was the old, familiar dream. She was standing beside a cement parapet watching a motorcycle crash through the guard rail and plunge in horrifying slow motion from an elevated highway to another freeway beneath. As usual, in the split second before she could lean over to see what had become of the rider, her cry wakened her.

"Aghhh!"

Brittany jerked up. Her eyes were large and moss-green with fright. Her shoe struck the floor with a thud. She was heaving, and the sound was raspy and harsh. Where was she? Was it real? Or was it the dream again?

Then she recognized her room—a tiny space that could easily have been mistaken for the site of a one-day sale in the Esprit department at Holmes's: strap sandals and paisley skirts and bright, raunchy caftans cluttering the floor and buried beneath towels and silk camisoles and medical smocks, the flat surfaces spilling hardback books on Japanese architecture and magazines, misplaced and forgotten coffee cups.

From his throne upon her chair, Jack opened his one cat's eye and yawned.

"The same to you, buster," she smirked and swung long, slim-calved legs over the side of the bed.

With a limber move she unfolded to her full six feet. She danced around in the disorder until she had succeeded in peeling off a pair of pants stained with disinfectant from the emergency room. Her cotton knit top was spotted where Mrs. Guillaume's baby had burped formula on her shoulder. She lifted it to her nose and sniffed. Gad!

Adding it to the collection on the floor, she walked, sweat-moistened and naked, to the air-conditioning unit and turned the thermostat as cold as it would go. When goosebumps rose on her front, she rotated and greedily chilled her back.

Across the room, in the mirror above her vanity, she caught a glimpse of pale, shadowed limbs—that long-waisted, streamlined body had been her curse when she was a foot taller than everyone else. Now, at twenty-eight, it was conveniently thin and facile as a gymnast's. A lot of years and disillusionment stretched back to the days when she'd stood so dreamy-eyed before her vanity on St. Charles Avenue. Then she'd been enamored with each tiny freckle that seemed to cover every inch of her body. And her breasts! Her hips! Life was a search for pleasure and acceptance, and the body was the key to it all.

What a delusion! Her body that she'd been so enthralled with hadn't made her accepted at all. But then, maybe nothing could have done that. Now her body was a tool, and like any craftsman worth his salt she cared for it well but for an entirely selfish purpose: without it she couldn't work, and if she couldn't work she would die. Clarity: pure, eternal.

"You will model, of course," Lilith had declared as far back as she could remember. *"We'll use my connections. You can't help but be a success."*

Reaching back to pluck the combs from her hair, Brittany shook her head like a dog shedding water. An extravagant mass of fiery red curls sprang out like a Christmas tree over her shoulders, offsetting, she thought, a mouth that was too large and a nose that was too long.

She crushed her temples between the vise of her palms. If there was an occupation in the world with a higher fatigue quotient than that of general practitioner, she didn't know about it.

Combat infantry? *Maybe.* Last night had been the appendectomy at Charity Hospital, and a fractured collarbone the night before. Before that? Mrs. Pintoro's stroke. Jake Gilliatt's gallbladder. Stella's baby. A junkyard dog got more sleep than she did!

And, speaking of dogs, one was setting up a ferocious racket out in the alley. From up the street, a window slammed against its sash. A man—he sounded vaguely like Mr. Duell, one of her patients—yelled out into the darkness.

"What'n th' sam hill's goin' on out there?" he bellowed. "Can't a fella get any sleep around here?"

Brittany stood wearily motionless. No, Mr. Duell, she could have told him. Not in a New Orleans ghetto that had been suffering from a tenacious September heat wave for more than three weeks. Perfectly sane people went a little crazy in heat like this.

From out in the alley drifted more sounds of scrambling and a groan. Protecting her bare breasts with an arm, Brittany slipped into the spilling folds of the drapery and pulled an edge of the blind aside.

This part of New Orleans was never truly dark, always blurred with taillights or headlights glinting off taxis, or garish shop windows, the flashing neon of "adult" bookstores and girlie shows only a few blocks away. This was the ghetto, a high-crime area where husks of men moved slowly and patrol cars prowled around the next corner.

Far out over Lake Pontchartrain lightning flickered, but the real news was the tropical storm brewing out in the Gulf. Meteorologists were predicting a hurricane. People would almost welcome one—anything to bring relief from the leaden skies and defeating, stagnant air.

Beyond the medical clinic attached to her apartment, Brittany saw garbage strewn from her Jeep to the street. "Damn!"

Releasing the drape, she groped her way across the dark room to a bureau. Inside a drawer she found a wilted T-shirt and a pair of crumpled shorts. She patted beneath the tumble of garments, groping and feeling. What she would *really* like was a cigarette.

She pulled on the clothes and racked her brain. Every time she quit smoking, she stashed cigarettes all over the house like land mines. She'd quit again just last week. If she could only find one . . .

Switching on a lamp, she removed a pair of glasses from her doctor's bag and pushed them onto her face. An earnest plunder of the nightstand yielded two prescription pads, a crumpled magazine picture of Kurt Russell, a book by Erica Jong and a Cross pen she thought she'd lost. Along with a picture of her mother modeling a gown back in the years when the name Lilith Garamond was practically synonymous with that of Christian Dior.

She moodily drew her fingernail down Lilith's gorgeous silhouette. *"No, Brittany, I will not put John's name on the invitation list. The boy's a commoner, for goodness' sake! What will our friends think? What will Sybil think?"*

Slamming the drawer shut, Brittany dragged off her glasses and threw them on the bed. She didn't want to start thinking about her mother, not at three o'clock in the morning when she was having a nicotine fit.

Another ambulance was shrieking in the distance now, and the helicopter was returning for another sweep. Brittany strode to the window and looked out again. What was going on out there? Nothing that she could see. But then, ghetto darkness was different from other darkness. It took special eyes to see.

Moving to her closet, she began slapping haphazardly at the pockets of her clothes for just one cigarette. No success. For a moment she stood chewing her lip, then twisted around to dump Jack unceremoniously from the chair to the floor.

"Sorry, Jack. Your nerves are better than mine." When she searched beneath the cushion and heard the cheerful crinkle of cellophane, she giggled. "Voilà!"

But upon bringing out the pack, she found it disgustingly empty.

"It's too late, Mother: I've already invited him."

"Then you just uninvite him, miss! If John Gallois shows up at that reception, I swear I'll call the police! For God's sake, Brittany, do try to be something besides a disappointment for once in your life!"

Scooping up the cat, Brittany pressed her cheek to his head. "After ten years it still hurts," she whispered as the recollections washed cruelly over her. "They had no right, Jack. I was only a child. I did everything they wanted."

She really had done everything. A frightened, lonely girl, she'd taken all the hosts of extracurricular classes prescribed by her mother and her aristocratic friend Sybil who'd said "Lilith, you must do *some*thing to bring that girl out of her shell!" She'd taken riding, swimming, ballet, piano. She'd gotten herself chosen as maid in the courts of the balls of the Krewe of Apollo and the Harlequins, a maid in the courts of the balls of Mithras, the Elves of Oberon and Proteus. She'd been presented by the Debutante Club and the Pickwick Club, also the Bachelors' Club and the Midwinter Cotillion—agonies, all of them. Then, at eighteen, she was about to be presented by Le Debut des Jeunes Filles de la Nouvelle Orleans. All she wanted was for John— her one friend in all the world, her only friend, her secret lover—to be invited.

Dropping the cat, Brittany darted to the bathroom and struck the light switch with a stinging slap. She frantically searched the linen closet. No cigarettes. She harriedly switched on a miniature television that was perched on the vanity. She dragged on her headphones and turned MTV to an earsplitting level, but as she turned away, her reflection in the mirror took her breath.

"It wasn't my fault, John," she whimpered and bleakly turned off the music, pulling off the headphones and dropping them to the tile. "It wasn't my fault."

From outside came another rough whisper. "Hang on, will you?"

"God, I'm trying. Oh, God, oh, God—"

Brittany switched off the light and waited, holding her breath. She should go outside and have a look. Someone was out there. But what did it matter? What did anything matter? She was too tired to care, and everything in the world seemed to be her fault.

Wanting only to block out the world with sleep, she stumbled back to bed and pulled the pillow over her head. She drew the sound of the air conditioner all around her and tried to imagine what it would be like to be a "regular" person, one whose life revolved around a family first and work second, one who could *live* life instead of tolerating it.

But all she could see was the motorcycle plunging through the guard rail. She could see John....

A siren screamed. Where was Mooch, anyway? His feet were the first to hit the floor at the slightest sound outside. Where was that child?

Whenever Hammer Curry's phone rang in the middle of the night, he was instantly awake.

He'd never taken the time to analyze exactly why this was so, but he suspected it had something to do with the divorce: for a year after he'd returned from Vietnam, he'd slept with one ear open, hoping with the naiveté of a dumb twenty-two-year-old kid that it was all some dreadful mistake, that Kit would call.

She never had, of course. Now, at forty, he didn't care. When the call came through at three o'clock, he knew it was an emergency. He was already kicking off the sheets and prying his skivvy-clad body off the bed by the third ring.

"Yeah?" he said as he pulled on his trousers. "What is it?"

A police dispatcher replied with her customary sterile tones. "Canal Street, Lieutenant Curry. We have an officer down."

Hammer's stomach turned apprehensively. "Officer down" was the worst thing any cop could hear, and he shifted the receiver to his other ear. "Who?"

"Patrolman Arnold Bates, sir."

"Get Patrick on the horn. Tell him I'll be ready by the time he gets here."

"Yes, sir."

By the time the dispatcher was pushing buttons on her console, Hammer was snapping on lights with swift economical movements. He pulled open a bureau drawer where a dozen clean shirts were neatly folded and stacked, their collars and cuffs as crisp as cardboard. As he lifted out a striped one, he also removed the telephone receiver from its cradle.

He punched in a number and scowlingly gripped the instrument between his shoulder and jaw while he shrugged into his shirt and left the tails flapping about his hips.

A woman's sleepy voice came on the line. "Yes?"

"Sandy, I've had a call."

Yawning, she hesitated for a second, then came fully awake. "Be right over, Mr. Curry. What time is it?"

"Just after three." Reaching around the door of his closet, Hammer stripped one of the ties from a rack that extended over an orderly row of shoes.

"Okay," Sandy said. "Just don't forget to leave the door unlocked."

"You got it. And thanks, Sandy."

"No problem."

Long ago Hammer had discovered the truth that every single parent has always known, that the baby-sitter is the most important person in the world. Sandy Gittis was paid handsomely and treated well. Except that the children weren't his: when he'd agreed to keep his brother's two youngsters, he hadn't dreamed that a few short weeks would turn into four years.

After a hurried brushing of his teeth and a dash of cold water in his face, Hammer glanced at his pleasantly ugly reflection, all five-feet-eleven-inches of it. He wasn't doing too bad a job of keeping it all together, he guessed. Not when a batallion of young New Orleans Police Department eager beavers with bodies like John Rambo's were casting covetous eyes at his job.

One day, when the time was right, he would make his move. He'd climb on up the ladder. But it would have to happen *his* way, on *his* terms. He didn't want a fancy job run by politicians. If a man couldn't belong to himself...

Maybe he was too much of an idealist. A dreamer. Maybe what he wanted didn't exist. Anyway, until the big day came he kept his rib cage taut and his chest flexible. He kept a waist that was the same as it had been in the army. He ran his five miles a day and weighed in at the usual one-hundred-eighty pounds.

Reaching over his head, he gripped the steel bar that dropped from the ceiling, and he chinned himself ten times. Then he splashed on some after-shave and skimmed a brush over the crisp brown hair that he wore very short and without a part—not a crew and not punk, sort of "early Road Warrior," the despair of his barber.

He leaned nearer the mirror to squint at his stubble of beard. One of the good things about being the ranking officer of the precinct was that he could have a car and driver whenever he wanted them. He'd shave in the car.

Stuffing his shirt into his trousers and rezipping his fly, he fit on his shoulder harness and slipped his service revolver into place. Not once in fifteen years on the force had he ever fired it at a human target. His sport coat was a lightweight cream-colored silk, tailored with his holster in mind. Shrugging it on, he gave himself a final inspection. He saw a rugged, lined man of strong, virile style, something that came naturally, but now he wasn't so sure about his edge on all those Rambo bodies.

"Face it, Curry," he said with a not-too-impressed grin. "You're getting old."

As soundlessly as a cat, he walked down the hall. He peered into the room of his niece, Alice, where she lay curled in an adorable nine-year-old knot, her long blond hair catching the soft beams of the nightlight. Alice was afraid of the dark, and together they had come to the conclusion that sleeping with a light was *definitely* not a mark of maturity.

Smiling, he bent to pluck a strand of hair from her face and placed a kiss upon her dewy forehead. "Nothing's going to hurt you, my darling," he whispered with gruff tenderness and prayed it would be true.

In the next room Craig, with the same blond beauty as his sister but sporting a barked cheek and a bruised jaw from his first fistfight, lay sprawled crosswise on his mattress. His mouth was open, and his ten years' worth of mischief was momentarily out of commission.

A sleek Irish setter looked up from her rug at the foot of the bed and started to rise.

"Stay, Duchess," Hammer murmured and wondered grimly, as he stooped to scratch the dog's ears, what he would do if Richard ever wanted his children back.

Once in the kitchen, Hammer tossed down a handful of vitamins and brought out the blender. In less than a minute he had concocted a perfectly vile-tasting drink that he sluiced down without breathing.

As he was finishing, he heard the soft rumble of a car pulling into the driveway outside. He gave a final glance around to appease his finely tuned sense of order, snapped off the light and walked out the door, making certain to leave it unlocked so Sandy could get in.

Patrick leaned across the seat to open the passenger door. Hammer smiled at the young detective whose freckles seemed to glow in the harshness of the overhead light.

Patrick Gilbert was a plodder, but he was an honest and competent and immensely likable plodder, which in the eighties was something. He was stocky but paunchless, and his square boyish face was as fair as a woman's. It revealed every flush, and he compensated by wearing a smudge of a rusty mustache like a merit badge.

Crawling in, Hammer shut the door. The police radio under the dash was crackling. Reaching for it, he said, "You're running a little late, aren't you?"

"Sorry, sir." Patrick swerved the car out into the street with a whisper of tire rubber. "Sally had to track me down."

Hammer chuckled. "Patrick, what I'm going to do is buy you a bed and have a sign welded into the headboard: 'Sleep Here.'"

Even in the darkness, the younger man's flush was visible. It occurred to Patrick that he could bring up the subject of Hammer's on-again, off-again affair with state Senator Deborah Keyes, but his boss was an exceedingly private man.

He was pushing the button on the spitting radio transmitter. "Car twenty-one-Baker, eastbound on Raleigh to Canal. Over."

Patrick said, "I gotta warn you, Lieutenant, this promises to be a nasty one."

Fishing out his identification badge, Hammer clipped it to his lapel. He removed an electric razor from the glove compartment and plugged it into the cigarette lighter.

"What have we got?" he asked as he worked the razor over his jaws.

"Bates and Wise took the call. A jewelry store alarm went off. From what I understand, Bates was supposed to have taken off down an alley. Wise said he heard the shot out by the street, but by the time he got there, it was too late.''

Hammer inspected his shave by touch. ''Has anyone told Bates's wife?''

''Not yet. It's gonna be a press case.''

Looking up, Hammer said, ''Not necessarily.''

''Wise heard scuffling and took off on a chase. Two juveniles, apparently. Wise yelled for 'em to stop.''

Hammer lowered the razor as dread tightened in his chest. ''Don't tell me.''

''Wise thinks he hit one.''

''Christ!''

For the past two years Patrick's duty in life had been to be Hammer Curry's man Friday. He didn't dislike the job. He admired his superior's extraordinary intelligence; Hamilton Curry III had an uncanny way of weighing and measuring a situation and could almost always come up with the right answer. It was nice to be on the side of a winner.

But Hammer was also a true, real-life straight cop. Too straight—a lot of officers on the streets these days weren't, and some of those who were disliked the way Curry had come up through departmental ranks armed with degrees rather than years of beating the pavement.

But Curry just so happened to be on the mayor's list when the big shuffle had come to give New Orleans a new image. Curry's job was to ''clean up the place.'' Another thing that didn't make him the most popular cop in town.

Now he was saying ''I suppose it's hoping for too much to have any identification on the two boys.''

Patrick shook his head. ''I don't think so, sir.''

''Well, let's begin by alerting the hospitals in the area.''

They were approaching Canal Street; the wide thoroughfare was a carnival of flashing red and blue lights. Hammer could see swarms of cars, patrol and unmarked. Uniformed personnel were dealing with the onlookers, but they weren't too much of a problem this early in the morning.

The photo unit was at work, as was the medical examiner. An ambulance was parked at an angle to an alley, and an ABC-TV press wagon was arriving from the direction of the World Trade Mart. Even a groomed chestnut horse was there with his patrol rider. Uniformed men were writing and talking and cordoning off the area with signs.

Sighing, Hammer replaced the razor, opened the door and got out of the car. As they both walked to the scene, he told Patrick, "If we've got two juveniles out on the streets and one of 'em is shot, I want you to get ahold of Melissa and have her ask the computer for a list of every private practitioner within a mile radius of Canal Street. Just in case. Get some men down here. Have them start knocking on doors."

"Yes, sir."

"And no phone calls. We don't know if the kids are still armed. They may force some doctor at gunpoint. Anyway, doctors have this thing about confidentiality. Have them check out the names in person."

"You got it."

Hammer shifted his shoulders against the bite of the holster strap. Drawing his palm over his bristly hair, he walked to where the forensic people were working.

A reporter spotted him and fell into step, his microphone extended. "Have you got anything for us, Lieutenant Curry?"

"Not now, Dwight," Hammer said and motioned him away. "When I get it, you'll get it."

Hammer raked his lower teeth over his lip. Already his clothes were sticking to his body from the heat. He had a bad feeling about this one, and he'd learned a long time ago to trust his feelings. It was going to be a long, long day.

* * *

Wearing a pair of drooping nylon swim trunks, nine-year-old Muchard "Mooch" Billiot tiptoed to the back door of the apartment where he had lived with Dr. Brittany Schellenegger for the past six months. His tread was light, springy with the ingrained caution of one whose life had been spent surviving on ghetto streets.

Cupping his small hands against the glass pane, he squinted into the night. The sirens were hushed now, and the sounds of scuffling outside had subsided. He knew the lay of the land out there like his own hand, and he grimaced to find his very own space strewn with trash from one end to the other.

He supposed it would be his job in the morning to pick it up. *Yuck!*

An urgent whisper from outside the window made him withdraw from the window and press his back to the wall.

"Hey, Doc. You in there? It's Devane, Doc. Hey, Doc!"

Mooch shuddered. He didn't like Devane. Six months ago he would have stepped outside and told him to buzz off, but now he stayed put on Doc's orders. Ever since she'd found him outside in this very alley, he hadn't dared commit so much as one sin. A single disapproving lift of Doc's eyebrow could put more fear into him than the whole New Orleans Police Department.

He walked to her bedroom door and debated whether he should wake her up. Doc never got enough sleep, what with the telephone ringing at all hours. But maybe Devane was having a heart attack. Maybe he was going to kick off.

Nudging open the bedroom door with a toe, he found her sprawled across the bed. Walking over, he lifted the pillow from her head and touched her wrist.

"Doc?" He found the lamp switch and turned it on. "Someone's at the back door. Wake up, Doc."

Brittany jerked up as if a jolt of electricity had shot through her. She let out her breath. "Mooch," she said, as if she were making an announcement.

"Sounds kinda awful out there," he gravely informed her.

"What time is it?"

He tipped up the face of her digital clock. "Ten minutes after three."

"Who's outside?"

"Devane. Want me to get rid of him?"

"No."

Mooch didn't argue. Sometimes he had a feeling that Doc was onto him. In the beginning he'd psyched her out, or so he'd thought; he'd reared back in his best shocked affront when she'd told him he couldn't stay at her house.

"You're goin' to throw me out on the streets, Doc?" he'd challenged, the corners of his mouth trembling expertly. "You? A servant of mankind? You want me to wind up a drug addict or somethin'? Don't you have no sense of decency, Doc? Didn't you swear no Hippocritic oath or nothin'?"

She hadn't stood a chance. The truth was—and he was possibly the only one to understand this—Doc couldn't make it by herself. Until he showed up, she would go all day long seeing patients without ever remembering to eat. If not that, the mortgage company would certainly have come and hauled her away, for she never remembered to pay the bills.

So he tried to be very good and very indispensable. He did the shopping down at Marty's Grocery, and he put the dirty clothes in the washing machine. When Doc's Jeep needed fixing, he found someone who wouldn't rip her off but just a little.

Now she stood to her full height and rotated in a groggy circle. He scrambled to find her shoe. After weaving back and forth on one foot, she finally got it on and tied.

"All right, all right," she called as the knocking persisted. She walked out into the tiny living room where the Hide-a-bed was opened for Mooch to sleep on. "I'm coming."

She made a detour by the bathroom to pour some mouthwash into a glass, and she rinsed, then doused her face with cold water. She was blotting her cheeks dry on the sleeve of her T-shirt as she trudged to the door. When she peered out and saw two teenage boys standing on her stoop, she struck the light switch with her palm.

Brittany recognized Devane Sadu at once. The other boy was sort of draped over Devane. When the glare struck them in the face, Devane waved his free arm for her to cut it off.

"Off, off!"

She doused the light and saw, upon opening the door, that the boy was considerably younger than Devane, seventeen perhaps. He wasn't a large boy, but he was well developed with wide shoulders and muscular arms, tightly sinewed flanks. One leg of his jeans was ripped open from hem to thigh to reveal a badly lacerated calf and knee. His shirt was a gaudy island print, and its buttons had ripped free. The hand he pressed to his body was stained with blood.

He attempted to raise his head and squint at her, but the effort cost him more than he could afford. He dropped his head, and a shock of thick black hair swung down over his face.

"Good Lord," she said under her breath, then called over her shoulder to Mooch. "Turn on the lights in the clinic, Mooch. Open the doors."

Together, she and Devane managed to get the boy inside, and Mooch scuffled ahead to obey. He knew the routine. He planned to be a doctor when he grew up, just like Doc was.

"And order out an ambulance," she told Mooch.

Alarmed, Devane reached across his companion and grasped Brittany's arm in a bruising grip. "No!"

She questioned him with disbelieving brows, and Devane jerked his head toward the boy draped between them. "My friend—"

"Your friend is seriously hurt. He has to go to the hospital, Devane. Order the ambulance, Mooch."

The younger boy groaned when Brittany took his weight upon herself, and he slid an arm about her waist. She strained to help him onto the examination table. "Okay, okay," she reassured him gently. "Just relax now. Let go."

With his teeth clenched, the youth released her by degrees. She finally extended him full-length upon the table and straightened his legs. When she made an attempt to lift his arm from his side, he sucked in his breath.

"I have to see," she urged him and wondered if she would ever treat one of these battered ghetto boys who didn't have John's imploring face.

"It's all right," she murmured. "You're here now. I'll help you." She lifted his arm away, then plucked the soaked shirt aside.

She knew immediately it was a gunshot wound, a bad one. The boy's eyes streamed sudden tears, and his mouth contorted with pleading. From a distance a siren wailed, and the looks of fright that passed between the two boys confirmed her guess that they were the reason for all the commotion.

What was going on? What terrible thing had happened on Canal Street?

She swiftly took note of the youth's Calvin Klein jeans and the Pierre Cardin label on his shirt. Ghetto boys didn't wear designer clothes, nor did they have haircuts as this boy had. She began cleaning him with swift, expert moves.

"What's your name?" she cautiously inquired.

Biting his lips, he shook his head in refusal.

Brittany had a moment's empathy for the boy's mother, whoever and wherever she was. Did she have any idea that her son needed her? Was she somewhere worrying?

It appeared to her that the piece of lead had passed through the boy's side rather cleanly. But there was really no way of telling what damage it had done internally. A lot of doctors would step back at this point and hold up their hands in a refusal to do more. She reached for her stethoscope and blood pressure gauge.

"Tell me about this," she demanded tersely of Devane as he lounged against a table and watched her check his friend's pulse, heartbeat, pupils, blood pressure.

Devane was one of the bronzely tanned young hustlers who made his money on Bourbon Street. His tank top showed off his biceps and the hair on his chest. Brittany guessed that what he hadn't done with women didn't exist. Every time she'd had dealings with him, he'd propositioned her.

She could feel his eyes hungrily stripping her, even now as his friend's life was slipping away. He threw his weight on the opposite hip in an attempt to catch her attention.

"Wal, you see, Doc..." he drawled.

Brittany ignored him. "I want the truth," she snapped and threw a glare over her shoulder. "What hit your friend? Besides the bullet? A truck?"

Devane moved a few paces closer and grinned. "Kinda."

"How can a truck 'kind of' hit a person, Devane?"

"Well, Doc, there was this...ah, a sort of holdup, you know? And Ger, here—well, he got shot."

"I can see that." Brittany swabbed a bottle of vitamin K with alcohol and pierced it with a needle. "What happened to *Ger*?"

"The police shot 'im. Hell, Doc, they didn't yell halt nor nothin'. Just shot him. And Ger, well, you can see he ain't even eighteen. You know what I mean?"

They never learned, did they? Always in trouble and always afraid. There was no way she could make them understand that nothing, *nothing* was worth this.

She added some vitamin B to the syringe and gave the boy an injection. From where she worked she could see Jacksborough Street across the creek. Traffic was picking up outside.

Mooch poked his tousled head around the doorfacing, his black hair flying from his head in all directions. He'd pulled on a T-shirt, and it was wrong side out with the label sticking out behind his neck.

"Pigs outside," he announced as lights flashed out in the parking lot.

"Police," she tartly corrected and knew a thrill of fear as she saw two uniformed men getting out of their car beyond her glass doors. *"Did you see the motorcycle when it went through the railing, miss? Do you know the boy who was riding it?"*

"Is the ambulance coming?" she asked.

"Yeah."

Brittany flicked him an understanding smile. "Then you can go on back to the apartment."

Mooch was religiously committed to the belief that one should have as little to do with the police as humanly possible. He gratefully disappeared.

Despite her fury at Devane, Brittany's heart twisted when the sound of slamming car doors visibly alarmed the two boys. She placed her fingers upon the underside of the injured boy's wrist. She could smell fear on him—the kind that bubbled out of the skin along with the sweat and couldn't be washed out of clothes.

Her eyes collided with those of Devane when the door buzzer sounded. She said, "I believe that's for you, Devane."

Devane was so high that he was quite reckless. He shoved Brittany back against the wall. Though Brittany was used to dealing with this element of the ghetto, her anger was displaced with a real fear. Devane was strong, and he was scared. His lips drew back to bare his teeth, and she could feel the heat of him. One of his hands closed upon her side.

But when the door buzzer sounded, the drugs—PCP, crack, whatever—made him too afraid to carry out his bluff. Releasing her, he laughed and skittered backward to the door that led to her apartment. He talked to his friend with every step. "Hey, man . . . hey, Ger . . ."

Brittany was outraged. How dare Devane throw his life away like this? Who gave him the right to destroy himself? And how dare he make her an accomplice, as John had done.

The buzzer's demand was undeniable. Hardly knowing what to do, Brittany placed an oxygen mask on the boy's face. She feared to leave him lest he try to make his own escape. He wouldn't get very far.

"Hold this in place," she ordered. "And don't move from that table."

Chapter Two

Brittany had never been certain, whenever she met people for the first time, if their surprise was because of her height or her face. Though she was much too intimidated by Lilith's glamour to consider herself beautiful, she wasn't ugly. People simply didn't expect to find a single woman who looked like she did to live where she did or to do what she did.

From the opposite side of the glass door she bore the inspection of the two uniformed men. One of them she vaguely recognized as Brian Gallagher. The other officer would have been much more at home on Saturday night wrestling than in uniform. His eyes were puffy slits and his jaw a ledge of beef. He was very much the hardware man with one hand resting on the butt of his gun and the other carrying a stick. As if to say *"Mess with me, and I'll punch your lights out."*

Both their uniforms were splotched with dark stains of sweat. Brittany opened the door. A blast of heat wilted her instantly.

The wrestler removed his cap, wiped the inner band and bent over his paunch to read the sign by her door. "Dr. Schwarzenegger?"

"Schellenegger," Brian Gallagher corrected with a commiserating grin at Brittany.

Brittany was used to the misnomer. She nodded to Officer Gallagher that they could come in. "I have an emergency," she said over her shoulder and headed for the examination room. "I don't have time to talk."

They followed her politely, but when the wrestler moved past the outer door and into the room itself, Brittany stopped him with a look of warning. He grudgingly inched back.

The patient appeared to be going into shock. Brittany swiftly checked his blood pressure. "Say what you came to say, gentlemen."

"There's been a shooting on Canal Street, Dr. Schellenegger," Brian Gallagher explained as she gave the boy oxygen. "We have reason to believe that this juvenile was involved. We'd like to ask him a few questions."

Brittany could hear well enough with the ear plugs of her stethoscope in place, but she pretended not to.

Presently Brian said, "Ma'am?"

She didn't look up. "Upon whose orders?" she finally asked and pulled the instrument from her ears.

The two men exchanged a shrug. Gallagher said, "Our police lieutenant. Hamilton Curry."

"Sounds like something in my kitchen," she blandly quipped and bent over the boy again.

Brittany, whose sympathies had always been with the underdog, anyway, was filled with compassion as the boy stared into her eyes and closed his bloodstained fingers about her arm. She understood not only what it was to be the doctor touching the boy, but because she had been there—a person who didn't belong, who clung to people who weren't friends because they were all there was—she understood what it was to be the boy touching the doctor.

"I'm afraid your questions will have to wait until this boy's vital signs have returned to normal, Officer," she said to Gallagher. "I've ordered an ambulance. He may have to go directly into surgery. After that, there'll be plenty of time."

The wrestler bulldozed his way to the head of the table and spread his legs as if he were planning to deal her a karate chop. "He looks okay t'me."

She couldn't believe what she was hearing. "My patient is not okay—" she read his nameplate "—Mr.... Officer Webster."

"Look, lady!" The veins were standing out on Webster's neck like ropes. Sweat was running down his face. "There's a police officer on his way to the morgue right this minute because of this punk!"

A policeman killed? Brittany felt nausea rise up from her stomach. A death, any death, pained her. But she couldn't turn away from this boy; she was committed to him now.

Outwardly she remained calm. She ripped off a strip of tape and secured a compress around the boy's ribs. Officer Webster stepped to the table and attempted to take the boy by the shoulder, but Brittany's empathy overpowered any fear she had of David Webster. She pulled herself to her full height and thrust out her hand.

The boy, his face glazed and streaming sweat, slipped beneath her arm and scrambled to the floor.

Officer Webster gloated. "Seems he's got a little life left in him, eh, Doctor?"

Revolvers suddenly appeared.

"Wait!" Brittany cried in horror as Brian Gallagher pushed the boy to the wall and frisked him roughly up and down the torn jeans.

Officer Webster began reading him the Miranda rights. "You are under arrest for the shooting of Officer Arnold Bates. You have the right to remain silent. If you do not choose..."

"We figure," Gallagher explained to Brittany as Webster rattled on and on, "any person able to attempt an escape is able to come downtown for questioning."

"I want to go on record here!" she blurted.

"Consider it done."

"You don't understand."

"No, you don't understand, Dr. Schellenegger. If we don't get a confession from this boy now, by the time the medical and legal people get through throwing a blanket over everything, he'll be back out on the streets again. An officer is down, ma'am. This boy's responsible."

She thought of Devane. Maybe Devane had shot the policeman, not this boy. "You're making a mistake."

"Hands behind the back, fancy man," Webster snarled as he snapped handcuffs on the patient.

Brittany moved quickly, but when Brian Gallagher laid his hand upon his revolver, she desisted. Webster shoved the boy ahead of him and goaded him out the door. The youth was doubled up and holding his side, but he didn't make a sound of complaint.

Cursing her helplessness, Brittany followed them outside where the boy was shoved into the back seat of their patrol car. "At least let me go with him," she begged.

"He'll be all right, Doctor," Gallagher said, and his look was one of disappointment in her.

"But the ambulance will be here in a minute. He would at least have oxygen. You could ride in it with him."

They shut the doors of the police car in her face and got into the front seat. Hating them, Brittany waited beside the fender.

Brian Gallagher rolled down the window. "Dr. Schellenegger, Curry'll have our behinds if we don't bring this boy in, and the police commissioner will get what's left. I'm sorry."

"You don't know what sorry is, Mr. Gallagher. Who did you say your superior was?"

"Ma'am?"

"His name, Officer Gallagher. If something happens to this boy, I'm going to file a complaint. I'm going to sue. I'm going to go to the press. I'm going to do everything. This is an outrage!"

That foolish statement earned her nothing but a series of hard, resentful looks. "Lieutenant Curry, Doctor," Brian Gallagher said and emphasized each syllable as if she were a retarded child. "Lieutenant Ham-il-ton Cur-ry."

Tears pricked Brittany's lids as the car whipped around and screeched out of her driveway. Through the rear window she saw the boy until he was no more than a shadow blending into a million other shadows. The blue-and-red lights whirled and swirled into the hot night.

Some part of her heart died. She hadn't tried hard enough, had she? She hadn't been skilled enough. As usual, she had failed, and she hadn't even known his name.

Like an old woman, she moved toward the clinic door.

"Some show, Doc," a voice murmured from the darkness. "But you did good, yes you did. Real good."

Brittany whirled. Devane Sadu emerged from behind the dumpster. He flicked his mocking glances up and down as he moved toward her.

"Look, Devane—" she extended one palm out, warning him to keep away "—it's late, and you're high. Just go home, okay?"

His hips swiveled sexily. "You didn't tell them about me, did you, mamma? Hey, I appreciate that. I didn't think you liked me, but I guess I was wrong, huh?"

"I didn't tell," she snapped testily, "because they didn't ask, but if they do, I will."

Devane closed in. For the kill, Brittany figured. Boys feared nothing down here. She threw up a barrier of glares.

He mimed a kiss. "Aw, come on, mamma. You don't have to put on that doctor act with me. Come on, let's go somewhere."

"Good night, Devane."

Surprisingly he didn't try to stop her, and when she practically ran for her back door, he bawled to her back, "Hey, there's no need to get all bitchy on me, Doc. I was just tryin' to be nice."

Much safer now, Brittany drilled him with a look that dispensed with status. "Look, Devane, I'm not your Doc, and I'm not your lady. I'm not even going to talk to you when you're like this. When you come down, if you want someone to be your friend, you let me know. I'll even help you get clean. In the meantime, *go home*."

His mouth curled in a handsome sulk. Without another word he slipped back into the shadows.

Before Brittany could get inside, the ambulance arrived, and she explained to the driver that the police had taken her patient. Shrugging—it was no skin off his nose—the man disappeared into the same gloomy night the police car had.

Brittany blotted her face on her arm as she stumbled wearily through the darkened clinic. She wished it was seven o'clock. Once the sun was up, the ghosts of her past were exorcised for another day.

"Oh!" she gasped.

The small mouselike rustle made her do a double take, then she laughed at Mooch peeping out from behind the examination room door. His dark eyes were baffled, and he was braced for a scolding. When he realized he wasn't in trouble, he grinned like the con artist he was.

Ruffling his hair, she walked side by side with him. "I thought you'd gone back to bed," she chided affectionately.

He swaggered. "Nah!" But he let her mold him into her side, and when his whisper came it was low and troubled. "What'll they do to What's-his-face?"

Brittany motioned for him to precede her through the door into the apartment. "They'll probably book him for first degree murder, Mooch. It's sad, isn't it?"

"Will Devane get it, too?"

"I have no idea."

"I hope he does. I hope they tear out his fingernails."

"Mooch!"

Silence.

Mooch waited until she shut the door. "Doc?"

"Hm?"

"What would you do if I got into trouble?"

It wasn't difficult for Brittany to remember Mooch hunched into a pathetic little knot outside her apartment, hiding beneath the eaves, shivering as the rain coursed down the gutters. Her first impulse then had been to scold. Or, maybe, if he came back again, to scrape up some odd chore for him to do. Then he'd fixed her with those sad, pleading eyes of his. Such a small creature to be so deserted by the world, she'd thought as he'd squared his thin shoulders like an old declining warrior who refused to stop fighting even though he knew he couldn't possibly win.

So she'd let him stay, and his gritty courage made her ashamed that she complained at all. Despite all her warnings to herself, she'd come to love him desperately. And she didn't ask herself the nagging question of what she would do if she got up one day and he was gone.

Hugging him, she buried her face in his mop of hair and placed a kiss there. "You're very important to me," she said with gruff tenderness. "So just don't you go getting into trouble."

"But I might," he argued contentedly against her stomach. "I got bad blood."

Laughing softly, she tightened her embrace until he yelped. "I'd be there for you." She sobered. *"For once in your life, Brittany, do try to be something besides a disappointment."*

She whispered, "No matter what happened, Mooch, I'd be there."

At nine o'clock the next morning Patrick Gilbert swung a blue sedan up to the curb of St. Charles Avenue. He and Hammer Curry sat for long, speechless seconds staring at the serpentine sidewalk leading up to one of the most celebrated mansions in the city—one of the two-million-dollar, well-guarded, well-taxed homes where nothing is ever parked in the drive except a Rolls-Royce or a Jaguar or a Bentley.

The house had been built in the 20s. Its four stories, seven bedrooms and eleven baths were set on an emerald-green lawn that kept a maintenance man busy full-time. The formal gardens were still glistening from the water sprinkler. Other oases surrounded the house—tennis courts, a swimming pool, a croquet court, a spa with its own separate building, an observatory, the servants' and deliverymen's entrances, and a guest house.

"Whew!" Patrick said. "Dipstick city. Poverty row."

Hammer drummed his fingers upon the ledge of the door. He didn't look forward to the task awaiting him. "Makes you wonder, doesn't it?"

"About getting good help?"

"How a person can get so fat."

"Don't look at me. I'm just poor white trash." Patrick laughed at his own joke.

Dark clouds were drifting in across the Mississippi River, ready to dump tons of water upon the city. To Hammer, it fit somehow—the ominous weather. Now his job was to get out of the car, walk up to the mansion and explain to Judge Sybil Wade about his pending investigation of her son Gerald's death.

A courtesy, really. When the son of a federal judge shoots a policeman and is himself killed by a policeman, the commissioner breaks the news. Bruce Clements had already talked to Sybil. He'd said, "Lieutenant Curry will answer all your questions."

"Give me a reason to call this off," Hammer said and drew back a cuff to consult the wisp of a gold wristwatch.

The younger man chuckled. "That's what I love about you, Lieutenant. You never ask anything easy."

"Then get me a date with a great redhead."

"Consider it done."

The theory was that the small talk was supposed to lessen the tension. It didn't. Hammer's reaching for the handle of his door was the cue for Patrick to reach for his. Together they swung out and moved up the long walk. Hammer took a breath to speak, then stopped.

"Anything else you wanted?" Patrick asked, glancing at the lieutenant. "Besides the redhead?"

"This doctor who treated the Wade boy?" Hammer absently stroked his short hair toward his forehead.

"Schellenegger?"

Hammer grimaced. "You know the gossip attached to that name, don't you?"

"Should I?"

He shrugged. "Maybe it was before your time."

"I *sort* of know, Lieutenant."

Hammer's own knowledge of the Schellenegger family was based primarily upon what he could remember of old newspaper headlines and bits and pieces of New Orleans gossip. "Lilith Garamond was a French model back around the time Bardot was such a sensation." He twisted his mouth. "Brigitte Bardot wasn't before your time, was she?"

"Aw, boss."

"The way I understand it, Edward Schellenegger was already a U.S. citizen when he married Lilith. I guess bringing a fortune in Austrian diamonds into the country makes it easier. Anyway, he set up housekeeping in a Fifth Avenue apartment. Then he married, and that made Lilith a citizen."

"Sort of Princess Grace in reverse."

"One or two notches removed, yes."

"How big d'you suppose the Schellenegger fortune is? Or was?"

"*Is.*" Hammer glanced at the closed drapes of the house. "And I doubt if anyone knows, but Sigmund Schellenegger willed that fortune, except for token amounts, to our Dr. Schellenegger over on Carondeleer."

As Patrick digested the information, he puckered his mouth. "That's what I don't understand. If Schellenegger's got all that money, what's she doing operating a clinic in a New Orleans ghetto? I mean, why doesn't she buy the Ochsner Medical Institution?"

Hammer pictured Brittany Schellenegger as a virginal tight-lipped spinster who looked like his seventh-grade homeroom teacher. "Maybe it's the missionary spirit," he mused uncharitably. "What would you do if you had a few million? Or billion?"

"Live somewhere besides Carondeleer. Maybe she'll turn out to be a cute missionary."

Grinning, Hammer shook his head. "I expect Brittany Schellenegger is your typical feminist bitch."

"But a rich typical feminist bitch."

"Very."

"She probably needs a good man," Patrick couldn't help adding.

"You, I suppose?"

"Hey, I could dig it."

"I'll just bet you could." Hammer laughed. "Well, she's all yours, laddie buck. I've got enough troubles of me own."

The door of the mansion loomed before them. Patrick reached inside his jacket to make sure his pen and pad were in place. "What are you going to tell Judge Wade?"

Hammer was organizing his thoughts. "The commissioner has already informed her about Gerald's death. What else do we know until the autopsy is completed?"

"That Dr. Schellenegger faces a possible charge of criminal negligence."

"I'm not ready to say that yet."

"Why not?"

"If I knew, I'd be ready to say it," Hammer snapped.

"But Gallagher and Webster both reported that Schellenegger gave the boy an injection before he died." Patrick climbed the steps to the portico that was secluded from the street by a lush bower of wisteria.

"That doesn't make sense," Hammer insisted. "Doctors are scared to death to do anything these days without a release."

"You think Gallagher made a mistake?"

"Brian's too good to make that kind of a mistake, either."

"According to both statements, the officers suggested that the doctor turn the boy over to them so they could get him to a hospital. She insisted on giving him an injection first."

Hammer grasped the clapper. "And the next thing they knew, he was dead. They took him to the morgue and signed in. End of report."

"So what are you going to tell Sybil?"

"I'll know when it comes to me."

As soon as Hammer banged out the announcement of their arrival, the sounds of huge deep-throated barking reached their ears. A series of complicated gratings and rattlings indicated the unlocking of the door. They waited patiently until it swung open.

A uniformed maid, astonishingly pretty, Hammer thought, but teary-eyed and rumpled, stood beside a huge Doberman that had dropped to his haunches, a hungry, no-nonsense rumble vibrating in his throat.

Great, Hammer thought and, keeping one wary eye on the beast, said kindly to the maid, "We've come to see Judge Wade."

They followed her into a great high-ceilinged room that was already breathtakingly restored but was in the process of being remodeled yet again.

"Wait 'ere," she said in a thick accent and vanished.

Most of the room's furniture had been gathered into clumps and covered with drop cloths. Swatches of expensive fabric and costly samples lay cluttered on the inlaid marble floor, and the odor of paint made Hammer want to sneeze. On one wall was an English fireplace with an original Picasso leaning on its side against the stone. Fine leatherbound books were stacked everywhere on the floor. From the ceiling, a hand-cut crystal chandelier dripped prisms that glittered like jewels—flashing ruby and topaz stones, sapphires and emeralds.

Sybil Wade hadn't been born to her money. Like Lilith Garamond, she had married it. Fleming Wade had been two decades older than she—a shipping magnate in his prime. In anticipation of his demise, Fleming had made plans for the immortality of his name. He insisted that his wife, then a mere trial lawyer, take the bench; Gerald would have respectability as a legacy, as well as money.

Whether Sybil had earned her distinction as a judge by merit of genius or from Fleming's connections, Hammer didn't know, but she was presently one of the most powerful people in the state. She had once deposed a governor. Some said she planned to have that office herself someday. More if she wanted it.

This tragedy, especially if it contained a scandal, could ruin any ambitions she might cherish for a political future unless she'd somehow manage to hush it up or capture a lion's share of public sympathy. If Hammer were a more ambitious man, he would be tempted to feather his own nest out of all this; the bald truth was, anyone who helped Sybil during this difficult time would not go unremembered when the time came to give rewards for services rendered.

Hammer looked around, spied a telephone and moved forward to brace his foot on a crate. He held the receiver between jaw and collarbone as he flipped through his notepad. When he came to the number of Dr. Brittany Schellenegger, he punched it in and met Patrick's questioning look.

"I think I'll find out just how big a missionary Brittany Schellenegger really is," he said.

"Today?"
At nine o'clock Brittany stood in her clinic, looking

briskly efficient in her flowing white smock and bright orange skirt that peeped chicly from beneath the openings. The neckline of her cream-colored cotton blouse was caught with a drawstring at her throat, and her soft leather sandals matched the color. A stethoscope was draped around her neck, and her ballpoint pens, clipped importantly to her pocket, were utilitarian and smart, as was her wristwatch with its black leather band.

On the opposite end of the telephone line, a man waited for the answer to his question: Could she spare a few minutes to talk to him about Gerald Wade?

No sooner did she hear the words "New Orleans Police Department," than Brittany froze. She hadn't reported the gunshot wound of the night before. Oh, well, she'd do it now.

"You want me to come downtown and make a statement today?" she repeated his request.

"If you could, we'd appreciate it."

From behind Brittany's left elbow, Henrietta hissed, "Who is it?"

"The police," Brittany said and covered the receiver with her hand.

Henrietta Triche was one of the older ladies from the neighborhood. She tended Brittany's appointment book and mailed out statements. Whenever Brittany needed someone to stay with Mooch, Henrietta did that, too.

Clucking, Henrietta sagely shook her turbaned head. "Confess to nothing."

Brittany twisted around in bafflement toward the woman. "I haven't done anything."

"Good. Then don't confess it."

With a roll of her eyes, Brittany returned to the telephone. "Who did you say you were?"

"I didn't. I'm Hamilton Curry, Dr. Schellenegger."

Who of human mortals could say which of the senses was more subliminally provocative? Sight? Sound? Smell? Brittany didn't know if it was the authority in Hamilton Curry's voice or the deplorable state of her confidence at the moment, but something threw a net over her feelings, trapping her and frightening her with the thought that perhaps she could not get free. She swiftly put together a composite of every overweight cigar-chomping stereotyped sheriff she'd ever seen in the movies or read about in novels.

Her mouth pursed with distaste. "Well, speak of the devil..."

"What?"

"I'm sorry, Lieutenant Curry," she said frostily, "it simply isn't possible this morning. Anyway, you could learn as much by talking to Brian Gallagher. Or David Webster. They were both here in the clinic last night. They know everything I know."

"We have talked to them."

"Well?"

"Since you were one of the last people to see Gerald Wade alive—"

The last to see Gerald Wade alive? His name was Gerald Wade? *Had been* Gerald Wade? And he had died?

Reality faded in and out for Brittany. "I'm sorry, Lieutenant Curry, I—"

"Do you know who Gerald Wade was?" His radar had picked up her discomfiture.

"I know, sort of know, who *one* Gerald Wade is...was."

"Gerald Wade's mother is Sybil Wade, a federal judge who—"

"Yes, yes." Disbelief was battling for Brittany's motor responses now. She was first hot, then cold. She gripped the ledge of the counter. It wasn't possible. She could remember seeing Gerald Wade several times when he was a baby.

"Then you knew—"

"I knew his mother," she quickly explained. "I mean, I know her. Sort of, a long time ago."

"I see."

I see, her brain mocked. *I see, I see.* What could Hammer Curry see? He was a cop. He was part of the system that had taken Gerald Wade away as he'd peered out the back window of a patrol car.

"Doctor? Are you still there, Dr. Schellenegger?"

Oh, yes, she was there. "I'll do everything I can, Lieutenant," she explained numbly. "But it'll have to be this afternoon. I have a room full of patients here."

"Of course. I understand."

He didn't understand. At nine o'clock on Fridays her elderly patients came early to get their weekend's medication before the heat of the day drew on. He didn't understand that to them she was "Doc." She was the drama of their lives, and they, whether she wanted them to be or not, were the drama of hers. She was privy to all their most intimate hopes and dreams, their most terrible fears and griefs, their happy triumphs, which were all too few and too far between, their demands that drained her until she sometimes thought she would die.

"I'll have someone pick you up at one o'clock," he was saying.

Her sudden weariness felt like a fever.

"Dr. Schellenegger?"

"I'm sorry. I mean, all right, Lieutenant Curry, one o'clock is fine. Yes."

"Are you sure you're all right, Doctor?"

"Yes," she said breathlessly. "Thank you, I'm fine."

"One o'clock, then."

She started to hang up the phone but found herself hesitating, holding the shiny instrument breathlessly to her breast, like a girl who had phoned a secret crush but is unable to speak his name or admit who she is.

Returning the instrument to her mouth again, she realized that he hadn't hung up, either. She said stupidly, "I'll be ready."

She waited for him to break the connection, but the silence went on forever—not quite a silence, for it had its own tacit voice.

Presently, from far away, he said, "Fine. Thank you very much, Doctor."

Another shattering pause.

"You're welcome," she whispered.

After a strange eternity, the click finally came.

The sound of her own breaths heaving made Brittany lean heavily against the wall, and when Henrietta cleared her throat, Brittany turned and stared at the woman as if she'd never seen her before.

"Is the news good?" Henrietta asked.

"What?"

"Is it good? Good—you know, not bad."

Henrietta was fifty but looked seventy, and when she wrapped her head in one of her usual gaudy turbans and put on one of her horrendous dresses and mumbled in a jargon of French, Spanish and New Orleans street slang, Brittany accused her of being an ancient Cajun queen, mixing voodoo potions for money slipped under the table.

Henrietta was plucking the receiver from her hands and hanging it up as if Brittany were an incompetent.

"Of course the news isn't good," Brittany said. "Whatever gave you that idea?"

"You don't usually smile when the police call."

"I'm not smiling. And the police never call."

Henrietta turned down the sides of her wrinkled mouth, which made her look like a prune. She leaned around the partition so she could call out into the waiting room. "Cookie?"

From across the room an old black man stirred in his chair, and jerked up his ancient white head. "Yas'm, Miz Henrietta."

"Just tell me one thing, Cookie. Is Doc smiling?"

Cookie's old black eyes twinkled as he pretended to ponder. And so did several other patients, eagerly conferring behind their hands and going through all sorts of facial gymnastics.

"Look lak a smile t'me," Cookie toothily agreed.

Henrietta lifted her bony shoulders at Brittany in triumph and snorted. Brittany knew the time had come when she must take up her role and give another Oscar-winning performance. Gerald Wade's death or Hamilton Curry's charisma could not change that.

Stepping around the end of the receptionist's niche where she would be in full view of her patients, she forced herself to plant a lazy fist upon the side of her hip. "You ask Cookie a thing like that, Henry?" she drawled. "Why, he's an old man. And half-blind to boot."

Everyone laughed, Cookie loudest of all. He slapped a knee and crowed, "I ain't that blind, Doc. I can still see a scam a mile away. Yessiree."

"Senility's getting to you, Cookie." Brittany reached for his wrist to take his pulse. Presently she walked over to Agnes, a middle-aged woman who should have been home enjoying her grandchildren but who was dying of leukemia instead. "Agnes, will you tell that old man I'm not smiling?"

Agnes dipped her frail head. "Oh, I don't as how I could do that, Doc."

This camaraderie was the real medicine they came for, wasn't it? And perhaps it healed them better than all her fancy free drugs.

Pretending to mumble to herself, Brittany strode back to the reception nook, her white tails flying. Once there, she turned her back to them and scribbled notes upon a pad. She exchanged a grim look with Henrietta.

"How's Cookie?" whispered Henrietta.

"Not good, but Agnes is worse," Brittany said under her breath and added, "You know that boy I was telling you about?"

"Who came to the clinic last night?"

Brittany nodded. "He died."

For a moment Henrietta didn't respond. Then she asked "What you want me to do?"

"Cancel all my appointments this afternoon, but don't let anyone pick up on the idea there's trouble. I may need you to stay here with Mooch, too. If you need the work, you can send out some statements."

The older woman tossed her head back, and her laughter was raucous and crackling. "And waste all those postage stamps?" she scoffed for the benefit of the patients. "You are one for the books, Doc, you know that? First you smile and then you tell me to send out statements. It's a sign. An omen."

Muttering some ancient Cajun antidote against curses, Henrietta crossed herself.

"Cookie?" Brittany called as she returned to the waiting room and motioned for the man to come with her.

The black man's face broke into a hundred happy creases. "Comin', Doc. Be patient, now. Remember I'm an ole man."

"Nonsense. You'll live to be a hundred-and-ten."

"Lawd, I hope not."

As Brittany walked the man slowly back into the same examination room, a strange, unsettling sense of expectation absorbed her. Should she hope that something was about to change? Something exciting? Something challenging? Just because of some unidentifiable something in a strange man's voice?

Nonsense! This was all there was in her life, and it had taken her long enough to accept that. "Come on, Cookie," she said gently. "Sit down and roll up your sleeve. Let's get this show on the road."

"Right on, Doc," he said with a laugh. "And some show it is."

Chapter Three

Even in her grief, Sybil Wade possessed a formidable glamour. When she entered the room where Hammer and Patrick waited, she stood poised in the doorway like a madonna—her face elegant with its high prominent cheekbones and regal nose, controlled with a discipline that came from a century's worth of aristocratic Creole blood.

Sybil Wade was the last of a dying breed, that of the old New Orleans, the elite *Vieux Carré*. The pure strains of blood that had produced the society before her, however, had become diluted with the influx of a mobile America.

Still, there did exist in the city a severely strict Victorian element. Sybil was its untitled champion. Today her lean back was rigidly erect. Her shrewd black eyes marked everything. Her grief, they said, like everything else, would be borne with impeccable dignity.

Grief had taken its toll, though, for her natural color was drained, and the half-moon shadows beneath her lashes were too dark to be camouflaged with makeup. Her lipstick made her mouth a bit too brilliant for Hammer's taste.

Yet she was impressively, if not unsettlingly, beautiful, and Hammer knew a moment of apprehension as he hung up the phone after talking to Brittany Schellenegger. A strange empathy that he didn't expect or understand buzzed in his ears.

From his position near the end of the divan, Patrick looked up to watch Sybil instruct her maid, who lingered behind in the corridor. From one side of his mouth, he murmured to Hammer, "Why didn't you tell her?"

"Tell her what?" Hammer kept his gaze riveted on the grieved woman.

"Schellenegger," Patrick answered. "Why didn't you tell her that Gallagher implicated her in his statement?"

Good question, Hammer thought. He had meant to, but things had been so out of focus. He told Patrick, "It didn't feel right."

"You mean she didn't believe you?"

"Oh, she believed me all right. I just don't know...."

"Don't know what?"

"I got the distinct impression she was surprised that the boy had died."

"That's impossible."

"Later."

Sybil had finished with her maid and was gliding toward them, her slender silhouette made more striking by the long black robe that created a rich susurrus upon the marble tile floor.

"Your Honor," Hammer said, stepping nearer and offering his hand, which she only perfunctorily touched before lifting the same hand to the cameo at her throat.

Patrick bowed respectfully but said nothing.

Piqued—such an aloofness might have been appropriate in a courtroom, but it wasn't here—Hammer went on to explain, "I understand that the commissioner has already been to see you, Your Honor. I won't add to what he's said, only to add our sympathies, Officer Gilbert's and mine. We'll do our best to get the answer quickly and as painlessly as possible."

Sybil Wade didn't thank Hammer for his concern. She moved about the grand room, pausing here and there as if to inspect the work that was going on or to remind herself of what lay beneath the drop cloths. She glided to a table where fine leathery legal books were stacked. Picking one up, she opened it without looking to see what it was.

"Actually, Bruce Clements told me very little about how the investigation would proceed," she informed them, gesturing with the open book. "Mostly he said what he thought I wanted to hear. I want you to tell me, Hamilton. Tell me everything you've got."

Sighing, she walked to a chair and, leaving her finger between the pages, she laid the book upon her heart as if it physically pained her.

Hammer glanced uneasily at Patrick, then back to the judge. "We can come back later, you know."

"*Now*, Hamilton." Taking her seat, she crossed her legs so that her robe fell open to display long, glamorous legs. "I want to know."

Shrugging, Hammer moved toward one of the covered chairs and lifted the sheet. He laid it aside and prepared himself to sit.

"No, not that one," Sybil snapped with sudden petulance and waved him away with her hand. "There, beside the fireplace."

The rudeness sent a shaft of white anger through Hammer. Patrick flushed darkly. Chalking her rudeness up to grief, though even that was no excuse, Hammer took the chair. Before he could begin what he'd come to say, the maid tapped at the door.

"Yes, what is it?" Sybil called in exasperation, throwing back her head.

The maid entered and placed a silver coffee service upon a table. Hammer watched Sybil uneasily—the subtle trembling of her hands as she laid the book in her lap, the crossing and uncrossing of her legs. Not a word was said as the maid poured coffee into large tissue-thin cups. Hammer held up a hand before she could place sugar into his own.

When she offered her mistress a cup, Sybil waved it away. "Brandy, Aimie." She didn't speak again until the girl had left the room. Then she leaned forward and, utterly without warning, said, "Brittany Schellenegger is guilty of criminal neglect, Lieutenant Curry. I know it, and you know it. I don't intend for her to walk away from this."

Her venom stunned Hammer. "I beg your pardon, Sybil?"

"You do know who you're dealing with here?" She caught him off guard again as she leaned forward, eyes flashing. "You do know *that* much, don't you, Lieutenant Curry?"

Bitch! Hammer had half a notion to get up and walk out. But then he thought of Alice and Craig and the perpetual three-figure balance in his checkbook. Now wasn't the time to alienate someone who could be important to his future.

A weight settled in his throat, as if he'd tried to swallow a stone and it wouldn't go down. "I'm sure the doctor acted in good faith," he said with a dull disappointment in himself. "We've had no indication that there was criminal neglect anywhere, Sybil. I'm sure—"

Sybil's interruption was not with a word but with a raw tossing down of the brandy. The two men exchanged a fur-

tive concerned look, and Hammer carefully drew a mask
over his face. There was something badly wrong here. Aside
from Sybil's power, something hidden and ugly was in the
room, like a dangerous virus.

"Hamilton," Sybil said, "I've been a friend of Lilith
Garamond Schellenegger since before Brittany was born."

Let her talk, Hammer told himself. *Lean back and learn
everything you can.* He placed one ankle across the opposite knee and lifted his cup to his lips in a gesture of encouragement.

"Back in all our younger days," she said musingly, more
to herself than to them, "the four of us were great friends.
What days those were—Lilith and Edward and Fleming and
myself, traveling all over the world together, seeing everything, doing everything."

She looked up.

Hammer smiled thinly.

"Brittany broke her mother's heart, you know," she said.
"Actually, she broke Lilith's in much the same way that
Gerald broke mine, but at least Gerald was passably normal. Brittany was always a strange child, an eccentric. She
never made friends. She never behaved predictably. Lilith
and Edward gave her everything. Even I tried. But how did
she repay us?"

During this recounting, Patrick watched his superior with
something akin to surprise. It wasn't often that Hammer
Curry let his emotions show through his professional crust,
and he never, never allowed it to happen in front of civilians.

Yet he knew Curry too well to interpret his reaction as
being anything else but stubborn resistance to Sybil Wade.
What had happened, he wondered, in the course of that
telephone call to Brittany Schellenegger?

"Parents and siblings, Sybil," Hammer was saying with a shrug that Patrick recognized as a tactful disagreement. "Every generation has its own."

"You should have known Lilith in those days. She was magnificent, Hamilton—the epitome of true French beauty and grace that few ever see these days. Why, it was like having the old New Orleans back—the one my grandmother used to tell about. Every hostess in town consulted with Lilith before they planned a party or an important affair. Women dressed like Lilith dressed. They went to the same places Lilith did, patronized the same stores, supported the same charities, ate at the same restaurants. And Lilith spent money as if it didn't exist. Everyone flocked to her feet. Oh, you would have to have known her to understand such charisma. No one was immune. And when the four of us did a thing..."

Sybil lowered her eyes to the book in her lap. Their lids were a sooty gray. "If you haven't already discovered the story about John Gallois," she said, "you will. No outsider at the time knew that Brittany was even involved with the boy. Lilith was very protective. She went to great lengths to keep it hushed up. Brittany, of course, blamed her mother for John's death.

"You know, Hamilton—" here Sybil looked up "—I honestly believe Lilith and Edward would still be together if it hadn't been for that child."

That much of the story Hammer was vaguely aware of. Edward had been the other side of his flamboyant wife's coin, much the same as Fleming was the opposite of Sybil. An Austrian by birth, Edward was a graceful, witty man who was a friend, not just of the powerful giants of Wall Street, but of people with names like Rockefeller and White and Lowell. Crushed by what he considered to be a treachery by his own father when Sigmund willed his fortune to

Brittany, Edward had returned to Austria at Sigmund's
death. People said he had taken over the operation of the
diamond business with an admirable defeat.

Hammer scratched his jaw. "Sybil, I will certainly keep
all these things in mind during my preliminary investigation."

Never had Patrick seen Hammer Curry caught so off-
balance as when Sybil Wade came to her feet. The book,
falling unheeded to the marble floor, made an ugly crum-
ple of pages, and her glass shattered the instant it struck the
floor, sending a shower of shards and brandy across the
gleaming surface.

Patrick winced as Hammer nearly spilled his own coffee,
but neither man made a move to help Sybil or to retrieve the
book and the glass.

A dull stain crept up the side of Hammer's neck. Patrick
stood stone still as Sybil threw back her head with majestic
power. Her black robe could have been the garb of an un-
touchable high priestess.

"Don't give me any speeches about what you intend to
do, Hamilton Curry!" she shrilled scathingly. "I will *tell*
you what you're going to do. And you will *do* it! If you
value your future at all, sir, *you will do exactly that*!"

Patrick guessed that Hammer could have ruined himself
then and there. Fine white ridges appeared beside his mouth,
and the blue of his eyes turned to coldest steel. He was prepared to lash out at Sybil with his pride and his incorrupti-
bility.

Patrick stepped swiftly forward to intercede. "Sir," he
said on a wavering voice as if sharing a confidence, "if I'm
not mistaken, there's another pressing matter that demands your attention."

The ridiculous part was that all three of them welcomed
such a ludicrous lie, even Sybil, who realized that she had

just humiliated herself beyond words. She became a statuette, icily imperial and remote.

"Sybil," Hammer began.

But her outburst was past. In a monotone, she said almost beseechingly, "Go now, Hamilton. Proceed with your investigation. You must prove that Gerald didn't shoot anyone. You must prove that she allowed him to die unnecessarily, and that had he lived, he would have been proved innocent."

For all his private ambition, Hammer wasn't going to allow Sybil Wade to dictate what he should or should not prove, but now was not the time. A gentleman didn't kick a hysterical woman.

He mumbled, "I will do my best to get at the truth about your son, Sybil."

The visit had come to a grisly end. Sybil Wade stood staring blankly at both of them, no longer beautiful with her crimson mouth turning downward and the pupils of her eyes blurred. Her hands were clenched into tight fists.

Hammer felt an excessive weariness wash over him, and he looked at Patrick and shook his head. No one spoke as all their heels echoed down the great corridor.

At the door Sybil hesitated and weaved slightly. Fearing she might faint, Hammer reached out a hand, but she waved his help away. "I'm all right."

Hammer cleared his throat and said helplessly, "I hope you'll let me know if there is anything I can do, Sybil."

"Thank you."

The maid and the Doberman appeared from nowhere, and the young woman moved forward to see to the door. The dog sat beside the flowing swirls of Sybil's robe and bared his glistening teeth.

"Brittany Schellenegger has waited a long time to take her vengeance upon me," Sybil said as Hammer hesitated before stepping through the portal into the depressing gray day outside.

Of all the statements she had made during this ill-timed interview, this was the first that truly gave Hammer a reason to wonder if Sybil bordered on madness, if her grief was pushing her to the brink.

He was vaguely aware of the sweeping marble staircase at her back, and the paintings mounted on the walls, of men portrayed in eighteenth-century dress and women resplendent in their jewels. Somewhere in the monstrous house, Fleming Wade lay in an invalid's bed. Did he know how his wife's sorrow was affecting her mind?

And where did this put Hammer with respect to Brittany Schellenegger? Just because Sybil was going off the deep end didn't necessarily mean that the doctor hadn't done exactly as Sybil had said.

He smiled inadequately. "This is such a trying time, Sybil. If there's anything we can do..."

She leaned so close that Hammer could smell brandy on her breath. She suddenly glowed with her unsatisfied hatred, her need for revenge.

"I want Brittany Schellenegger," she said bitterly. "I mean to have her. And if I don't get her, you will be the one who pays. You do understand, don't you, Hamilton?"

Apprehension pulled Hammer as taut as a wire. "Yes, Sybil. I understand perfectly."

For the first time since she had walked into the room, the tension around her eyes relaxed. She smiled. "Good."

There was nothing left to do but walk back out into the humidity. Hammer sensed Patrick immediately behind him, and once they'd be in the car, they would compare impressions, but now he must get a grip on his own feelings. No matter how scrupulously honest he intended to be in the

Gerald Wade investigation, he didn't for a minute underestimate how easily Sybil Wade could break his back.

The woman was a federal judge, for heaven's sake. Who in their right mind would not believe the word of a federal judge? Anyone with a brain the size of a pea would consider the consequences of disloyalty, would pacify Sybil with a passable performance, then conduct the best investigation possible.

But such a pretense would be a lie: a hypocritical, fawning, self-serving lie. And if he didn't lie? Goodbye to everything. And to any good that he might have done. The end justifies the means? Good God! How had his life suddenly come to this?

Leonard Bowles was a contented man. A fifty-year-old high school graduate who was thirty pounds overweight and whose cholesterol was sneaking to the danger point, he happily cherished his prejudiced law and order of the old days when a woman belonged at home and in the kitchen.

For the best part of the afternoon, Brittany had sat in the man's cramped, windowless office and watched him abuse a cigar and a perfectly good typewriter.

"Now, Dr. Schellenegger," he said as he looked up from the keyboard with his cigar anchored neatly in the side of his mouth, "you say you had seen the two officers around your clinic from time to time?"

Brittany didn't understand. Why in the name of heaven was it taking the police so long to ascertain her own small part in the tragedy? She'd been making the same statement to the detective for hours. He wasn't listening.

She struggled to keep exasperation out of her voice as she answered the question again. "Yes, Mr. Bowles, I had seen Officer Gallagher before, driving around the ghetto at night or something. I'm not sure where I saw him. Around. Just around.''

While he typed her reply, pausing every few words to let her prompt him, Brittany rested her left arm upon the top of his desk. Her fingers drummed out an irritated percussive roll.

He looked up through a blue cloud of smoke. Brittany immediately stopped her drumming. He removed his cigar with stubby fingers, flicked the ash from its tip then replaced it. She fanned her neck and plucked her damp blouse from her body. When he smiled, she smiled back and presently consulted her wristwatch.

Enough! Rising, she cautiously formed her departing speech. ''Ahh, Detective Bowles, I'm afraid I miscalculated about how long it would take to make this statement. I have a few patients who need to see me today at the hospital. Surely you have everything you need by now?''

Before he could reply, she gathered up her bag and settled it upon her shoulder.

The detective leaned back and laced his hands behind his head, and as Brittany moved toward the door, she wasn't too surprised to hear his feet strike the floor. ''Before you go, Dr. Schellenegger,'' he said predictably.

From outside, Brittany could hear the faint jingle of telephones ringing and typewriters clattering. She turned back. ''Yes, detective?''

He held her pinned with no more than a look—a butterfly to the board. With an economic movement he reached behind himself for the receiver of a telephone without even glancing at it. He placed it to his ear. Without giving it time to ring or to be answered, he said one word. ''Okay.''

He hung up.

Every nerve in Brittany waited for the roof to drop. She chewed apprehensively at her lip for a moment. ''Who did you call?'' she presently said, every nerve in her going on red alert.

"My lieutenant.'' He smiled. "I think you're gonna want to talk to him."

Wrong! Now Brittany became aware that the palms of her hands were wet. The doorknob was slippery when she clasped it and pulled the door open. "I don't want to talk to anybody, Mr. Bowles. I have to go now. I'm sorry."

"I think it would be a good idea if you waited a few more minutes, ma'am."

"Why?"

"I just think it would be a good idea."

Brittany knew how to fight. Sometimes she was even good at it, but it was nonetheless a skill she had learned by default and now, trembling, she wanted only to be away so she could nurse her cowardice in private. She took the first step through the door, and when Detective Bowles moved more swiftly than she, much more agilely than she imagined a heavy man could, she grew recklessly desperate.

"Look!'' She raised her voice as she spun around to face him. "I've answered everything you asked me, sir. I've spent a great deal of time that I can't afford, and I've cooperated to the fullest extent. What more do you want?"

Without a shred of emotion, he said, "We'd like to see if we can't clear up a certain discrepancy between your statement and those made by Officers Gallagher and Webster."

Brittany's heart jerked painfully. Tipping her head, she blinked at him. Discrepancy? *What* discrepancy? In a low, alarmed voice she said, "What are you saying?"

"I'm saying that the statements filed by two of our officers state that Gerald Wade was alive when they arrived at your clinic at 3:08 on the morning of September twelve."

"I know what day it was!" she shrilled frantically at him. "And of course the boy was alive! What's the problem here?"

"Dr. Schellenegger, would you like to come back into my office?"

"No, I would not like to come back into your office! And you either say what you've been hinting at, or I'm not saying another word without an attorney."

His smile was the most terrifying thing Brittany had ever seen. He yanked up his sinking girth, sucked in a huge breath and chewed his cigar for several seconds. "Based on the reports filed by Gallagher and Webster, the boy died in your clinic approximately ten minutes after you gave him an injection."

Brittany's first impulse was to turn around and run as fast as she could. She wanted to fly through the air and disappear like a mist. But she was rooted to the floor, nailed there by the weight of her own horror.

"I'm afraid there's been a serious mistake here," she said, hardly recognizing the sound of her own voice.

"Yes, ma'am, I'm afraid there has."

Removing the cigar, he held the stub of it between his second and third fingers. He waved his hand as he talked. "I can understand how you might not've wanted to say that Judge Wade's son died in your clinic, Dr. Schellenegger, seein' as how it turns out that you knew the woman and all. But you surely see that the conflicting statements here raise some question as to—"

"No question!" she snapped, feeling the fire of hysteria burning the back of her throat. "There is no question here, Detective Bowles. No question. *No question!*"

"But they said—"

"I don't care what they said! They're lying!"

"Ma'am, the two officers involved wouldn't lie. They're good officers—"

Helplessness was also nothing new to Brittany. She had felt it when she'd leaned over the parapet and stared down in horror at John Gallois. She had known it when her mother stood up at the reading of Sigmund's will and declared that she no longer had a daughter. But the helplessness that overwhelmed her now was the worst. Malpractice? She could see it coming a mile away. Yet it was more than that. Much more.

She did the only thing she knew to do. She bluffed with every grain of energy in her entire body. She took the necessary steps until she stood nose to nose with the hefty detective, and for once in her life, she was glad for her six feet; it made her taller than he was!

"I'm not talking to you anymore," she declared through gritted teeth. "I'm not talking to anyone. I'm walking out that door, and you're going to have to shoot to stop me."

"Ma'am, you're making a mistake."

"Mistake!" she shrieked, past caring. "*You're* the one who's making the mistake, sir!"

Even as she cried the words Brittany could feel the futility pressing heavily upon her scalp. She reeled slightly. How simple it was. Perfect, absolutely perfect. The policemen had accidentally let the boy die, just as she had warned them he might, now they were liable, and they needed a way out. A scapegoat.

"Am I under arrest?" she asked tightly.

His expression said that her naiveté was a complication he could do without. "Lady, you're not charged with a damn thing."

She curled the sides of her mouth. "Then I'll tell you something, Detective, since I'm not being charged with a 'damn thing.' If that young man who died this morning hadn't been the son of a federal judge, your officers wouldn't be desperate for a patsy. If that boy's name hadn't been Wade, I wouldn't be here. You're out on a head hunt now, Detective Bowles. There are boys where I live who could be lying on a slab at the morgue, and everyone would be saying that they got what was coming to them. I see these boys every day, and no one gives a rip about what happens to them—whether they're hot or cold or hungry or scared. Well, I care, and I'm not going to stand by and watch years of work go down the tubes. So you either arrest me, or take your hands off. But if you arrest me, you better have a damn good case because I'll fight you down to the wire, Detective Bowles. I'll drive you into the ground. Now, please excuse me, sir! I have more worthwhile things to do than argue with someone who's proved me guilty *without benefit of a trial*!"

Drained, defeated, desperate, Brittany feared she'd waited too long and said far too much. She wanted to get away from the insanity of it all now.

"And you can tell your famous Lieutenant Paprika or whatever his name is," she added as a final gritty thrust, "that I'm not coming back down here. If he doesn't know how to use the telephone, he can take his bloody 'discrepancies' and . . . stick 'em in his stupid ear!"

Brittany whirled around and stared, dumbfounded, at the portal of the office door. Its space was filled by a man—a tall, striking, self-contained man whose expression wavered somewhere between amused mockery and anger, a man who she knew, without a shred of doubt, was Lieutenant Hamilton Curry III.

Chapter Four

He could have been a renegade riverboat gambler passing himself off as a gentleman. Or next year's candidate for state senator. Or both.

Hamilton Curry's scowl, Brittany thought, suggested a major impatience with fools. As did his stance with his feet planted strongly apart. The height of his forehead revealed a superior intelligence, and the breadth of his shoulders showed a fondness for athletics. The look in his eye was that of a man who thrived on competition, on being at the center of things.

Tough? Definitely. The lines in his face left no doubt. She couldn't imagine anyone else turning such ridiculous hair into an asset as he did. His eyes were the most striking thing about him: as blue as water rushing over stones, their yes meaning yes and their no meaning no. Eyes like that would never lie. They would never divulge secrets. And they would never give in.

All her best self-justifications settled to the bottom of her chest like a rock. "Excuse me," she mumbled and wondered ludicrously if she could save herself by fainting. "I was just leaving."

He remained in her path like a force field. "*You* are Dr. Brittany Schellenegger?"

With a superhuman effort, she arched her brows and peered loftily down the bridge of her nose. "You don't mean to tell me, Lieutenant Curry, that there's something you don't know?"

His look was enough to warp steel. Without relinquishing one millimeter of her with his eyes, he said to the man standing beside him, "Correct me if I'm wrong, Bowles, but I think I sense trouble upon the horizon."

"It wouldn't surprise me a bit, sir," Bowles dryly replied.

"I always said this would happen when you didn't maintain a gestapo."

"People just up and say anything they want to, sir."

"Social deterioration, Bowles. This world is going to the dogs."

The detective, amazingly amicable now, shook his head with comic woefulness.

If, in that moment, she had had a gun in her hand, Brittany thought she could happily have shot them both. They thought this was all some kind of huge joke. They thought she could be cajoled into being all sweet and docile and cooperative. Imbeciles, both of them!

As gracefully as a dancer, Hammer Curry ambled to Bowles's desk and picked up her statement, skimming it as he talked.

"You're right, Doctor," he agreed and glanced up to flash her a smile. "I do know who you are. Actually, you've been the center of my entire day in one way or another."

She swore she would kill herself if she responded to that smile. "I'm afraid I don't find that fact particularly comforting, Lieutenant Curry."

He chuckled. "And what you're thinking is true." He continued to read Bowles's account as he talked. "I keep asking myself what you hope to gain by lying. It isn't a criminal offense for someone to die in a doctor's office, you know."

"Gerald Wade didn't—"

"In fact, we wouldn't have any problem at all if the statements agreed, and that's the truth."

"The problem—"

"It is, however—" he stopped her with perilous blue eyes "—a criminal offense to lie under oath."

Brittany slumped dejectedly. "I think I know what's criminal and what's not, Lieutenant Curry."

"Good!" He laid a hand upon the trimness of his waist, as if satisfied at last. "And I hope you know what obstruction of justice is, too, Doctor. It'll save us all no end of time."

She certainly knew what a no-win situation was! With grim tenacity, Brittany moved toward the door before her knees betrayed her and she really did faint.

When he was only barely in her line of vision, she saw him waving the statement. "Are you sure you wouldn't like to amend this, Dr. Schellenegger?"

No, she would not like to amend it. She would not like to stay in this office any longer. She would not like to match wits with this terrible man, and she didn't at all like the fact that she'd come off looking like an incompetent when she had probably done more for Gerald Wade than anyone else could have under the circumstances.

"Not by so much as a period," she snapped.

"Ahhh." He thoughtfully tapped the end of his nose with the paper. "That's too bad. I was hoping—"

"It's unhealthy to hope too much, Lieutenant Curry." She paused in the doorway. "Please excuse me."

After his interview with Sybil, Hammer had thought he had Brittany Schellenegger at least halfway pegged. It would have been vastly more convenient if she had stayed that way—the tight-lipped spinster who looked like his seventh-grade homeroom teacher.

But she had turned out to be a strikingly lovely young woman caught in a situation for which she had no expertise, and her charming dirndl skirt and loose full-sleeved peasant blouse reminded him of beachcombing on a lazy Saturday morning. At the same time, it gave off unmistakable vibes: *Don't see me as rich or having sex appeal.*

How silly—the sex appeal part. The more she tried to disguise it, the more it showed. Her luscious hair was a half-dozen shades of red and gold that made him envision himself burying his hands in it. And her eyes? He wasn't sure what shade of green they were; they kept changing—at the moment sort of mossy, but they'd changed twice since he'd walked into the room.

Looking at her now, past her magnificent height and her dynamic anger, he could imagine the toothy and leggy, awkward colt she must have been as a girl. Perhaps that was part of the problem; the ugly duckling had turned into a striking swan, hadn't she? Perhaps the swan and her gorgeous mother had vied for the love of the same man, and Lilith had lost.

But that didn't really ring true. She seemed too proud to fight over a mere man. But what besides love was strong enough to create such a publicized schism between mother and daughter?

And there were his instincts, which were rarely wrong. Brittany Schellenegger did possess some dark, menacing secret, all right. Something was buried beneath her icy femininity that was much out of the common order of things, but aside from his strange need to take her into his arms and thaw that ice—the eternal male challenge: a good man could bring you off that, lady!—he felt nothing to warrant any suspicions.

When she reached the office area where one could see into half-glassed conference rooms and niches and carrels and desks crammed back-to-back, he called after her in his best official voice. "Oh, there was one more thing, Doctor...."

A number of people glanced up from computer terminals and typewriters. Some curiously covered the receivers of telephones. Brittany Schellenegger arranged her face in a smile that had to come straight from Lilith Garamond's famous genes.

"Oh, come on," she countered, her tone dripping honey, "I thought you were supposed to be one of the good guys, Lieutenant."

Hammer's smile felt silly. "Well, ordinarily I would be, but as you can see, a white hat wouldn't match my jacket."

Her expression was suddenly as cold as marble. "That leaves you no choice, then."

"How so?"

Her eyebrows lifted regally. "You'll have to torture me."

Brittany guessed, when she saw the grimness of Hammer Curry's smile, that he had been giving that possibility some thought already. He took several menacing steps toward her, and the lines at the edges of his eyes tightened.

"Am I to assume, then," he asked slowly, "that you have no intention of amending this?"

Though it took all the courage she possessed and every shred of drama she had learned in her lifetime, Brittany

threw back her head and brushed a clinging ringlet of hair
from her cheek.

She flashed him a sudden smile and tipped her head.
"Oh, all right. I give up. You've got me, Lieutenant, fair
and square. I guess I have no choice but to make a full
confession."

The silence wasn't really a silence at all but the hiss of a
fuse racing to a keg of dynamite.

With a flick of his fingers, Hammer Curry motioned to
Bowles to see to the machine on his desk. Turning, touch-
ing the knot of his tie, he said guardedly, "Carry on,
Doctor."

So badly was Brittany quaking that she had to wipe her
palms on the sides of her skirt. But, wetting her lips, she
arranged herself so she addressed the machine. She hadn't
the faintest notion of what to say into it. She knew only that
she wanted to make as big a fool of him as he was making
of her.

She cleared her throat and smoothed the waistband of her
skirt. Taking a deep breath, she said, "My full name is
Brittany Cecille Schellenegger." Hesitating, she tipped her
head in Hammer Curry's direction, innocence ludicrously
large on her face. "I don't take any credit for that name. My
mother is French, you see, and my father lacked imagination."

His scowl was deadly. Oh, God! Brittany concentrated
shakily on the tape recorder. Oh, God!

"When I was eighteen," she said, "my grandfather died.
His name was Sigmund Schellenegger. I was more surprised than anyone to learn he had made me his heir. I
thought there'd been some terrible mistake. I'm still not sure
there wasn't. Grief, I didn't even get a lawyer."

"Ahem!"

She shot the lieutenant a startled glance. "I'm sure there's a point to all this," he said with saccharine patience. "Somewhere."

"You have to understand the kind of man my grandfather was," she objected tartly.

"I'm trying to, dear."

Bastard! She would never intimidate this man! She gave him an expression that was much more honest. "Listen, you're not interested in all the sordid details. Why don't we just give up?"

His smile was terrifying as he moved closer. His voice was a sandpapery rumble. "I might be interested . . . Doctor."

Was his macho posture a technique he used on all the women he questioned? Or just her?

Brittany threw back her head, determined to see it through now that she'd started it. "Well, a person at least has the right to an opinion about the things he's forced to bear, doesn't he?"

"What?" Confusion filtered momentarily across his face.

"That's why Grandpapa—Sigmund—made his will the way he did. Dammit, Lieutenant, it was *his* money, he had the right to do anything he wanted to with it."

"Money?" His squint conveyed a distinct bafflement.

"Oh, that's what this is all about, and you know it. Bottom line equals money. Well, the terms of Sigmund's will didn't set too well with dear Mummy and Daddy, and they made their opinion known around town. Almost everyone in New Orleans bears me a grudge, sight unseen. It's inevitable. I'm the poor little rich girl, don't you know? Even Detective Bowles isn't immune to it. You aren't immune to it either, Lieutenant."

Hammer took a step to the recorder and slammed his fist angrily upon the stop button. The tray containing paperclips skittered across the surface of the desk and slammed against a vase. Now he saw her tactic. She'd been playing him out on a line, like a prize trout.

He ground out his words. "In case you don't take this seriously, Dr. Schell—"

"Wait!" She threw out a splayed hand, as furious as he now. "That's not all I want to say."

"Say it then, woman!"

Brittany unconsciously drew her bag to her bosom and hugged it. "When you had me brought down here," she continued, speaking to him now as to a man, any man, "I didn't know what this was all about. I thought you really did want my help about Gerald Wade. But I learned you were trying to trick me into saying something that didn't happen, Lieutenant. You don't want a statement from me: you want a patsy. 'Well, what could it hurt? She's got all that money. She can get some fancy lawyers and won't even feel the pain.' But I do feel the pain, Lieutenant. Why don't you get someone else?"

A woman in uniform passed the door: Marie Trudeau, her nameplate said. Her glance inside the office was a mixture of curiosity and feminine commiseration, and Brittany wished she dared follow Marie.

Through his teeth, he said menacingly, "Such nasty words coming out of such a nice mouth, Doctor."

"Nice?" she cried. "You don't know what nice is. Have you asked yourself why on earth I would want to lie about Gerald Wade? For fear of being sued? I can afford to be sued, Lieutenant Curry. I can afford anything I want. I can afford the best lawyers this city has to offer. I can afford the best lawyers this *state* has to offer!"

The whole ground floor of the building seemed to grow as quiet as a crypt. Brittany imagined ears pressed to walls and fingers held to lips.

Her throat constricted, and she compelled herself to finish what she'd started. "I can also afford to sue the pants off you and the city of New Orleans," she added coldly. "I could charge you with false arrest, Lieutenant Curry. I could buy myself a newspaper and ruin you. I'm telling you the truth."

She couldn't believe what she was saying, and she irrationally wanted to reach up and touch the angry lines marking Hammer Curry's face. She wanted to smooth them away and murmur that she didn't mean any of what she'd yelled at him.

"You have not been arrested," he snarled.

So much for sweet caresses! She twisted her face into a look of mock shock. "Defamation of character, then."

"Your character has not been defamed."

"Harassment!" she cried and flushed, for she was presently doing most of the harassing. "Mental duress!"

Oh, she wished she'd never begun this! She wished she could run away, but all she could do was stand perfectly still while he circled her like a wolf moving in for the kill.

"You know, Bowles," he said with malicious shrewdness as he folded his arms across his chest until his silk jacket was strained to the limits across the shoulders, "I think the good doctor could use a bandwagon to climb onto."

Brittany narrowed her eyes to slits of green. "And I think I just marked you off my list of people I'd like to know!"

Grinning, he lowered his arms, as if her outburst was proof enough. "I'm crushed."

"Besides," she mumbled lamely, "I cooperated with Detective Bowles."

"Then cooperate with me."

It wasn't the mockery smothered in his words as he turned away—though it was there, ridiculing her with its confidence and expertise—it was his sex appeal. It was not an

assumed trait found in his eyes or words or his body, but
something deep inside his genes, an aura, an utterly internal quality that Brittany found staggeringly magnetic. This
man whom she was battering with her words was a good
man, an honest man. It had been a long time since she'd
been around someone who attracted her with their goodness as well as their masculinity, and she didn't want to ad-
mire him or respect what he did or what he was. She didn't
want to wonder if, under other circumstances . . .

She told herself to start walking and not to stop until she
was in the street. What could he do if she left? Shoot her in
the back?

She could almost hear the hammer cocking as she stepped
across the threshold of Bowles's door. Tears were stinging
her eyelids, yet she forced her head to remain erect, her
shoulders to stay back. And if it hadn't been for the ele-
ments outside—an act of God, some would have called it—
she would probably have pulled off her grand exit.

At the precise moment when she moved out among the
offices, a huge ball of fire literally shot out of the sky—like
something a cartoonist would sketch, an angry Zeus hurling lightning bolts toward earth. A flash of flame was followed by a peal of thunder that rocked the building to its
foundations. Some of the front windows shattered out into
the sidewalk.

Later she would learn that such occurrences weren't un-
common when the environment and the pressure were right;
electrical storms had been brewing around New Orleans for
the past three weeks. But as an anticlimax to her confron-
tation with Hammer Curry, it was horrifying.

She jerked back toward him with a naked expression:
*Please don't take this the wrong way. I'm just making sure
you're still there.*

I know, his eyes telegraphed kindly. *It scared me too, and I am here.*

"Jesus!" Leonard Bowles lunged away from the wall where he slouched, and he strode into the doorway, his expression one of disbelief.

Hammer Curry, though he moved more slowly, followed him. A hush had fallen upon the entire office area, and people waited with almost comic expectancy for more to follow. When nothing did, they looked at each other and laughed nervously.

"You see, Doctor?" he murmured huskily from behind Brittany's left shoulder, "even heaven thinks you should stay."

Something white-hot touched the ends of Brittany's nerves. Without thinking, she looked up at the line of his jaw and gasped, "Are you sure that heaven didn't catch a whiff of something rotten in your precinct?"

His laughter, when he tipped back his head and let the merriment ripple out of him like music, was magnificent— a deep-from-the-gut Tommy-Lee-Jones laugh that cut through all the superficiality. Somehow, some way, he'd slipped past her defenses, and Brittany wondered, before she could slam the door of her heart shut and brace it with timbers, what it would be like to smile and slip her arms around this man's waist and lean her cheek contentedly against his chest, to close her eyes and to sigh and rest for just one tiny moment in the safe sunshine of such a laugh.

"I'm afraid," he said, his blue eyes dancing as he tried to smother his mirth by degrees, "that what heaven smells is my luck, Dr. Schellenegger. I left my car windows down."

"Oh, great," mumbled Bowles, oblivious to anything now but his search through his pockets for his car keys. "I think I did, too."

"Well, get mine while you're at it."

She must go. The reasons were too complex to understand, but Brittany knew she had to get away. Her life depended upon it.

"I'm not planning to leave the city, Lieutenant Curry," she said quickly. "You can reach me at home if it's necessary for us to speak again. God forbid it should be. Good day, Lieutenant Curry."

By the time she finished delivering her speech, she was moving away, and her soft skirt was swirling in and out between her legs. Hammer appreciated the flexibility of her waist and the strong, assertive bones of her pelvis that created fascinating ridges on each side of her belly.

But she couldn't walk out of his life like this. Quickly he said, "Then would you do us the favor of signing your statement, Doctor?"

Before he could step forward and give her the paper, she spun on her heels and walked back. With anger flashing from her eyes, she snatched the statement from his hand and slammed it to the outside wall of the office and, holding it there with one hand, dug around in her bag for a pen.

He lamely offered her one, but she furiously disdained it. After a pause during which half the precinct seemed to take a second look, she found the pen, scrawled an unreadable tangle of marks across the bottom of the page, then shoved it at his chest.

Her eyes were a blaze of brilliant, fiery emerald. Hammer compressed his lips, gazed at the paper and laughed briefly. "*This* is your name?"

She jerked the statement from his hand, scrutinized it and once again searched at length through her bag. This time she fished out a pair of reading glasses, minus any kind of case, and poked them onto her face. Once again she scrutinized the paper then slammed it to the wall. She flamboyantly crossed a *t*.

Patrick Gilbert was stepping out of an office as the farce was taking place. Spotting him, she thrust the statement into his hands.

"Can you read this?" she demanded.

Patrick, with a silly shrug at Hammer, seemed only too eager to help out. He studied the handwriting, then studied her. "Oh, yes, ma'am," he said enthusiastically as he grinned.

"Thank you." She withered Hammer with a look.

"I've taken a course in calligraphy," Patrick went on energetically to explain. "You see this little curl right here?"

"Patrick," Hammer tried to interrupt.

"That means—"

"Detective Gilbert!"

The younger man's brilliant blush would have stopped traffic. "Yes, sir?"

"Detective Gilbert—" Hammer forced a smile through his strained patience "—perhaps you would be so kind as to type the doctor's name beneath her signature."

"Of course, sir."

With near-comical obedience, Patrick accepted the paper and marched briskly into the office where Bowles's decrepit typewriter hunched on the desk. As the keys clattered, Hammer and Brittany stood glaring at each other.

When Patrick returned, Hammer privately promised himself that if the upstart clicked his heels he'd have his badge on the spot. Patrick neither clicked his heels nor saluted, and Hammer looked at the statement without seeing a single word of it. When she asked him if he was satisfied, he dipped his head in a sullen dismissal.

"That," he said testily, "is all, Doctor."

"Thank you, Lieutenant."

"Thank *you*."

"You're quite welcome."

He did insert a small nod at this point.

"Good." She gave him a nod equally meaningless.

"Yes, well..."

Brittany felt like Pavlov's dog. Lilith Garamond, if she had been brought downtown to give a statement to the New Orleans Police Department, would never have given an inch. Lilith would have created a national incident first. She would have thrown back her head like an abbess and had all the officials down on their hands and knees groveling with apologies. Which was why she was Lilith Garamond, and Brittany was the disappointment.

Submerged in a cloud of self-pity, Brittany desperately closed the distance between herself and the outside doors of the precinct house. It seemed like miles.

Now, of course, she could think of a dozen magnificently clever things to say. Oh, yes. If she could do it all over again, she would be Joan of Arc, champion of the downtrodden. She would bring Hamilton Curry to his knees!

When she was twenty feet from the doors, her compulsion to flee was suddenly too much. She didn't look over her shoulder as she gripped her bag and lunged for the wide steel bar spanning the door.

Too late, she saw someone doing the same thing—a fleeting movement from a corridor that she hadn't noticed was there. And then a hand was coming down powerfully upon her own, and her momentum was throwing her against a silk-covered arm until her breasts were crushed against it.

She gaped mindlessly at her own bosom pressed to a man's wrist. She couldn't move. Then she jerked up her head, her green eyes liquid with fright.

"Where did you come from?" she gasped.

His smile touched a dozen different parts of her. "I materialized. It's a talent I have. I can also transform myself into a wolf or a bat."

Her courage began to wilt. "Please—"

"If you fight me," he warned with a chuckle, "I'll bite your neck." Squinting, he leaned nearer, and Brittany swore he memorized every pore of her skin. "Has a man ever told you, Dr. Schellenegger, that it's disconcerting to look straight across into a woman's eyes on the same level as your own? There's nothing wrong with it, though. Actually, it's quite nice. Actually, I like it."

Which broke the spell, naturally, as he had meant it to do. Brittany drew on her best armor and prepared for war.

"If I hadn't just happened to leave my wooden stake in my other purse, Lieutenant Curry," she said through a deadly smile, "I'd drive it into your vile heart."

He laughed, and she felt his aura engulfing her again, casting an irresistible spell.

"And if you think I doubt your ability to do it, you're wrong. No, the truth is, Doctor, I made that up. I can't really change myself into a wolf. I don't know why I say things like that."

What charm! His combination of grin and grimace was virtually hypnotic. He must have a whole string of women who sat at home waiting for their telephones to ring.

"Then please list your reasons for following me in order of importance," she mumbled, "and get out of the way."

"One, to take you home," he said and rolled his eyes drolly upward. "Two, to find out why I like you in spite of the fact that you're obviously going to be difficult about it. Three, to humiliate myself before you in this revolting manner."

Brittany had to literally brace herself against the warmth that his teasing triggered. It spread over her like sunshine, and just because he looked all-American with that haircut and that wicked tan, and just because his eyes squinched at the corners when he laughed...

She said, just to let him know that she was no one's pushover, "I find all this friendship highly unethical, Lieutenant. I'm your main suspect, remember. Criminal negligence, or something on that order. Sorry. See you around."

As she was galvanized into sudden action, Hammer rehearsed a dozen reasons for turning around and walking in the opposite direction. Brittany Schellenegger was a sharp-tongued troublesome piece of baggage. *Unethical?* Dammit! He didn't need that.

She darted out into the street, and he swore an oath under his breath. A gust of wind swept up the debris from the street and hurled it against her, nearly knocking her against the building.

He took in the street in a glance—the telephone lines that were swaying and shuddering like children's swings in the wind, and pedestrians who stopped where they were and looked up in consternation at the sky. Clouds were scudding into each other and tightening into a dangerously beautiful mass overhead. The long-cursed heat wave was just about over.

"You won't get far," he yelled to her back, his words snatched by the wind. "It's going to flood."

She turned to look at him as if he were a severe disappointment. "I'm a championship swimmer, Lieutenant Curry."

Let her go, idiot! "Do you have a car?"

"I'll take a bus."

Feeling like the world's biggest jerk, Hammer started doggedly after her, and he tossed a glance over his shoulder, half expecting to find the police commissioner taking notes of the ridiculous yelling match.

She stepped off the curb, and the wind filled her big skirt like a sail. When she tried to place her back to the gusts, Hammer was reminded of the famous picture of Marilyn. He had a glimpse of deliciously long legs, firm, flashing thighs and filmy bikini panties.

"Hey, lady!" a masculine head leaned out the window of a passing car and bawled, "Great legs!"

Then the great hissing wall of rain cut him off. People began running in all directions for cover, and metallic lines of buses, taxis, trucks and cars threw on their brakes. By the time Hammer reached Brittany, they were both drenched to the skin.

"Don't be a fool!" he yelled and took her arm roughly. "Come on."

"Leave me alone!"

"You can't catch a bus in this rain!"

"Go play with your gun, Mr. Curry!"

Pulling her into the curve of his body against her will, Hammer half ran, half stumbled with her to the parking lot across the street where his unmarked car was waiting. He protected her against the downpour as best he could with his back, and she shrank into the haven of his body as he groped in his pocket for a set of keys.

Brittany guessed she knew before he did when it started happening between them, but maybe her decade of single life had attuned her more closely. Maybe being a woman made her more susceptible. Maybe the hunger for compassion made her too ready.

She was suddenly aware of his legs straining against her own and the side of his hip that pressed into the concave of her groin. In turning, his pelvis molded to hers.

She was no stranger to a man, but her expertise was that of a healthy woman to a sick male. Brittany felt as if she'd been in a prolonged state of sleep for years—a character in a science fiction movie who'd been programmed to come awake after a decade of suspension. She shivered violently.

Even if he was less swift on the uptake, Hammer knew human nature somewhat better. He glanced down at his aroused state in disbelief. Water was sluicing off his hair and into his eyes, over his cheeks, into his mouth. He blinked at her.

In those first seconds, Brittany thought he would dip his head and kiss her, and she flashed him a look that said she was too vulnerable now. He smiled and swiped at his face with the back of a hand.

He jerked open the car door with that same hand. "Get in."

She couldn't tear her eyes from his face. "I can't."

"It's okay. I don't go around biting the necks of lonely women."

"I'm not lonely!"

"Get in!"

She said, as nastily as possible because she feared her own emotions, "This is the wolf part, right?"

"No." His lips pulled back, baring his white teeth. "This is the liking-you part. Dammit, will you just get in?"

Brittany let him bundle her inside. The second they were seated, the windows steamed up, and she, with chattering teeth and shivering limbs, sat hugging herself as he slid beneath the wheel and began shrugging out of the silk jacket.

His shirt was wringing wet. His tie was dripping, and the leather of his holster was darkened with dark stains of water. He thrust the jacket at her. "Here, put this on."

She made no move to obey.

"Take it, Brittany."

His insistence was even more of an intimacy than being pressed against his body or having her thoughts read. "I'm really quite all right," she protested feebly.

His frown accused her of everything from naiveté to insanity. "There aren't any strings attached, darling," he said more gently. "Will you take the bloody jacket?"

Snatching the jacket, Brittany drew it upon the front of her body and pulled it high over her shoulders so that only her head showed over the collar. "It's not a very good fit," she mumbled inanely.

He had begun rolling the sopping cuffs of his shirt. He paused to scrutinize what he could see of her—her scrunched shoulders and her tightly pressed knees beneath her clinging skirt.

Grinning, he wiped his face dry on his sleeve. He turned so that his knee was between them on the seat. "It looks better on you than it does on me."

Brittany stared at her hands and said nothing.

"About what happened," he ventured.

She refused to look up. "Forget it."

"Now, that does surprise me."

Well, he'd asked for it. She threw the events of the whole afternoon into his face, but more than that, she threw at him the feelings they both had had. "Because I can resist it, Lieutenant?" she challenged, eyeing his revolver. "Because I can resist you?"

When he slammed both hands to the steering wheel and absorbed the impact clear into the bones of his shoulders, Brittany knew a moment of real fear. This man was not Cookie. He was not Devane. He was a man's man—a real live hot-blooded flesh-and-blood man, and he was used to having control of a situation.

She braced herself for a battery of obscenities. When they didn't come, she braced herself for his insults. When they didn't come, she slid a slow, cautious look to see what had gone wrong.

He was studying her with an oddly plaintive look on his face. Her heart skipped a beat and made her snatch a quick breath.

"I think we should start over from the beginning," he said and lifted a hand to his hair, sleeking it down toward his nose. "I hope you don't mind a short detour first. I have to pick up my kids."

Chapter Five

When Hammer married Kitty Lomand fresh out of high school in Lake Charles, Louisiana, he'd planned to be married for the rest of his life. He'd given the matter a good deal of thought. Everything was in his favor. He was an honor graduate. He came from a good family: Delbert Curry was a second-generation railroad man of sound stock. Why wouldn't some nice girl be eager to make such a catch?

But he'd returned from Southeast Asia in the early seventies to find himself divorced and the brother of a good kid in the neighborhood who'd turned bad. He inherited Richard's children, and he never saw Kitty Lomand again.

It was then that Hammer learned several hard lessons very quickly. Life as he knew it had changed. It would never go back to the way it was. Living alone wasn't the absolute worst thing in the world, and to have women friends overnight was great. But to fall in love made one vulnerable.

Once a man wanted something that much, he was already a victim.

Up until now Hammer had lived in relative peace with that philosophy. His affairs had come and gone with the passion of a healthy single male who thought women could take their liberation and let it keep them warm on cold nights. Besides, cops made terrible husbands.

Gradually he'd stopped having affairs at all. They cost time and money and precious adrenaline. By the time he was forty, neither he nor Deborah Keyes really understood how they kept breaking up and wandering back together again. It hardly seemed worth the trouble.

For those reasons, he didn't understand his strange attraction for Brittany Schellenegger. It was not only inconvenient and badly timed, but also it was unprofessional. The policeman's first commandment: thou shalt not lust after civilians in the line of duty.

He stole furtive sidelong glances at her and wondered if what Sybil said could possibly be true. He'd known some consummate liars in his day, and most of them had been women.

But when he'd made the remark about the children, her mind had been all too easy to read: *Oh, you're married and have a family,* she seemed to say as the tension about her eyes relaxed. *Well then, that puts everything into a much safer perspective, doesn't it?*

He should correct her misconception, but he was unwilling to lose the pleasure of watching her draw her arms from beneath his jacket and begin her toilette, first combing her wet hair with her fingers and arranging her wet clothes. She was innocent of knowing how provocatively her wet blouse was clinging to the planes of her back and the shadowy suggestion of her breasts. Her cheeks were wet. She blotted them dry with her hands.

"What a mess," she said, grimacing as she took stock of herself.

Grinning, Hammer shifted on the seat. "Not from where I sit."

The compliment caught her by surprise. Hammer could feel her weighing it, to see if it was proper, considering that he was now a married police lieutenant on the way to pick up his children from school.

Her features lost some of their gaunt edges. "Why, I declare, Mr. Curry," she affected a shy but friendly tease, "the age of gallantry lives on."

"A delusion of the young, I'm afraid."

She tossed her head coquettishly. "I'm not so young."

"Compared to myself, I meant."

"Oh?" Her smile hovered somewhere between Mona Lisa's and Delilah's. "Then, yes. You're very old, Lieutenant. Quite past your prime."

He tipped back his head in a laugh. "Ouch! I thought doctors were supposed to relieve pain, not cause it."

"Age is a fact of life."

"Just what I need, a fatalist."

She smiled at her hands folded primly in her lap. The interior of the car was warm now and filled with the sensual allure of her fragrance. Hammer turned down St. Charles Avenue. Innumerable drivers had pulled to the sides of the street, and the tops of trees were swaying wildly in the storm, swooping nearly to the ground. Utility wires flapped and whirred and strained to the breaking point and gutters couldn't handle the overflow.

Presently she broke the silence. "How many children do you have, Lieutenant?"

"A boy and a girl." He coughed lightly and concentrated on the street.

"Ah."

She, too, leaned forward to peer through the opaque wall as if she must help him watch. She rubbed at the condensation on the windshield.

"And you live on St. Charles," she said. "On a policeman's salary, too. Very good."

"Actually, I live on Raleigh Street. The kids go to school out here. Considerably more than I can afford, but what the heck? I can always eat after they get out of college."

She laughed. "Yes." A more solemn irony slipped into her speech, then. "Parents must see that their children get the best life has to offer, mustn't they?"

There were a number of retorts he could have made to such a loaded remark, but suddenly he didn't want to talk. He felt as if he'd stumbled upon an unknown weakness in himself, as if he subconsciously wanted to be this young woman's fool, to ruin himself for her. The thoughts of such a self-destructive streak were frightening.

"What does your wife do?" she asked with an innocent lack of preamble.

He mumbled another lie about the family making do on one income. Quickly then, to steer the sticky conversation away from himself, he said, "Your mother lives somewhere out here, doesn't she?"

Distance wrapped around her like a mist. "My mother lives out by the university. In one of the mansions by Tulane."

His reply was a long, thoughtful stare.

Her brows chided him. "I didn't take *all* the money, Lieutenant. My parents have more than they can spend for the rest of their lives."

"Hey, come on, did I ask you that?"

"You didn't have to. Ever since you first laid eyes on me, you've been wondering."

Piqued, because it was true, he divided his attention between her and the street. "Do you have any idea of the enemy you have in Sybil Wade?"

"I don't think I should talk about Sybil Wade to you."

"Would you take some advice if I gave it to you?"

She narrowed her eyes. "That depends."

"I think you should make peace with your mother."

Her laughter wasn't the kind that made a person feel good. It called to mind wasted dreams and broken hearts. She looked away. "You don't ask very much."

"Are things that irreparable?"

"Even if I would make peace, she wouldn't."

"This . . . whatever it is between Sybil and yourself might just boil down to a matter of credibility. And you have to admit, Doctor, you don't go out of your way to create a diplomatic image of yourself."

Her protest flashed back to him. "I've never been a hypocrite."

"I'm not saying you should be a hypocrite. I'm saying you shouldn't make it harder than it has to be. Mending fences with your mother will make you look good."

"For a change?" She blushed, becomingly he thought.

He laughed. "For a change."

She took some time to digest what he'd said, and she gave him a long, pondering measuring look. "I suppose your family is one of those marvelous well-balanced and emotionally healthy ones where the grandmother makes Easter eggs and everyone brings food on Christmas Eve."

"Yeah, I guess so." He smiled. "We're pretty normal. My brother's something of a pain, but other than that . . ."

"I do things with my family, too." Her tone lost its sparkle as she resumed her scrutiny of the street. "Every October I go to Vienna and meet with the board of Schellenegger Enterprises. My father meets me at Sacher's, and we have coffee and pretend to like each other. It's not particularly good, but I guess it's not bad."

"I'm sorry, Brittany."

She flinched, as if his use of her name pained her. "It's not your fault." Shrugging, she reached up to pull at a tendril of hair that framed her cheek. "I don't know whose fault it is."

"Maybe it's Sybil's."

She drew her brows together, then she tipped her head to the side and laughed. It was a laugh that Hammer found utterly irresistible—a slow, deep-throated disillusionment that hinted at a much more complex woman beneath what he had seen so far. He wanted badly to know that woman.

"If you don't stop making remarks like that, Lieutenant," she said, "I'm going to get the idea that you believe I'm a little bit innocent."

"Did I say I thought you were guilty?"

"You didn't have to."

"Well, if it's any consolation, I'm keeping an open mind." He chuckled.

"I don't want an open mind," she said with a sudden startling gravity. "I want..." She looked down at her lap and gathered the folds of her skirt tightly about her knees.

Finish! Hammer wanted to yell at her. *Say you want me to believe in you!*

But she reached into her handbag and took out a pair of dark glasses even though the sun seemed lost forever. He debated about telling her what Sybil had said.

"Brittany, why would Sybil Wade make the statement that you have always wanted revenge upon her?"

She didn't reply. She hardly even moved.

He cleared his throat. "At the risk of leading you to believe I'm pumping you for information, would you just answer the question?"

Her shrug was mistrustful and afraid. Well, hell, he thought. Maybe Sybil was right. Brittany was a misfit. The girl, the woman in her had a deep psychological need.

But didn't everyone? Really? The question was, then—and this was what he'd been driving toward all afternoon—was that psychological need threatening enough that Brittany would lie about Gerald Wade? Was she so insecure about her place in the world that she would commit perjury and obstruct justice? Would she deliberately let a boy die?

When he reached over and pulled off the dark glasses, she fixed him with a sad, unchallenging look.

"It was a long time ago," she said. "Actually, it didn't even happen in this country. We were in Vienna at the time. What happened was one of the reasons my grandfather left his fortune to me instead of my father and Lilith. He was very old by then, you see, and he didn't have the strength to force them to listen, to stand up and knock them down if he had to. The money was the only weapon he had."

"Weapon for what?"

"To protest against a life-style he didn't approve of, I guess, though that seems outdated now. You have to understand that the four of them—my mother and father, Sybil and Fleming Wade—were inseparable in those days. Sybil and Fleming were as much my family as anyone. I was taught to call them 'Aunt Sybil' and 'Uncle Fleming.' They weren't all mature and decorous like they are now, you understand—younger, in the process of sowing their wild oats."

She grew wistful for a moment, and Hammer gently prompted her. "What wild oats?"

Her finger idly followed a seam in her skirt. "I was too young then to appreciate the impressive man that Fleming Wade must have been. And my own father—well, he was brilliant and sophisticated and charming. He knew how to deal with the officials of foreign countries and bankers and jewelers and waiters and the most difficult concierge. The four of them, along with my nanny and me, traveled all over Europe, the Riviera. Nothing but the best for Mummy and Daddy. The four of them attracted attention everywhere they went, and they spent money like water. Parties and yachts and lots of scandal.''

She glanced up, her mouth twisted prettily down at one side. ''Those were the days when this country would blacklist you just for having a child out of wedlock. And especially here—the *Vieux Carré*, with its strict, conservative ways. Sybil's family went back for generations and generations. It was whispered that she was getting a reputation abroad.''

A long line of traffic had forced them to stop. The thunder and the rain upon the roof and the hood almost drowned out her words. Her nerves seemed stretched very thin now, Hammer thought.

He raked at his upper lip with his teeth. ''Are you inferring that this four-sided friendship was mutually... sexual?''

Her shoulders drooped. ''To an outsider, it was probably difficult to tell who was married to whom. One time I barged into my parents' bedroom—I don't even remember why—and Sybil and my father were in bed.''

''Jesus,'' Hammer said under his breath as his foot touched the accelerator once more. ''And your mother? Did Lilith know?''

Her laughter was bitter and pitiless. ''I can only assume that she was in her bed with Fleming. She's never forgiven me for knowing.''

Hammer was caught in the middle of two conflicting claims. Her story made sense to him. But she would be less than human if she didn't want to make Sybil Wade pay her dues. Maybe it *was* true. She certainly had motive enough. Maybe Brittany didn't even realize how much she wanted revenge upon Sybil Wade.

The telling of the story had drained the color out of her face. She gazed out the window again, the strong, assertive woman having retreated somewhere inside the complex network of her facades. A truck was stalled sideways in the street, and he was forced to back up and go around it. She had crossed her arms over her waist, and the damp cotton of her blouse was drawn tautly over her breasts. He could see their small, firm swells, their budded nipples, even the paleness of her skin, the delicate freckles, the caressable slopes of soft curves—half girl, half woman.

She seemed to sense the desire in him, and she jerked away. Presently, though, their looks fenced with each other again. This time the ground had already been broken and the awareness already established. The engine rumbled and traffic waited. He leaned over and clasped her jaws in his palm.

Surprisingly, she didn't shrink from his advance. Several wisps of her hair were blowing gently about her face. He wanted terribly to brush them back.

Kiss her, his senses clamored. *Whether you trust her or not. Get it done with.*

"I'm not married," he bluntly admitted. "I'm divorced. And the children aren't mine. They belong to my brother. I've had them four years."

Disbelief flared to emerald life in her eyes, but she still didn't strike his hand away. She had only the dazed look of a victim who realizes she's in trouble but doesn't yet know how badly.

"Why, then?" she whispered.

Releasing her, Hammer shook his head and moved the car along in traffic. "I don't know. Why did you tell me about Sybil and your father?"

"I don't know," she whispered, lifting her hand to shield her mouth and turning so that he could see no more than a profile.

But they both knew the answer. Hammer knew they were both standing over Pandora's box and that to do anything except walk away was to invite disaster. Brittany knew that the forces they would unleash, once they were out in the open, would be radioactive and irrevocable.

Hammer wished he was thirty years old again. He wished he could possess Brittany Schellenegger with no questions asked for one hour. He would change the world.

When Hammer Curry carefully nosed his car beneath the wide red-tiled roof of the school's canopy, Brittany didn't have to read the sign attached to the austere Edwardian brick exterior: John James Elementary School, Private. This elite building was as familiar as her own apartment. She had gone to school here herself, and it had hardly changed at all in those years.

School hours were over now, but Wednesday, as she recalled, was the day for band rehearsal. Hammer squeezed his car into the parking area alongside a dozen or so other waiting parents. He signaled offhandedly to someone in another car, and hardly had he killed the engine than the double doors beneath a pillared portico opened.

A medley of bright yellow slickers flashed through the gray rain like twinkling fireflies. Hugging instrument cases and backpacks, the children skittered along the open canopy to the parking area, screaming goodbye to their friends with arms and legs flying.

"You really take this fatherhood thing seriously, don't you?" Brittany asked.

He seemed eager to talk about his children. "My parents help out a lot on the school bills," he confessed with a fond smile. "Actually, they would have taken the children when Richard skipped out, but I couldn't let them. They've paid their dues. They deserve a rest."

He also took his parents seriously, she noticed with a deepening respect. "You feel that guilty, huh?" she quipped to cover up.

The lines beside his eyes crinkled. "I was a model son. Richard, however, was a rat. Still is."

"I went to school here," she said quickly. *If you had a wife, she would be doing this. I... she would have brought the station wagon to pick up the children. She would chauffeur them around, then rush home to prepare dinner.*

Surprise was open on his face. "You're kidding."

"Don't look so surprised," she chattered nervously. "I do have *some* balance in my past."

"What you have, Brittany Schellenegger," he mused and slid his hand along the back of the seat, calculating the distance between his fingers and her shoulder like a teenager at a drive-in movie, "is a nasty mean streak."

Other parents, wet and irritable, were climbing out to place instruments into the trunks of cars and to herd children into back seats. When a girl of approximately eight and a boy some two years older dashed up to Hammer's car, he swung out into the rain without hesitation.

The children fell into the back seat, armed with a clarinet case and a French horn. "I thought Jared's mom was going to take us home," the girl said.

"I changed my mind," Hammer told her with a sharp, guilty look at Brittany.

Brittany smothered a smile. Why, the wily villain!

Muddy droplets splashed on the carpet of the car, but Hammer didn't scold. He swiveled around and leaned over the back seat to help them settle, the muscles and springs of his length perfectly coordinated to push and pull and make adjustments.

A deep yearning settled in Brittany as she watched his large hands deal gently with the girl. When she couldn't climb in as quickly as her brother, dropping her bright vinyl bag in the process, Brittany reached back to help, too. It felt good, brushing hands and shoulders with Hammer Curry in something as mundane as settling two children.

"My teacher said I talk too much," the girl cheerfully announced as they picked up dropped books and tried to get the umbrella shut. "He said if I don't learn discipline, he'd be..." She questioned her brother with wide blue eyes. "What did he say?"

"He'll be forced to take action, *nerdo*," the boy supplied with a disparaging groan.

"He hurt my feelings," she concluded with a sniff for Hammer. "He's a mean man. He broke my heart."

Hammer tipped back his head in a laugh that captured Brittany's senses all over again. "I'll break the man's kneecaps, if he tries," he promised and seemed not the slightest bit self-conscious about retucking her little top into her pants where it had pulled free and giving a tug on a loose tendril of hair.

Oh, Lord! Brittany swiveled around to stare blindly at the streaming windshield. Why couldn't Hammer have been an awkward father who was making a mess of everything? Why couldn't he be superficial and shallow? Why couldn't he try too hard?

"Hey, Hammer." The boy leaned forward and braced his elbows on the back of the front seat. "We're gonna take a band trip."

"Yes," his sister chimed in. "And we have to raise money."

Groaning with pretended agony, Hammer turned and fit his long legs beneath the steering wheel and unconsciously adjusted his trousers where they cut into his crotch.

The girl giggled. "We're gonna sell candy, Hammer. Your favorite kind. The kind that makes you fat."

"Cruel child." Hammer rolled his eyes at Brittany.

"Oh, he don't care about that, stupid," the boy scolded his sibling.

"*Doesn't* care, Craig," Hammer calmly corrected and started the car with a roar.

"I know that," yelped Alice and plopped her clarinet case emphatically upon her lap. "I'm not stupid."

"Of course, you're not," Hammer said.

Craig was absorbed with more practical matters. "We gotta raise eight hundred dollars by next March. If we can't raise it, you gotta pay." And, indicating Brittany, he asked, "Who's she?"

Hammer grinned. "Brittany Schellenegger. And be nice—she's a doctor."

Screwing up her pretty face, Alice revealed a mouth full of missing teeth. "All the doctors in our book at school are men."

"That's why you have eyes and ears along with your books." To Brittany, Hammer confided, as if it were a secret, "The rude one is Craig. The one with no teeth is Alice."

All her life Brittany had picked up on the reverberations of love such as this—a rational, unartificial, unshakable commitment. All her life she had coveted it until, in desperation, she had turned to John Gallois who, as disturbed as he obviously was, at least soothed part of the hunger. Now, after believing that envy was safely behind her, she found herself once again on the outside looking in. She felt as if she were in a country where she didn't speak the language. She hated it.

She huddled against her door and tried to shut it out, but Hammer's silence tapped her on the shoulder. When she refused to look at him, he said, "You didn't really go to John James, did you?" Which meant *It's okay. I'm still here.*

She smiled at him like a robot. "Yes, I did, for years."

"I didn't think you really meant it."

Alice, bringing her toothless smile nearer, leaned over the back of the seat near Brittany. Before Brittany realized it, she was reaching out to arrange a tress of fallen hair. She asked the girl, "Does the door by the gym still have the three steel bars across the window?"

Even Craig's attention was caught. He lunged forward. "Hey, yeah. It does. Why?"

Brittany laughed. "I'm the reason why."

"What d'you mean?" Alice asked.

Pushing up her sleeve, aware of Hammer's approving eyes, Brittany showed them a three-inch scar in the smooth flesh between her wrist and elbow. "One day I shoved my hand through the bottom glass. The next day the maintenance man was busy installing the bars."

"Wow," Craig breathed, enormously impressed. "Hey, I've got a scar. Wanna see?"

"Craig," Hammer cautioned, "I think Dr. Schellenegger knows what an appendectomy looks like."

"Oh," the boy said, unperturbed as he threw his feet up against the back window and resumed his argument with his sister.

When Hammer pulled into a driveway and pressed the button on a remote control so that a garage door rose, he drove the car into a neatly organized two-car stall. The in-

stant he turned the key in the ignition, both children tumbled out with a maximum of noise and bedlam and raced for
the back door.

Twisting on the seat so that his hand lay casually between them, faintly brushing the side of her thigh, he suddenly cleared the air. "To say how well that went would be
an anticlimax," he murmured. "Will you come in?"

Brittany was too aware of the nearness of his hand. It
would have been better if he'd taken hold of her, then she
could have resisted.

"I can't," she whispered lamely. "I shouldn't."

"Why not?"

She focused on his teeth glistening between his parted lips.
How would it be to be overpowered by that strong, sensual
mouth? Have everything taken out of her hands so she
didn't have to feel blame later?

It was a dangerous thought. She looked quickly around
at the garage. It was a work of art, like an advertisement in
Popular Mechanics with its rows of baby food jars filled
with nuts and bolts and screws and washers. A pegboard
extended the width of one wall with all the tools hanging on
their neatly specified hooks.

Sitting in the second stall was a car that she had to guess
was a 1957 Chevrolet—one of the models that young men
give their eyeteeth to collect and restore. The years of tender loving care were evident in the lacquered red shine and
the rolled and pleated upholstery. It must have taken Hammer years to find the original pieces of chrome and the
steering wheel, the lovely dashboard.

"I suppose this makes you the natural envy of the com-
munity," she said.

He didn't reply, and instead laid his hand upon the top of
her leg with a suggestion that an idiot could not have mis-
construed, and it was the mistake Brittany had been wait-

ing for. She jerked up her head, eyes flashing with
accusation, as if she had known all along that it would come
to this.

"Now, don't you look at me like that," he warned and
leaned so near that the male smell of him assaulted the hollow of her emotions. "You know, and I know—"

As his other hand found her shoulder and turned her
around, drawing her ever closer, Brittany heard her own
breath growing harsh and rough. She didn't resist or push
him away but let her head snap back on its axis.

Her words, when she got them out, sounded as if she'd
had too much to drink. "So you're going to kiss me now?
Hm? Mr. Police Lieutenant? You're going to make the big
move now?"

It was an outrageously bitter thing to say. With his head
bent low over hers and his mouth within an inch of her own,
he froze.

"Oh, you'd like for me to, wouldn't you?" he said, his
smile more knowing now as he moved his eyes over every
feature of her face, searching for her very thoughts. "You'd
like for it to be taken out of your hands so you could enjoy
it and then blame me?"

"You're crazy."

He shook his head. "Not good enough." He dropped one
palm to the arched curve of her throat and touched his lips
to the other side where her pulse throbbed violently.

"Tell me not to do this, then," he whispered. "Tell me
you hate it."

She had lifted both hands to his chest, and she couldn't
even gather the resistance to push him away. He flicked the
tip of his tongue over the lobe of her ear. She felt her own
fingertips betraying her by melting against the rippling
muscles beneath his shirt.

"I don't hear you," he muttered, his own voice distorted now by the heat that was generating between them. He closed his teeth onto the tiny lobe. "What did you say?"

A gasp rushed from her throat. *"Must you be a disappointment?"* *"Did you see the accident, miss?"*

"I *said*—" Brittany heard her own voice struggling with the words "—I said that it wouldn't work. This thing, I don't know what it is . . . but it won't work."

She expected him to snap back with a sharp, blistering retort. Instead he lifted his head, though he did not let her go, and a crooked grin spread over his face.

"That's better," he murmured and suddenly slid low upon his spine and unexpectedly dragged her down with him. "I'm glad we had this little talk."

Lying on top of Hammer Curry was like stretching out on a steel slab. He was incredibly fit, unbelievably hard, and when he boldly lifted his hips in a thrust, a ridge of aroused masculine anatomy made its own daring statement.

Even as she thrashed in her mind for something to say, he started making amends for being so brash. He arranged her more comfortably, shifting onto his side and settling her deep within the sliver of space between the seat and his own warm body.

His breath fanned her cheeks, and Brittany could smell her own heat and arousal.

"You're right," he murmured against her hair. "It wouldn't work. There are a dozen good reasons, the main one being we don't even trust each other. But I've been wanting to kiss you since the minute I laid eyes on you. I'm not going to, though. You know why?"

All she knew was that she was so dizzy with her own heat and the male impact of him that she could scarcely hold her head up! He was touching the dip of her waist and drawing his palm along the span of her ribs. He was stroking her side, inching around to find her spine and to move up the center of her back.

She breathed the word "why?" against the swell of his shoulder, but she wasn't certain he heard.

"Because this is too much trouble," he answered his own question.

"Yes."

"And I don't want you blaming me."

"No."

"And you would."

"Yes."

"I'm forty years old."

"Yes."

"And I don't need this."

"No."

"What's so great about one mouth touching another mouth, anyway?"

"I don't know."

Fullness, hot and throbbing, had spread to the center of Brittany's breasts, exuding an ache clear to the depths of her belly. Her common sense had flown somewhere it had never gone before, and though she tried to retrieve it, all she could really find was the sensation of his legs pressed against her own, his hands curving over the slope of her hip. This couldn't be happening. Scenes like this were years and years behind her.

She stirred in his arms, battling for one elusive point of clarity to hang on to.

"Oh, hell," he muttered and turned his face so that his mouth all but touched her own. "Don't make me do this by myself."

End it now, her last rational thought warned her. But she couldn't, and she whimpered and tried to turn her mouth away. "I—"

His tongue touched the corner of her mouth, and a surge of tremors raced up Brittany's spine.

"Say yes, dammit," he muttered into her parting, turning, reaching, yielding mouth.

"Yes," she said helplessly. "I . . . yes."

His kiss hovered somewhere in the fragile boundary of experimentation and a total loss of control. He seemed to be questing as he slanted his lips more securely, but then he drew in a long, deep breath and tightened his arms as if he planned to kiss her forever.

How many times had she been kissed in her life? Brittany didn't know. By how many men? Boys? She couldn't remember. Had any of them rocked her to the very roots as this man was doing? No. Why, then? She had no idea. Even his hands buried in her hair made her half-delirious with longing. His struggle with his own restraint made her mad with desire.

He strewed velvety kisses along the line of her jaw to the tip of her ear, and raped the tiny shell. She moaned softly, and, as if that were a signal he'd been waiting for, he pulled her deeper and deeper into his embrace.

"I can't take any more," she heard herself confessing. "Please."

"Please yes or please no?"

"Please . . . don't hurt me."

The desperation in her words, something she didn't totally understand herself, jarred him. He stilled his caresses and drew back to look at her.

"I wouldn't hurt you," he said in surprise.

"I meant—"

"I know what you meant. I won't hurt her, either . . . the woman inside."

Not ever in her life had anyone mentioned the woman inside, the woman that she never let show but who was as real,

perhaps even more real than the woman who was known as
Doc and who marched into police stations and raised a big
ruckus. That he should have that knowledge, that sensitiv-
ity, Brittany supposed, was what pushed her over the brink.
In that moment she knew she had never truly trusted a man
in all of her life, not even her own father. Especially her own
father. She knew, too, that she wanted to trust Hammer
Curry with every facet of her soul.

She deliberately let her body melt against his until her legs
were tangled with his, their bones converging. She groped
for one of his hands and slid it between them, surrendering
her breasts. He eagerly accepted, slipping his hand beneath
her blouse and making the silk of her camisole rustle with
sultry promises.

So it was all her fault that it got out of hand. No man
could have reciprocated the demands she had just made and
not have been strained beyond his limit. Hammer groaned
from far down in his chest, and he flexed his hips and moved
gently, rhythmically against the side of her thigh. She plea-
sured him by placing her hand upon his hip and pressing its
tension.

If Alice hadn't belatedly remembered her manners and
returned to the back door, announcing her arrival a mile
away with slams and calls that brought them both rocket-
ing back to their senses, Brittany didn't know how it would
have ended.

She returned instantly to reality.

"Damn!" he muttered and straightened, even swifter on
the uptake than she.

By the time the slash of light from the kitchen was
streaking across the garage, they were both sitting in the car
with an absurd equanimity. With the exception of Hammer's hand, which remained, trembling, upon her own on
the back of the seats between them.

The child bounced innocently down the back steps and positioned herself beside Brittany's window, smiling and bobbing in the polite little curtsy the girls were taught at John James Elementary.

"Hammer says I have terrible manners."

"Such an obedient child," Hammer murmured murderously between his teeth.

"It was nice meeting you, Dr. Schelle . . . Sch—"

She was adorable. Brittany couldn't keep from reaching out to touch the sweetly plump cheek, and as she did Hammer released her hand and pushed open his door to climb out.

"It was nice meeting you, too, Alice," Brittany said and reached for her own door.

"Will you come back?"

"Why, I—"

"Of course she will," Hammer said. "Go change your clothes, problem child."

"I'm not a problem child."

"Of course you are. Scat!"

"See ya!" the girl cried and scampered up the back steps again.

Hammer adored the sight of her retreat for a moment as she tore away, then he turned back to view Brittany's fragile composure.

Brittany had climbed out of the car and leaned upon the roof to catch her breath. What shocked her more than the fact that it had happened at all was the knowledge that if it was to occur again she wouldn't run away from it. It had been a long time since she'd been so knowingly self-destructive.

For long moments he watched her, his face taut with control, his weight thrown to one hip, one elbow braced like a pivot on the hood of the car.

"You're lucky we have this car between us," he said with a wry, self-deprecating smirk at himself. "How do you feel?"

She smiled and forced her head to remain upright. "Like an idiot. How do you feel?"

"Like an older idiot," he confessed and, grinning, reached across the distance to touch the place in her chin where a dimple might have been but wasn't. "I want you to know something."

The honesty of his blue eyes was painful to watch. Brittany began connecting the raindrops on the roof of the car with a fingernail. "There's no need to—"

"There's every need." He stopped her foolish hand with his own, and she was forced to look up. "I don't run around finding beautiful female suspects, Brittany, then try to seduce them. It's important for me to know that you believe that."

"You're a free agent, Lieutenant Curry—"

"Dammit, don't call me that again, and don't play a game with me. This is important."

To hear his voice raised at her was also painful. She tried to remember the seconds when he could hardly breathe from desire of her. It was gone, and it wouldn't return.

She grimaced and looked blindly at the organized garage. "It was a fluke, something with the barometer. Everything's been off-kilter for weeks."

"Oh, is that so?"

He gave his head a shake and motioned her toward the back step of his house. "In that case, I need to talk to my sitter before I drive you home. There's no need to wait out here. Come in. Make yourself at home. Pretend it never happened."

Just for that, she thought, she would. "Pretend what never happened?" she asked innocently.

The interior of his house was merely an extension of his garage, neat and organized, and Brittany wouldn't have hesitated to eat dinner in the garage any more than the kitchen. It wasn't the kind of fanatical orderliness and sterility where one didn't want to touch anything, like an operating room—a setter padded out and cordially sniffed her hand, for pity's sake!—but one knew upon strolling through the kitchen that it wouldn't be possible to reach under the bed and find a forgotten nacho container from Mazzio's Pizza with an inch of prime penicillin growing in it. The children's pajamas would be fresh and sweet-smelling. The sheets would be clean and scratchy and crisp.

"May I get you something to drink?" He was dragging his shirttails from his trousers as he moved casually through the door, complimenting her by taking her for granted and flipping through the mail as they passed—as if they'd done it a million times before.

"No, no." Brittany carefully arranged her expression as she gestured vaguely toward his clothes. "Go ahead and...change or whatever. Make your call, Lieutenant. I'll browse."

He headed for a room down the corridor that ran the length of one side of the house, his voice drifting richly back. "Turn on the television if you want to. Or put on some music. The kids'll be out in a minute."

In the space of a few seconds, Brittany saw his strategy. By leaving her alone, he was forcing her to think about him whether she wanted to or not.

She strolled to his stereo and, glancing guiltily over her shoulder, began flipping through his albums. She winced as she saw the complete works of Mozart, albums of Beethoven, Rachmaninoff, Chopin, Bach, Stan Kenton and Scott Joplin and what? Albums autographed by Andre Previn and Eduardo Mata, Pablo Casals. How different could two people be? She with her blaring MTV and David Lee Roth and a room that looked as if a hurricane had whipped through it?

"D'you want to see my school pictures?" piped a small voice.

Gasping, Brittany laughed down at Alice who had changed into a pair of garish purple shorts and a T-shirt that had to be Hammer's, for it struck her laughably below the knees. With some gratification, she saw the mark of an ancient stain on the chest. Well, hooray for that! She'd found a flaw in Hamilton Curry at last!

"I was hoping you would ask me," Brittany said and walked easily to the stuffed sofa where she very quickly found herself overpowered by the family album, along with Alice's generous commentary about the circumstances of every shot.

Many of the photographs were old, and the child had obviously sat many times with another adult who had recounted the stories. They were anecdotes sprinkled with old outdated phrases she'd memorized. Trying not to appear abnormally curious, she scrutinized shots of Hammer and a younger man who had to be Richard. They were captured as two muscular youths in high school football uniforms, two young men in out-of-date suits and stiff smiles beside a pleasantly mature woman and a tall, thin gentleman with glasses.

"Is this your father?" Brittany cautiously queried as she indicated the darker and more handsome of the two boys.

Alice blinked. "Yes," she said simply and traced Richard's outline. She looked up and showed the spaces in her mouth. "He's my father. Hammer's my daddy. That doesn't make much sense, does it?"

A wave of warm compassion made Brittany hug the child, and she lingered a moment to bury her face in the sweet-smelling hair. How wonderful it would be to have children who stayed with you at the end of the day, who didn't go back to their own terrible living conditions where they were yelled at and deprived of food and love.

"It makes perfect sense, darling," she whispered.

"Is this some kind of conspiracy in the making?" murmured a deep voice as Hammer fit himself onto the arm of the sofa and angled one leg so he could lean over Brittany's shoulder and see the album spread upon her lap.

At his appearance, Alice giggled at her uncle and immediately pounced on him with a dozen reasons why she must run next door this very *instant*, because it was *terribly* important, and her life would be *ruined* if she didn't.

Brittany found herself left stranded with the photograph album clasped awkwardly to her bosom, her thumb marking the place.

"Well, don't leave the umbrella over there," Hammer called toward the scuffling commotion at the front door, then added, "since Duchess ate the other one."

"I won't," drifted the fading reply.

He had changed into razor-creased jeans and had pulled on a tennis shirt of white terry—tucked in, naturally, so that it was difficult to avoid noticing the hard network of muscles that banded his waist and the flatness of his belly. If she had a hundred dollars to throw away, she would bet that she could peel Hammer Curry down to the buff, and he would be solid brown, with no white strips anywhere!

Another opposite: if she tanned at all it was in hideous blistering, peeling patches. In fact, all the opposites in her whole life seemed to converge in this man.

She rose to her feet without realizing that she did so. She moved to the table where she laid down the photograph album. She left it open at the page where Alice had been telling about the last time her father had paid them a visit.

The last snapshot caught her eye as she was in the process of turning away—not a terribly good picture, slightly out of focus, but its recentness couldn't be denied for Hammer was wearing the very same shirt he was wearing now, and he looked exactly the same. His arms were wrapped around a stunningly pretty woman, some inches *shorter* than he was, and they were laughing at each other and posing for the photographer, who had probably been Alice.

But that was none of her business. She had no claims on Hammer Curry. She didn't even *know* Hammer Curry. She spun around, keeping her eyes on the floor and deftly avoiding any proximity where she might be forced to confront the blue eyes that had been taking her apart, molecule by molecule.

"She's lovely," she said without meaning to, then flushed redly.

"What?" he said.

Brittany jerked up her head. "It's getting late. I need to go. I need . . . to go."

"Yes."

He spoke the word on a heavy sigh. When he motioned for her to precede him, Brittany moved rapidly to the back door, not pausing to look to the right or to the left. She didn't see him take a step backward and throw a look over his shoulder to the open photograph album, nor his gaze move over the memorized page and come to rest upon the snapshot Craig had taken when they'd first bought the Nikon.

He smiled a small smile to himself; his own thoughts had no such complexities as hers. He wasn't experiencing the first rush of a sexually blossoming man. He wasn't even experiencing the rush of a sexually aroused forty-year-old man. He was experiencing the slow, certain knowledge that life does not make mistakes in such matters. Be it happy or sad, frustrated or sublime, his dealings with Brittany Schellenegger would not end with this day.

And that excited him. As nothing had excited him in a long time.

Chapter Six

If meeting Hamilton Curry had been a caprice of fate, it was Brittany's opinion that saying goodbye should be a snap. As he swung off Carondeleer Street and veered the car into the flooded parking lot behind her clinic, she arranged her best common sense and logic and prepared herself to make quick work of it.

He cut the ignition and doused all but the parking lights. Raindrops were pummeling the roof, billions of crystal pebbles, and the erotic swish, swish, swish of the windshield wipers was a rhythm out of sync with her own heartbeat.

For long rain-drenched moments he sat pondering his hands upon the steering wheel. The sight of them, so strong even in repose, threatened Brittany's resolve.

She wanted to tell him to say *Goodbye, Brittany*.

But she didn't. She thought instead of the years after John—blurred years when she was still rabid with pain and was determined to fall into step with the rest of the female race. She'd thought about how everyone was having such terrific fun back then, sleeping around, making blasé remarks about it. Freedom was such a catchword; she'd decided to "find herself."

The nearest she'd come had been a medical degree, and then she'd learned the hard way that there was no such thing as freedom. To think that she could find it by waking up and wondering whose face was on the pillow next to hers was a nightmare she never wanted to live through again, no matter how short-lived.

Say goodbye, Brittany.

But the interior of the car was too seductive. Like a glass of fine wine and a fireplace on a cold night.

Sighing, she made a small production of settling her bag upon her shoulder. Her signals of finality made no impression on him. He turned his silent regard upon her.

She shrugged. "I think they made a movie out of this."

"*Friday the 13th*?"

"Ray Milland was the star. Or was it Dana Andrews?"

"*Laura*," he said presently, his voice managing to convey every texture from velvet to sandpaper. "With Dana Andrews and Gene Tierney. He thought Laura had been murdered, remember? And then she turned up alive."

Laughing, Brittany dipped her forehead to her fingers. "I remember the music mostly. 'Laura is the face in the misty night,'" she half-heartedly sang, embarrassed. "He suspected her of being the villainess for a little while, didn't he?"

"And she fell in love with him."

Their glance was for the length of a flickering eyelash only, but again and again they found themselves looking back, then away, then back—a necessary ritual of the species, she supposed.

"Well!" she exclaimed too brightly. "I do appreciate your bringing me home, Lieutenant Curry. I, uh...I enjoyed meeting your children. You're doing a first-rate job with them, you know. I really mean that, and as far as this thing with Sybil Wade goes, once she gets over the grief, I think..." She lost her train of thought and touched her fingers to her lips. "I mean, your men will see...the autopsy will show..."

"Don't do that."

The authority in his voice was not negotiable. The hard command of it brought Brittany up short. "I was only trying to—"

"I know what you were trying to do."

Swiveling on the seat, he faced her. "Don't pretend," he said more gently. "Don't admit it if you don't want to, but don't pretend."

"I wasn't pretending," she said and bent her head until her words were barely audible. "I'm just out of practice, that's all." She let her shoulders round. "The truth is, I'm not really sure I ever knew how."

He didn't reply to that. He reached over and flicked on the tape deck and pushed a button. Soft classical piano music made clarity out of the silence.

Presently, he said, "At least you don't have to walk into a dark house."

Brittany studied the soft glow of lights behind her venetian blinds. Henrietta would have put Mooch to bed by now. "Yes. There are few things worse than walking into a dark house, all right."

"Well, I suppose..."

The silence began to throw barbed quills at them again. When he didn't finish, she couldn't resist prompting him "You suppose what?"

"I suppose that you have a housekeeper. A live-in. And everything."

And everything? Now she understood. He was fishing. The man was fishing! And as much of a surprise as finding the father behind the cop had been, finding the possessive male behind the father nettled her—as seeing the photograph in the album had nettled her.

"Why don't you just come right out and ask if I have a man living with me, Lieutenant?" she curtly asked.

He leaned so near that his lie-detector eyes penetrated her facade as if it didn't exist. "Do you have a boyfriend living in, Brittany?"

"A boy lives with me." Her resentment was a rasp in her throat. "He's nine years old, Lieutenant Curry. No housekeeper, no boyfriend, just a nine-year-old boy. Are you satisfied now?"

No! Rubbing at a groove between his brows, Hammer wasn't satisfied with anything—not the way he had handled himself from the very beginning, nor with the way this woman's feisty prickly-pear stubbornness kept wrecking his best intentions. If anyone else had been sitting in her place, letting him know with every pulsebeat that they wanted him to leave, there would be a city block of tire rubber between them right now.

Yet he still didn't know if there was a man in her life. "Then you're not seeing..." His voice trailed damnably away from the question.

Brittany scooped up her bag and threw it over her shoulder. She didn't know if she was angry because she wasn't seeing anyone or because she must now admit that she wasn't.

She snapped, "I don't have to answer that."

"No, you don't."

"And you have no right to invade my privacy, either, to violate my rights."

"No, I don't have the right to violate your rights."

Brittany took the door handle in a death grip. She had one last defiant point to make. "Okay. The bottom line is that I'm a private citizen, Lieutenant Curry. I really don't understand your attitude, considering what you have done to me today. You've taken me away from people who really need me and dragged me downtown, for what? To answer a bunch of stupid questions that you'd already made up your mind about? And now you expect me to be a...what? A potential conquest?"

Hammer couldn't remember when anyone had driven him over the brink as she had just done. When she leaned on the door and prepared to dart out into the storm, he pressed a button on the panel at his fingertips. The lock on her door snapped down with an imperative click!

Brittany gaped at the tiny chrome cylinder, then at him. He was leaning forward, a finger pointing irately at her nose, and in an attempt to avoid it, she arched back.

Her head struck the windowpane. Lightning flickered outside. A pause spun out, a silence waiting for the crash of a falling tower, and she didn't know which happened first— the thunder making the car shudder or his hands closing about her shoulders.

"Brittany—"

"If you say one more thing," she gritted out the words, feeling the pressure of his grip not in her bones but deep in her belly, "I'm going to scream."

"Will you stop being an all-fired tough lady for just one minute?"

Why didn't she fight him? She could have flailed around in the silliest, most meaningless ways, and he would have let her go. She could have released a barrage of blistering verbiage upon him, and he would certainly have refused to argue.

But his eyes were raping her in the darkness, tearing her clothes off, and she found herself remembering the sweetness of his mouth and the way his hands had moved upon her back, the fire of his mouth upon her throat.

"It's begun," he muttered huskily. "It can't be unbegun."

"Don't say things like that," she whispered from her daze, which meant *Please say things like that to me.*

"You think it's just a matter of wanting?" He reached up to part the curtain of hair that had fallen about her bowed head. Her thoughts were spinning too quickly to think anything. His breath was so warm upon her jaw, so sweet, and her bones felt as if they would melt.

"Are you listening to me?" he whispered.

Her eyes fluttered closed. "Yes, yes, I'm listening."

"I want you to get yourself a lawyer, Brittany. First thing."

"I will. I mean, I intend to do that."

"And make it a man, not a woman."

She struggled to recapture her thoughts. "That's none of your—"

"Sybil's paranoid right now. Not only because she's a grieving mother but because she doesn't like you. A woman lawyer might just push her over the brink."

She was hardly listening. She'd asked such a little of love in the past, not even love really, just comfort, nothing complicated—a little holding, a little caring. All she'd ever asked of a man, John or any man, was to hold her and make her feel as though she mattered, that she was important, good for something: no commitments, no obligations, no sex, just simple caring. Was that so much?

His palms were closing upon her jaws. He was tipping up her face. "Do you have any idea just how dangerous Sybil Wade is to you?"

"What d'you care?" she mumbled.

"What?"

With a tremendous expenditure of will, she concentrated on what he was saying. "You don't believe I'm telling you the truth about Gerald Wade," she said, bracing herself. "How do you expect me to believe you care?"

In that moment, Brittany's commitment hit Hammer like a piece of lead pipe to the head. In his reluctance to let her walk out of his life—in keeping her here, in doing everything he could, he had done her the worst service of all. He had looked at her as he would have looked at Deborah Keyes. Or even Sybil Wade. Because Brittany Schellenegger did the world a service, he looked at her excellence and not at what that service had cost her—many times the price Deborah would have ever, ever paid. Or Sybil.

And he was shocked to find his hand trembling as he released her face. He drew back, holding himself away, a car's distance away, a world away.

Argue with me! she wanted to scream. *Kiss me to shut me up! Do anything! Don't push me away like this!*

But he did nothing, and she knew then that the moment was gone. Her hand felt as if it weighed ten stone as she lifted it to the door. Why hadn't she kept her big mouth shut? Why hadn't she just let her body do what felt right? Did it matter whether he believed her or not? Must she always be so... *correct*?

She forbade herself to weep as she leaned her weight against the door. She'd made her choices, dammit. At least she could leave with some dignity.

So haggard was Hammer's face when he jerked her back inside the car and slammed the door shut on the hissing, slashing rain that she hardly recognized him.

"But you see," he muttered as he crushed her in his arms, "I do care. I don't know how to tell you how much."

His was a fierce, wild kiss that dispensed with all the fine art of seduction. "Hammer!" she choked, saying his name for the very first time, only to have him smother her outburst with the hunger of a savage and misunderstood frustration.

Because of some residual independence, she thrashed weakly at his back, but he grasped her hand and drew it between them, to the raging part of him. "This is going to happen sooner or later," he muttered as he rained kisses upon her eyes, her throat, her hair. "What's to be gained by waiting?"

Pride, she could have groaned. The self-esteem, the luxury of practical reasoning, all of which she couldn't conjure up as she felt the wildness of desire burning through him and into her. But what good would pride do here? Reason? How many people wanted her? In any form or fashion? Lilith? Her father? John?

It was a moment not for lovers but for people driven. Brittany knew what he wanted, and she gave it. When he wanted her breasts, she yielded them. Her pleasure was in the giving and not in herself. In this moment he craved the sensations and the pleasure that her body could give him more than anything else in the world.

And if another body could do as well, hers was still the only one around. When she felt his manhood hurling him to the perimeter of self-abandon, when she felt him hesitate and want to reassure himself that he wasn't misusing or abusing, she forced him to continue. She told him with the demands of her mouth and the aggressive arch of her body that she was accessible, willing.

Her hands took him and awkwardly, painfully showed him the path to her soft center.

It was an incoherent moment that ended too quickly. Once done, Brittany began to withdraw, as was her habit in every other instance of life, so as to leave room for things more necessary, both for him and for herself.

She tried to wriggle free and was stunned when he trapped her in the narrow wedge of the seat.

"Where are you going?" he whispered in amazement, his voice still raspy and thick with sex.

Embarrassed now, and unbearably self-conscious, Brittany tried to hide behind logic. "Inside," she whispered.

"Uh-huh."

Surprised, she squinted at him through the film of frustrated years. Baldly, she demanded, "You want *more*?"

He scowled. "I want Brittany Schellenegger," he murmured as he folded her deeper into his embrace and began the slow, laborious process of searching for the woman that had completely eluded him, "I want the heart and soul of you, for an infinitely more extended period of time than that was. Do you think that this, your body—as much as I like it, don't get me wrong—is enough to pacify me?"

Brittany didn't know what to think. Her blouse was still unbuttoned. Her skirt was still twisted around her waist, and she could feel the naked part of him that pressed against the naked part of her.

He shifted his weight so he could see more of her, and she expected him to touch her, to indulge himself, to twirl her nipples or squeeze her breasts or do things that men liked to do with breasts. But he didn't touch her at all, and she was surprised. When he very delicately drew a fingertip across the angle of her collarbone to the center of her throat and only gazed down, watching her face and not her breasts, she slowly lifted her eyes to his in astonishment.

"What I just did to you, darling," he said softly, "was unforgivable. It was right out of the caveman era, and if I wasn't feeling the compulsion to do the same thing all over again, I'd plead temporary insanity."

It was too bad that she had no such eloquent posture available, she thought. Never in her life had she discussed sex with a man except in the ignorant way teenagers tormented each other, or as a doctor to a patient. And she had no intentions of doing so now.

"I need to go in now, Hammer," she lied quickly.

"Even I'm not that gullible."

"I'm not comfortable with this."

Chuckling, he kissed the cloud of her hair. "Thank you."

Drawing back, Brittany looked at him with mingled respect and a touch of hostility. "For what?"

"For calling me by my name."

What a strange man he was. His soft, seductive talk—a strategy, of course, yet it was like a drug. And the way he held her—not pawing her, not sating himself, not using her.

"Hammer?" she whispered and turned her head so that her cheek was pressed against the swell of his shoulder.

"What?"

"All this talk about 'making love.' Do you really believe that?"

"What d'you mean?"

"Doesn't it scare you that our generation talks about love, love, love, and all it turns out to be is sex, sex, sex, and divorce, divorce, divorce? You know, we've done more right here than a lot of our great-grandparents did in their whole lifetimes, and frankly, I think they were happier."

Only the sound of his troubled breathing and the rain reached her ears.

"I'm the wrong person to ask, Brittany. I was a kid when I got married the first time, but I think I went into it with an honest heart. I knew that the rush and the feelings were an evolving thing. I would've worked myself to death to make that marriage work, but I... All I know is, my parents have been together thirty-nine years. Whenever one of them starts talking to me, do you know what it invariably boils down to?"

She shook her head in spirit only, for even with the talk of love in the abstract, she was aware of his thudding heartbeat, and of her own aching emptiness.

"They talk about each other," he murmured pleasantly. "They kinda drive you crazy with it sometimes. My mother's a peaceful woman, but you don't say anything bad about Daddy in her presence—not Richard, not me or one of the kids. Mom would take your head off for that. Ninety percent of her life is wrapped up in that man, you know, and I think that must be it. It never seemed like an unbalanced equation for either of them, and it's worked. I think our generation thinks it's a sign of stupidity to go into a contract without at least a fifty-fifty split. We're afraid we'll get cheated. Or maybe we're just afraid. Ninety-ten isn't very good odds, is it?"

"No," she whispered.

"I don't think my parents knew that."

As he talked he toyed with the curve of her spine where it tapered into her waist, and Brittany could sense the radiant heat of his strength reasserting itself. It wasn't over with this man. He would want to do it all over again, and this time he would let her take all the time she needed. She didn't know if her pride would allow her to expose herself so much. Her fulfillments had never been in the presence of another human being, and she'd never said it, never explained.

As if he had read her mind, as he nudged her face upward with his chin, he whispered, "It's okay. Kiss me."

It was a gentle lover's kiss, his first with her, and she flicked her tongue shyly to his and thrilled to his subtle artistry.

"You're a naughty man, did you know that?" she teased and turned in his arms so that they faced each other.

"And you're an elusive woman, did you know that?"

"Yes."

But she didn't want to be. Yet when his fingers trespassed the fragile boundary of her panties and curved about one hip, reaching far deeper until he found the tangled curls, she stiffened in a taut protest.

His catching breath was his refusal to accept it, and his hands were exceedingly clever. They made her brain spin, and he learned more about how to seduce her this time. His moves were slow and controlled, and with no effort at all Brittany found herself holding on to him and closing her teeth into the ridge of shoulder—as she'd done before when the wind had been whipping her hair and she had been hugging a young man's waist and the roar of the engine had been filling her ears.

Yes, Lilith had called the police. Or maybe Sybil had done it. In a quiet corridor they had come for him—her young lover. And he, wearing his best dark suit, pale as death, had been escorted out of the building into the hot darkness outside. She had run after him in her beautiful billowing dress, and she had fought her way onto the terrible black machine, trying to cry explanations into his ears that he didn't want to hear, didn't want to believe.

They had roared through the streets of New Orleans, and the flames of hell itself had boiled out of the exhaust. He had raged and cursed and blamed her. She had tried to make reparations, but she'd been so young, and his eyes had glowed as he'd roared his threats—wild, violent words, and then his fury had turned upon her, too. They would pay, and she would pay most of all. He had put her off, then, and he had spun the machine in its final screaming pirouette and had gunned it with every drop of man-created power to go sailing over the parapet like some giant prehistoric bird that had never learned to fly, and it floated down, down, down....

"Did you see the motorcycle when it went through the railing, miss? Do you know the boy who was riding it?"

When Brittany came to herself in Hammer's arms, she was weeping. This was why she could never win, and why it would never work with Hammer Curry.

"Shhh," he was murmuring and cradling her like a battered child. "It's all right. It's my fault. I'm sorry. It's my fault."

But it wasn't, and she thought she would have given everything she had at that moment to rid her heart of such scarring guilt. But some things couldn't be explained, and some scars never really healed.

When she had finally made herself presentable, he said miserably, "I can't let you go like this, Brittany. It's not right."

"It's perfectly right."

"Then why do I feel awful?"

"Because you're a decent man. It's not your fault."

"Like hell."

"No one made me do what I did," she reaffirmed to herself.

"That's neither here nor there."

"What is, then?"

"I never meant to hurt anyone."

"You didn't hurt me."

"Then why are you crying?"

"I'm not crying. Please, Lieutenant Curry, forget it."

"Don't call me that."

"What do you want me to call you?"

"Darling would be nice."

"Please—"

"I'm sorry, I'm sorry. May I call you?"

"No."

"Why not?"

"It wouldn't go anywhere," she futilely snapped.

"Does it have to go anywhere?"

"Then why call?"

"Dammit, Brittany, you're twisting things."

"Twisting is my specialty, don't you know. If our paths ever cross—"

"Oh, they will cross, sweetheart. Make no mistake about that."

"Pretend you don't know me when you have to serve the warrant."

"Come off that."

"I'm sorry."

"Oh, hell."

Chapter Seven

Nothing had changed. The next morning Brittany was confronted with her usual "jet lag" and her usual lack of energy as she tumbled out of bed and staggered groggily to her feet. Her agony of awakening was par for the course as she propelled her body to the shower where she would depend upon the hot water to shock her brain into functioning enough to put herself into her clothes.

But as she stood beneath the scalding spray and tipped up her face to its painful heat, she realized that her memories of Hammer Curry and the night before were disturbingly intact. And then a strange sense of disorientation consumed her—hazy recollections of good things ending badly, and the soreness between her legs that was a grim reminder of the effect a man could have upon a celibate woman. If, indeed, she'd ever really known.

But she wasn't Lilith's daughter for nothing. She would not fight what could not be won.

She stepped out of the shower and dressed herself without paying any attention to what she was doing. It occurred to her to wonder, when she was about to walk out of the bedroom into the cramped little kitchen nook, if Mooch and Henrietta would be able to tell that something had happened.

But she was certain that was a figment of some novelist's burned-out imagination.

She heard water being poured into the coffee maker, and Henrietta's head suddenly appeared from behind the partition, wrapped in a blinding fluorescent green turban that set Brittany's fragile nerves on edge.

"What's the matter with you?" she demanded bluntly.

Brittany flushed. "What d'you mean, what's the matter with me?"

"You look different."

Brittany ducked her head and mumbled something about the rain.

"You've got a hundred telephone messages from yesterday," Henrietta said. "I finally gave up waiting on you to come home. You'd better have a cup of coffee before you look at this morning's paper."

Brittany fetched herself a cup and saucer and folded herself onto a chair. She opened the rather soggy edition of the *Times Picayune* and stared in horror at her own face.

"John Brown!" she breathed and raked her stunned eyes over the accounts of Arnold Bates's shooting and Gerald Wade's part in it. "What in the—"

"Local Doctor Questioned in Death of Gerald Wade," read one of the smaller headlines. As she scanned the article, she saw Hammer's name where he was quoted saying "As in any incident where a juvenile is shot by a police officer in the line of duty, a full investigation is on-going."

And again, in another place the police commissioner was quoted saying "The deceased boy did seek help from one of the local physicians."

What about Brian Gallagher and David Webster? she wanted to cry out. Why weren't they mentioned?

"I told you to have some coffee first," Henrietta reminded her.

Mooch came to stand solemnly beside her knee. "Are you arrested now?" he asked somberly. "Are you goin' to jail?"

"Don't be ridiculous," Brittany said as her stomach began to knot. But her tone lost some of its resilient edge. "At least, I don't think so. Drat those reporters. They could have at least told the whole story. Here they tell just enough to make it sound like I'm guilty of something."

"Sue, I always say," Henrietta said unhelpfully as she poured coffee. "Sue the pants off 'em."

Brittany's knowledge of police procedure left her at a total loss. She didn't know what her next step should be, only that there must definitely be one.

Sipping the hot coffee and burning her tongue, she started when the phone beside her hand rang. After the second ring, she snatched up the receiver. "Hello!" she shrieked. "Who is this?"

"Zees es your mother, dahling," purred a luscious mother-of-pearl voice. "I see you've caught a glimpse of zee front page."

To look at her, no one would guess that Brittany's life went on hold. She spoke, she moved and she functioned. She was rationally aware and in control of all her motor responses. But she was invisible as only Lilith could make her invisible. It was a phenomenon that she had always known and never understood. And if she'd ever try to put it into words, people would look at her as if she were crazy.

As her mother made meaningless small talk, Brittany thought, *Hammer told me to make peace with this woman. Do I trust him that much? Do I trust him at all? He's standing behind his men, not me. And after what happened between us last night. How could I even consider loving a man who thinks I could let someone die?*

Love? Had it come to that terrible word now? All that talk about ninety-ten? But he had said she should make peace with her mother, and, if she had to put a reason to it, she guessed it would be his remark about not hurting the woman inside.

"Do you have a lawyer?" Lilith was asking in a surprisingly congenial way.

Brittany wet her lips and raked back a tangled mass of her hair. When Henrietta placed a fresh cup of coffee into her hand, she looked at it and set it down untouched.

"No, Lilith," she said quite formally. "Actually—" she cleared her throat "—I haven't looked into it yet. I, uh . . . I just this minute got up and saw the paper."

"Well, zee first zeeng you do is get a good attorney. Appearances are everything now, dahling. Would you like for me to call Franz?"

Brittany closed her eyes. Franz was the senior partner of a law firm that Sigmund had retained for many years. It had served Lilith and Edward all the years of their marriage. After the divorce Lilith had kept the firm on, but Brittany hadn't seen the old man since the reading of the will. At Sigmund's death, the location of the firm's main offices had changed from New York to New Orleans, and Franz had moved with it. But she still hadn't seen him since.

Brittany stared down at her body in the plain cotton pants and plain blouse. She was due at the hospital in an hour. Would Franz even remember her? *Oh, Hammer, why did you have to come into my life and screw up my head? Why couldn't you have at least reminded one of those reporters that I was innocent until proven guilty?*

"Yes, Lilith," she said quietly. "I guess I would like for you to call Franz for me. Thank you."

Her mother let a dramatic silence spin out over the line. Then she said, "Have you spoken to Sybil, dahling? Have you tried to straighten zees out at all? Zees just isn't like her. I don't understand—"

"Oh, Lilith, you always were so gullible...." In horror, Brittany covered her mouth and didn't dare utter another word.

"Well," Lilith said with her beautiful, martyred tone, "never let it be said zat I interfered. We'll let Franz decide what your posture should be. Zee funeral, you will attend that, yes?"

The funeral! Brittany made her reply meek and respectful. "I haven't even thought about it."

"Well, I know you don't want my advice, but you'd better go, dahling. Everyone in zees whole town will be making bets about whether any of us will show up. But we'll let Franz decide about zat, too. Shall I have him call you?"

Glimpsing the confounded look on Henrietta's face, Brittany flushed and whirled around so that her back separated them. "Well, I think it's not going to come to that, but all right, all right. Tell Franz...tell him that I suppose we'd better talk. But I really..."

A pause hung on the line, filled with misunderstandings that seemingly could never be healed.

"Brittany?"

"Yes, Lilith?"

"Are you all right?"

"Yes," Brittany said slowly with a vacant stare that took her back to the stolen moments when she'd lain in Ham-

IT'S A JACKPOT OF A GREAT OFFER!

- 4 exciting Silhouette Special Edition novels—FREE!
- a folding umbrella—FREE!
- a surprise mystery bonus that will delight you—FREE!

Silhouette Folding Umbrella— ABSOLUTELY FREE

You'll love your Silhouette umbrella. Its bright color will cheer you up on even the gloomiest day. It's made of rugged nylon to last for years, and is so compact (folds to 15″) you can carry it in your purse or briefcase. This folding umbrella is yours free with this offer.

But wait . . . there's even more!

Money-Saving Home Delivery!

Subscribe to Silhouette Special Edition and enjoy the convenience of previewing new, hot-off-the-press books every month, delivered right to your home. Each book is yours for only $1.95—55¢ less per book than what you pay in stores! And there's no extra charge for postage and handling.

Special Extras—Free!

You'll also get our free monthly newsletter—the indispensable insider's look at our most popular writers and their upcoming novels. Now you can have a behind-the-scenes look at the fascinating world of Silhouette. It's an added bonus you'll look forward to every month. You'll also get additional free gifts from time to time as a token of our appreciation for being a home subscriber.

TAKE A CHANCE ON ROMANCE—
COMPLETE AND MAIL YOUR SCORECARD
TO CLAIM YOUR FREE HEARTWARMING GIFTS

If offer card below is missing, write to:
Silhouette Books, 120 Brighton Road,
P.O. Box 5084, Clifton, NJ 07015-9956

Did you win a
mystery gift?

Place sticker here

Yes! I hit the jackpot. I have affixed my 3 hearts. Please send my 4
Silhouette Special Edition novels free, plus my free folding umbrella
and free mystery gift. Then send me 6 books every month as they
come off the press, and bill me just $1.95 per book—55¢ less than
retail, with no extra charges for postage and handling.

If I am not completely satisfied, I may return a shipment and cancel
at any time. The free books, folding umbrella and mystery gift
remain mine to keep.

CJS 037

NAME _____

ADDRESS _____

APT. _____

CITY_____

STATE _____

ZIP CODE_____

SILHOUETTE "NO-RISK" GUARANTEE
• There is no obligation to buy—the free books and gifts remain yours to keep.
• You pay the lowest price possible—and receive books before they're
available in stores.
• You may end your subscription anytime—just let us know.
Terms and prices subject to change. Offer limited to
one per household and not valid for
present subscribers.

PRINTED IN U.S.A.

Mail this card today for
4 FREE BOOKS
this folding umbrella and
a mystery gift ALL FREE!

mer's arms and hungrily returned his kisses. "Yes, I'm perfectly fine."

As Brittany gently replaced the telephone, she refused to meet Henrietta's accusing glance. From the front of the clinic, so distant that she almost didn't hear it, the doorbell buzzed, and she wanted to shut it out. She wanted suddenly to shut out everything and go into her room and sit in the quiet privacy of her memories of Hammer Curry.

She slumped.

"You want me to get the door?" Mooch volunteered.

She smiled lovingly at the child and shook her head. "Fix us some toast while I'm gone."

"I could eat a horse," he said.

"Not in this house," Henrietta declared.

"Oh, Henrietta," wailed his complaint as if both of them believed she were dead serious.

Their familiar quarreling gave Brittany a sense of normalcy as she opened and shut doors on the way to the front. That's why her patients enjoyed hearing her bicker with Henrietta, wasn't it? It made them safe.

Making her way toward the persistent buzz, she peeped through the glass door out into the rainy parking lot, and her feeling of normalcy gave way to a new and fresh dread. A county sheriff's car was parked outside. Its parking lights were on, and the windshield wipers were moving back and forth.

Oh, Lord! Brittany stopped dead in her tracks. What would happen if she didn't answer the door?

"Dr. Schellenegger?" the deputy asked when she finally slid the glass panel aside and poked her head outside only enough to speak to him.

"What is it?" she asked apprehensively.

"I've been asked to deliver these papers to you, ma'am. You'll have to sign for them."

"What papers?"

"Would you just sign here, Dr. Schellenegger?"

It was the doctor's nightmare. Brittany knew it in the same way she'd known that Gerald Wade was in terrible trouble. Taking out her anger on the deputy sheriff was meaningless.

Removing the pen from his hand, she scrawled her name on the form that was clipped to his board. He handed her the envelope containing the declaration of a lawsuit. Brittany took it without a word and shut the door in his face.

With an odd self-control, she walked to the desk where Henrietta kept the books. Placing the envelope upon the desk, she pulled out a drawer and felt around in the back of it until she located a pack of cigarettes.

Removing one, she calmly lit it. She tried not to think until she had drawn the smoke deep into her lungs. Only then did she open the envelope.

The suit for malpractice had been filed, not by Sybil Wade, but by Fleming, her husband. How clever, she thought numbly. How very clever of the attorneys who represented Fleming: Throckmorton and Pruitt. They just happened to be one of the best law firms in the country.

Hammer Curry, damn him. Why couldn't he have believed her?

To look Franz Knoble directly in the face, to view his infant-smooth pink skin and pretty rosebud of a mouth, one saw an aging boy who was five feet and three inches tall.

Franz was seventy years old. Every day he did precisely the same thing. He rose, put on a three-piece black suit, ordered room service to his suite and drank two cups of coffee with cream and two lumps of sugar. At a quarter of eight he stepped into the elevator with the *New York Times* folded and in his attaché case. At eight-thirty he arrived at his office and read the paper. At nine o'clock he called Austria and spoke with his partner.

On this particular day, he skipped the *Times* and the Austrian transatlantic telephone call. With his case clutched primly beneath his chin and his umbrella extended so that the driver could make a tunnel for him to step onto the curb of Poydras Street, he disembarked from his white Mercedes-Benz coupé and peered up through the downpour.

The skyscraper towered above the street for twenty stories and commanded one of the most spectacular views of New Orleans. It was owned by the young woman whom he'd sworn to Sigmund Schellenegger upon his deathbed to protect for the rest of his life—though that fact was known to no one besides himself. For all intents and purposes, he was retained by Lilith Garamond Schellenegger.

Even though Brittany took no interest in Schellenegger Enterprises, her company was well diversified, thanks to Franz. With diamonds being the foundation stock, they dealt in oil and gas, gold, sulfur, nickel, copper, potash, uranium, phosphoric acid and geothermal energy. It employed nearly five thousand people all over the world, including eight hundred in New Orleans and another eight hundred peppered over the rest of the state. It operated in ten other states and four foreign countries. The past year its revenues were eight million dollars with assets valued at over two billion. In Franz's opinion, Brittany could afford her little charity down on Carondeleer. He had a team of two lawyers who did nothing but keep the IRS off her back.

Once he was on the twelfth floor, Franz passed through corridors of lavender and aquamarine that were flanked and enhanced by lustrous wood paneling. He himself had had the floors inlaid with marble and mahogany. As he passed conference rooms filled with men from around the world in dark suits and striped ties, he did so with a sense of pride

that he shared with no one. Schellenegger Enterprises could
carry on its profit-making if Brittany never came near it.
Actually, she had probably been in these offices a dozen
times in the past ten years.

He nodded to the attractive woman sitting behind a plush
reception desk, then to the one sitting beyond her at an even
more dramatic desk.

"Have they arrived?" he asked the secretary.

"Yes, Mr. Knoble," she said respectfully. "They're
waiting for you inside."

Franz entered the door as if he were a visitor himself.
Once inside, however, no one doubted who would be con-
ducting the meeting.

Eight attorneys rose instantly to their feet. They had all
been contacted personally by Franz himself within the past
hour, and they were experts in the area of malpractice. They
had been offered a fee that convinced them they should drop
everything they were doing and report to him immediately.

"Gentlemen," Franz said in his quiet effeminate voice,
motioning for them to resume their seats. "For the first order of business..."

"The first order of business," Hammer told Patrick as he
stood before the window of his office, his feet planted firmly
apart and his hands clasped behind his back, his hair clinging close to his scalp and his neck sporting an angry red
mark where he'd cut himself shaving, "is to get at the truth,
no matter where it lies."

Patrick was exhausted. Not only was Hammer pushing
himself to the limit over the Brittany Schellenegger affair, he
was pushing Patrick, too.

They had spent most of the morning trying to locate Devane Sadu, and when they finally found him—Hammer
being sure that he would corroborate Schellenegger's state-

ment—Devane had shocked them both by backing up Gallagher and Webster's statement to the hilt.

Then Hammer had had an ''altercation'' with a reporter at the newspaper, and Patrick had borne the brunt of that, too, for the telephone call he'd gotten an hour later had just about burned his ear off.

''They got to Devane Sadu,'' Hammer was mumbling from his place before the window. ''The little punk, they got to him.''

''But you can't prove that, sir,'' Patrick felt compelled to remind him.

''Maybe not.''

Patrick was no fool. He'd never seen Hammer so personally driven on a case before. First off, he'd come to work looking like death. He'd shut the door in everyone's face, and all the people in the department were walking around on tiptoe, throwing funny looks at each other.

''You really think she's innocent, don't you?'' Patrick said, guessing it would do Hammer some good to talk about it.

Turning, Hammer reached up to pinch the bridge of his nose. ''Don't you?''

Patrick wasn't sure what position to take. ''Brian Gallagher is one of our best men.''

''Don't you think it's awfully neat, Pattie? Doesn't it feel too neat to you?''

Patrick considered Devane Sadu and shrugged. ''Well, of course the little junkie could very well be lying. Probably is, as a matter of fact. He'd probably sell out his own mother for a joint. But the ambulance driver...''

''I'm going to talk to those people again. In person. Myself.''

Patrick hoped he wasn't around when that happened. The dispatcher at Children's Hospital had already disclaimed any knowledge of a request coming in for an ambulance to Dr. Schellenegger. Hammer had demanded that they put the dispatcher's name in the computer.

"Brittany looks too guilty," Hammer was saying, having returned morosely to the window. "Guilty people don't look that guilty. They look innocent."

Patrick shrugged at his superior's back. "If you don't mind my saying so—"

Spinning around, Hammer skewered him with a piercing look. "Well, I do. I know I'm overreacting, Pattie. Just let me do it in peace."

"Sorry, sir."

"No, I'm sorry. Hell, Pattie, you heard Sybil ranting and raving yesterday."

"Yessir."

Shrugging, Hammer buried his head in his hands. "Don't mind me. I'm just going a little bananas here. But dammit, she's not lying. She just can't be. I would know."

Feeling soggy and mildewed—he hadn't slept the rest of the night but had sat up thinking about Brittany and what they'd done, what he wanted to do to her again at the first possible moment, and the infuriating impossibility of that— Hammer jammed his hands into the pockets of his trousers and flexed his back against the bite of his holster.

Five hundred miles out in the Gulf of Mexico, the tropical storm was now Hurricane Helen, and all the meteorologists along the coastal states were speculating about where she would decide to come inland. The local radio and television stations were talking about statistics of past flood damage and about property integrity.

"Pattie," he said softly.

"Yessir?"

"There's something I want to know."

Patrick didn't move from where he waited, but he studied the subtle shift in Hammer's shoulders, the opening and closing of his large hands. "Yessir?"

"I'd like to know what Gallagher and Webster talk about when they're alone together."

There was no doubt what Hammer Curry was asking him to do; Patrick just wasn't sure about the finer ethical points. He walked to the opposite side of the room and idly adjusted some files stacked on a cabinet. He cast Hammer a furtive, sidelong glance.

"I, uh . . ." He cleared his throat noisily. "I don't see too much of a problem with that, sir."

"Good."

Then the two men looked at each other. They'd worked together a long time. There was trust, and there was support. But if anyone got in trouble, it would be Patrick who got hauled in to answer questions.

"Is it really that bad, Hammer?" he murmured sympathetically.

Hammer brought one side of his mouth down in a wry curl. "I've never had anything hit me so hard in my life."

Patrick suddenly grinned. Brittany Schellenegger must be some woman. "Good enough for you, boss. Maybe now I'll have a sign made for the head of your bed."

Shortly before noon, Brittany met with the lawyers whom Franz had retained for her. Before she had finished answering their questions, she wouldn't have been surprised if one of them had asked what she and Hammer thought they were doing parked on the asphalt lot behind her clinic at 10:43 in the evening.

* * *

At one o'clock, after Hammer returned from eating a tuna salad that he didn't remember tasting a single bite of, the phone on his desk jarred him out of a stupor.

"Hello," he said.

"Hammer?"

Dismay hit Hammer like a clip on the jaw. "Deborah?"

A hesitation. "Hammer, are you all right? I saw your name in this morning's paper. It reminded me of how long it's been since I've seen you."

"Sure, sure." Hammer cleared his throat and adjusted his tie. "Of course I'm all right, Deborah. How are you?"

"Lonely."

There had been times when Hammer had thought he would have given every cent to hear such words coming from Deborah Keyes. Now he forced a smile into his voice.

"Ahh, you always did have such a fantastic way with words, Senator Keyes."

She laughed—the rich, confident woman's laugh Hammer knew Brittany would never laugh. She purred, "Is it raining at your house, darling?"

"It was the last time I was there."

"Rain is so romantic, don't you think. It always does such strange things to me."

Hammer laughed wryly. "If I didn't know better, Senator, I would think you were propositioning me."

"Maybe I should come over tonight and remove all reasonable doubts."

Hammer wiped a sudden line of sweat from his forehead. Why not? To imagine that anything would come of what he and Brittany had done was not only stupid, but it was also unwise. Deborah Keyes was safe, and he was a man who valued safety above all things.

Yet, even with Deborah's voice in his ear, and it was the voice of a woman whose body he knew as well as his own, Hammer was seeing Brittany and remembering her awkwardness that thrilled him so, her uncertainty, her bristling resentments and her flaming pride.

Even now desire rose in him like a phoenix. Something was changing in his life, and he thought, with a great sense of loss, that it would never be the same with Deborah again. How had he managed to do this to himself?

"Ahh, Deb," he said, trying to keep the failure from showing in his voice, "it's been a bitch of a day. I—"

Coldness froze the telephone wires stretching between them. Hammer envisioned Deborah's brown eyes glowing with anger that she was too professional to allow in her voice.

"It's all right, Hammer, darling. I'll see you. Or better still, call me sometime."

Hammer thought he hated Brittany for the hurt in Deborah's voice. "Deb—"

"Goodbye, Hammer."

Goodbye, Deb, he thought to himself as he slowly and sadly hung up the phone.

"For since it was a man who brought death into the world, a man also brought resurrection of the dead. As in Adam all men die, so in Christ all will be brought to life."

For blocks, on both sides of the street, the elite serpentine twists of the drives at Oak Haven were lined with cars. Many of them were chauffeur-driven limousines, some of them vintage names registered in the names of Louisiana senators and high officials, plus other local district and federal judges.

A few of them, however, were the cars of the local police department. The city officials were anxious to see the fu-

neral finished before the hurricane grew capricious. All
through the night the rain had unfurled like sodden ban-
ners. Flood warnings were given everywhere in the low-lying
areas.

It was only nature's trick, of course: the lull, but the rain
blessedly slackened, which may have been the reason more
than the usual number of press people were in attendance at
the service. Not unnoticed by them was Franz Knoble,
attorney, and even more interestingly, Brittany Schellenceg-
ger and her famous mother. True, they were old friends of
the family, but it was the first time the three of them had
been seen together since the reading of Sigmund's will in
Austria a decade before.

Hammer had had little choice about whether he would
attend.

"The department has a certain obligation to Judge Wade,
Hammer," Bruce Clements told him when Hammer mentioned he had other things he could do, like having an im-
pacted wisdom tooth extracted. "You especially, Lieutenant. The judge has singled you out as the one handling
the investigation. For the record."

"A favor I could have done without."

What would the commissioner do, Hammer wondered, if
he guessed that Patrick had tapped Brian Gallagher's telephone, upon his own order?

"Sit with Babe and me," Bruce encouraged with a slap on
Hammer's back. "We'll pick you up."

Hammer dryly warned Patrick to check the condition of
his own dark suit. "I'm not suffering by myself, partner,"
he said. "If I go, you go."

As he stood listening respectfully to the service, however,
Hammer felt something even more disturbing at the back of
his neck. He felt restless and out of place, as if he were about
to catch a chill.

Lifting his head, he searched Sybil's veil for the answer. Then he turned and ran his eye over the crowd for the dozenth time. There, at the far opposite end of the canopy where the drizzle was falling upon those standing along the outskirts, Brittany was gazing straight at him.

She was wearing a black summer suit. Linen, he thought, with a high-neck collar and a slim skirt. A wide-brimmed hat had been settled upon her hair, which had been severely restrained into a chignon. One side of the brim dipped low, almost covering one eye and cheek.

Hammer wondered if Lilith Garamond had any idea of how the two of them compared when they stood side by side. Brittany would never have the exquisite disdain that lent Lilith her model's presence; on the contrary, Brittany seemed to almost disappear inside herself.

Hammer spotted a photographer drawing a camera from beneath his rain slicker and, holding it close to his chest, silently capture a picture of Brittany.

She never realized it, nor did Lilith beside her. Hammer suddenly remembered the sweet taste of Brittany's fingertips in his mouth. He closed his eyes briefly, shutting out the sight of her and willing the thoughts to go away.

The last person on earth Brittany had expected to see at Gerald Wade's funeral was Hammer Curry. When she first spied the closely cropped hair, she didn't believe it. Yet those were undeniably his shoulders, spread so broadly in the dark summer suit. She would know that neck and those shoulders anywhere in the world.

Beside her, Lilith stirred, and her green eyes sharpened with consternation.

"What's zee matter?" she whispered behind a gloved hand.

"Nothing."

With a sharp glance at Hammer, Brittany lowered her umbrella and tried to concentrate on the words of the service. Her grief for Gerald Wade was deep and real.

The service was over much too quickly. Before Hammer had decided on a way of contacting Brittany, the crowd was breaking up, and he, not free to leave, darted a swift look at Patrick.

The younger man didn't need words. He discreetly scanned the crowd, and when he found himself staring straight into the open green eyes of Brittany Schellenegger, he understood.

He grinned at Hammer.

With a troubled scowl Hammer watched the trio leave the protective canopy. He had no idea of who the old man was, but the fact that Brittany had made the effort to reestablish some kind of relationship with her mother pleased him enormously.

He watched the photographer step near and speak to the small man. Brittany turned swiftly away, and the camera caught her again, like a celebrity avoiding publicity.

By the time Patrick plowed his way through the crowd to reach Hammer, Brittany and her mother had nearly reached the white Mercedes. Hammer pinched the bridge of his nose. ''Ahh, Pattie...''

Patrick grinned. ''I don't mind, sir. What d'you want me to tell her?''

Hammer looked over his shoulder for Brittany again. She had lifted her head to look for him. *Don't leave yet,* he begged her. *Stay there, stay there.*

Why are you with Sybil Wade? her eyes accused.

I want to explain.

She turned away.

"Tell her..." Hammer ground his teeth in frustration, and for the first time in their relationship Patrick was delighted to see Hammer flush while he stood grinning.

"Tell her..." Looking up, Hammer saw the grin. "You bastard," he growled, chuckling. "Tell her anytime, anywhere."

"In case we miss connections—"

"I'll find you. Don't worry."

Just as Brittany was reaching the Mercedes, Patrick was reaching Brittany, and Hammer, smiling unhappily at Bruce Clements, watched Brittany listen to his partner. As he expected, she looked up.

Please come, he begged her, his stare penetrating. *Forget everything that went before. Just come.*

Behind his back, the commissioner called his name. Sybil was leaving, and those in attendance were clustered around her like drones around the queen bee.

Hammer held Brittany's eyes as long as he could. The inside of his shoes were getting wet. By the time the cluster of people had migrated to the Wade limousine—her friends, her family, the members of the funeral staff—Brittany had gone.

"Hamilton?" Sybil Wade said as the Oak Haven administrator assisted her into the lush crimson interior of her limousine. "Come with me."

Heads turned to look at Hammer. It was the last thing he wanted, and his mouth compressed with distaste.

Sybil smiled, assured of her victory. "Get in the car, Hamilton."

He could tell her to take a flying leap, he thought. He could tell her that he was going to bring her down because she was treading on someone who could be...who *was* very important to him.

"I'm sure you're exhausted," he muttered with stiff politeness while, beside him, the police commissioner cleared his throat.

"I am, but hearing what you have to say will make me feel better. Get in. I just want to drive and clear my head. I'll have Jacobs bring you back to your car."

Once within the smoke-glass enclave and settled into the plush pearl-gray interior, he declined the drink Sybil offered him. The great car pulled smoothly away with a hissing whisper of wet tire rubber.

Sybil poured herself a healthy glass and took a long swallow. Closing her eyes, she lowered the expensive crystal goblet and laid her head back upon the seat until the anesthesia of the bourbon did its work.

She had unclasped the heavy jeweled frogs at the top of her black silk cape. Her nails had been done since he'd seen her, Hammer noted. She appeared to have had a facial, and her hair had been gleamingly arranged. When she crossed her legs, the black stockings and black suit made her skin look like the finest china.

How many lovers had she had besides Edward Schellenegger? he wondered. Had she really loved Edward or had she been playing a boudoir game, common among the very, very rich and bored? Or was she tempted by all those Austrian diamonds and calculatedly hoped he could lure the jeweler from his French wife and ensure herself a bountiful future?

To his dismay, Sybil reached into a silver box and drew out a cigarette and handed him the lighter. Over the flame, he met her cool, calculating eyes.

He cleared his throat. She had buried a son today. How could she be so involved with personal selfishness? "How's Fleming taking it?"

She blew smoke at the ceiling and told the driver to take the causeway across Lake Pontchartrain. "He's heavily sedated. God only knows if he will survive."

Hammer smiled sympathetically.

Taking another sip of her drink, she said, "Tell me about the investigation. It's the thing that's kept me going—just knowing that there's something I can do. By now I suppose you've talked to..."

"Yes." Hammer had been anticipating the question. "I questioned Dr. Schellenegger at length, as a matter of fact."

"Do you see what I mean?"

"About her being an incompetent physician?" A chill went through Hammer, as if a goose had just walked over his grave. "On the contrary, Sybil. It's my opinion that Dr. Schellenegger did everything she could for the boy. It's her sworn statement that she had no idea who he was."

"That's a lie, of course."

"I'm not sure of that, Sybil."

The black of her eyes glistened. "But you are sure of the statement sworn by your policeman. Even if she didn't know who he was, she let him die."

He hadn't expected to cross her so soon. "Off the record, Sybil," he began.

"Don't give me any of that off-the-record business, Hamilton! Are your men lying or not?"

He sighed dismally. "They stand by their statement, Sybil. My point is that I've talked to the doctor, and there's been some breakdown in communication—"

"Does Gallagher know that the doctor accuses him of falsifying his statement?"

"He says that she's the one who's lying."

Stubbing out her cigarette, Sybil laughed cheerlessly. "This Sadu boy that Gerald was with that night? Has he made his formal statement yet?"

She knew full well that Devane had made the statement and had backed up Gallagher and Webster, Hammer thought angrily. Damn her, why was she putting him through this? To grind in the truth? To make sure he knew that she was running this investigation behind the scenes? That she would have his job if he didn't cooperate?

"Devane Sadu is a scared, spaced-out little junkie, Sybil," he said carefully. "The police are much more of a threat to him than Brittany Schellenegger could ever hope to be. He would perjure his soul to hell and back if they told him to."

Sybil's eyes were a triumphant glittering onyx now. "Hamilton, I've retained Throckmorton and Pruitt to handle the suit for me. Harold Throckmorton will be contacting you. This is just from the malpractice angle, you understand. I expect you to prove in a court that she is guilty of criminal negligence and obstruction of justice, falsification of testimony pertinent to manslaughter. I want it to be a strong case, because there'll be a natural resistance, my being a judge."

Feeling quite old and bone tired, Hammer wished that he were home wearing a pair of old jeans and puttering around in his garage on his old car while the rain came down. And that Brittany was in the kitchen with the smell of freshly-baked cookies.

He rubbed at an aching place in the center of his forehead. "Are you sure this is what you want?"

Her hand lifted in the manner of a ballerina. Hammer watched the fire of its diamonds. She turned on the seat, leaned forward and touched the tip of a scarlet fingernail to his chest.

"You disappoint me, Hamilton. I expected better things of the mayor's number one boy."

"You're treading on dangerous ground here," he muttered.

All the pretended civilities between them abruptly ceased. Sybil Wade narrowed her eyes until they were little more than malicious slits. "You are giving me advice about the law, Lieutenant Curry?"

"I'm saying, Sybil, that you've had a terrible thing happen in your life. I'm telling you that you're too close to this. Let Throckmorton handle it. Let your wounds heal."

The most frightening thing of all, Hammer thought as a numb reaction set in, was the way Sybil took it. He honestly expected a tantrum. Sarcasm, at least.

But her scarlet lips turned up at the edges, and her smile was the most terrifying thing he had ever seen. "Why, I appreciate your concern, Hamilton. I really do. And I'll take that into account."

He felt as if he had just turned over a dead body at his feet.

She went on, "I don't really expect that Bruce Clements will be overjoyed when I tell him that you don't believe the word of the two policemen involved. That will bring on an investigation of an altogether different nature. Internal affairs will have a field day. What did you really intend to do, Hamilton? Did you hope that your men would have a change of heart and waltz into the precinct and say 'Oh, by the way, we lied.'"

"Sybil—"

"Consider yourself off the case, Lieutenant!" She was cold now and icily furious. "I don't want someone working with me who can't give one hundred percent."

Not trusting himself to speak, Hammer reached for the bottle of bourbon on the bar. He splashed the liquor into a glass and tossed it off in a gulp. Then he tapped at the glass that separated them from the driver.

They were coming to the end of the causeway. "Take me back," he called.

The chauffeur nodded. Hammer sank back to his seat, exhausted.

"Well," she said, lifting a beautiful shoulder as the big car nosed onto the highway that would return them to New Orleans without recrossing the Lake Pontchartrain causeway. "That's that. You know, Hamilton, the mayor's a close friend of mine. The governor, too. If I were you, I'd be very careful what I said to people from now on."

Now that he'd effectively burned most of his bridges and come very close to shucking his entire career, Hammer wondered if Brittany would ever know or care that he had laid himself on the line.

He curled his lip at Sybil Wade. "Oh, I don't know, Sybil. I figure everyone can be forgiven once for telling tales out of school."

She paled slightly. Hammer felt like Cain, playing dirty with a woman who had just buried her son. But, dammit, she was ruining him.

"What tales?" she demanded through her sparkling teeth. "Just what are you driving at?"

"I'm not driving at anything, Sybil. I simply know human nature, and I daresay that if I started poking around in Gallagher's past or Webster's past, even your past, that I could come up with things that would be better off remaining underground."

Sybil hadn't gotten where she was by being stupid. She knew exactly what Hammer was warning her about. "You son of a bitch!" she said raspily. "You dare talk to me like that? I'll bring you down if you so much as try, Hamilton Curry. I'll break your back. You won't be able to get a job as a security guard when I get through with you."

"Somehow, Sybil," he replied with resignation as he wondered, as only a man with perfectly good intentions can, how his life had gone so quickly awry, "that's just what I expected you to say."

That afternoon the rain stopped. The sky turned yellow. As the hours wore on, it changed to a dull and heavy gray once more.

The weather service issued warnings and cautious predictions. Schools were closed from the severity of the thunderstorms. As people were evacuated from the bayous, the weather station gave reports of tiny coastal villages already incurring flood damage. Creeks and canals all along the southern fringe of the Gulf states were overflowing and pouring out into the marshes.

At twenty minutes past three, five hundred miles out in the Gulf, Hurricane Helen lifted her arms skyward and executed a perfect fouetté. As if she had been particularly grieved, she tightened her exquisite silver clouds about her and raced, shrieking and screaming like a banshee, toward Louisiana.

Chapter Eight

He was out of his mind. Hammer Curry told himself this over and over as he plowed at twenty miles an hour along Poydras Street through water up to his hubcaps.

If he weren't out of his mind, then he was approaching some terrible male crisis. He was behaving like a forty-year-old bloodhound on a relentless scent, and it wasn't like him. He didn't go after women. They came after him.

He swerved into an underground parking lot and drove through the cement cavern until he reached the security booth where a burly guard watched him park and get out of his car. He wrote something down as if Hammer were a criminal.

From force of habit, Hammer consulted his wristwatch. He was five minutes early. "Nine o'clock," Patrick had said. Brittany would meet him at nine o'clock in the parking lot of this building.

For what seemed a futile length of time, Hammer paced up and down. The sound of his own heels set up a motif that wove in and out of the cement columns and warned Hammer the odds were high that he would get stood up.

Maybe he should do it to her before she could do it to him. He could leave and call Brittany the next day with a perfectly true story that something had come up.

When he heard the sound of her Jeep, he had to laugh at himself. Nothing in God's green earth could have made him leave, and when he saw her turn off the engine and get out, the pulse pounded in his temples as if he were eighteen again and was dreading making a fool of himself before the prettiest girl in school.

"I'm late," she said and smiled.

"It's permitted."

"I teach a class on Wednesdays. Preventative medicine. Everyone's gotten so used to it, not even Hurricane Helen could keep them home."

The smile continued to play charmingly around her lips, and she hardly resembled the woman at the funeral at all, Hammer thought. She was wearing slim cotton pants and strap sandals. Her blouse, tucked in, was nothing special— a soft floral print with tiny pearl buttons down the front and slim capped sleeves. Her hair had been tied at her nape with a scarf, but it was pulling free, and raindrops still glistened on it. Her lips, unglossed, were pale and pink.

Upon one shoulder she had drawn a huge tote bag that was gathered on two sides around large bone hoops. It rattled mysteriously when she locked the door of the Jeep.

He murmured, "Helen couldn't keep me home, either. He might, though."

"Everly?" She laughed and dipped her head in the direction Hammer faced. "He's my friend. Why don't we go up?"

"To what?"

"To my…" With apprehension appearing suddenly in her chin and the color of her eyes, she glanced around the space. "This building is part of the Schellenegger conglomerate, Hammer."

With a long sigh that acknowledged everything he'd been looking at for the past half hour, Hammer let out his breath. It figured, didn't it? She even paid the security guard's salary.

"You own all this," he said. It wasn't a question.

She grimaced. "Do you mind?"

"Does it intimidate me, you mean? Hell, yes, it intimidates me."

"It intimidates me, too."

"It's not quite the same," he dryly retorted.

She walked lithely toward Everly. The man was one of the largest men Hammer had ever seen—not fat, but a great wrestling bear of a man. She playfully thumped his arm with her fist.

"Everly," she teased. "I thought you'd died."

"Now, Doc." His high-pitched whine was ludicrous, considering his incredible size. "That's the most uncharitable thing I've ever heard."

"I'm still upset because you beat me at arm wrestling."

"Did you come for a rematch?"

She laughed. "No, I'm a rat, looking for a sinking ship. How's the blood pressure, Everly?"

The huge man flushed. "Doc, you know I like my steak and potato."

"But do they like you? *That* is the question."

"I'm gettin' on in years, Doc. There ain't no sense in depivin' myself of a few final pleasures before I die."

She wagged her finger at him. "Final may be right," she warned. "And then you'll be nagging at me from the great beyond, down on my case to beat the band."

"Doc, did anyone ever tell you that you take the fun out of everything?"

With a wink at Hammer, Brittany laid her hand upon the man's leather belt where it strained to fit about his middle. "Skip the steak, Everly, and have the potato. Do you know Lieutenant Curry of the NOPD?"

The older man's face underwent a total transformation. The bushy brows lifted, and his white mouth of great teeth broadened. "Lieutenant?" He extended his hand reverently. "Why, I'm real proud to meet you, sir."

Fascinated, Hammer obligingly inclined his head. "I'm glad to know that someone's taking good care of Dr. Schellenegger."

"Wal," the man drawled, "it's easy 'cause she don't come around here very much. She thinks we're not good enough or somethin'."

"Be nice, Everly," she playfully scolded.

Not until they reached the private elevator and she had given the secret code did Hammer speak again. She asked for the twelfth floor, and he leaned back against the wall and indulged himself studying her. His stare finally wrecked her composure, and she looked over at him, then flushed and lowered her eyes.

"How much did you give him?" he asked.

"What're you talking about?"

He grinned. "The bill you palmed, Diamond Jim. A twenty?"

A pause. Then she said, "You don't miss much, do you, Hammer Curry?"

"About you? I suspect not."

"It's no big deal." She brushed her generosity off with a shrug. "Everly won't keep his blood pressure prescription filled if I don't make him, that's all. His wife's health isn't good, and what money he has he spends on her."

"Another one of those ninety-ten situations, I suspect."

She slid him an enigmatic smile. "You're a strange man, Hammer Curry."

"Me? Strange? You got real brass, girl."

The elevator made a soft, reassuring sound as it settled gently to rest. The silence was filled with the hum of a venting fan. Brittany looked, not at Hammer, but at the fan.

She asked softly, "Why did you insist on seeing me tonight, Hammer?"

"Insist?"

"Patrick Gilbert said that if I didn't meet you, you would send the sheriff to pick me up."

Hammer laughed. Presently he said, adoring her, "What will it take to make you fall in love with me?"

If he had said any word besides "love," Brittany thought she could have regained her lost equilibrium. But the doors of the elevator were opening onto a world that was strange to begin with, and she was so abruptly paralyzed, so out of her element, that she helplessly watched it whisper closed again.

"What did you say?" she asked, hardly daring to look at him.

His slow inspection from the top of her head to her feet was its own reply. "That I want to kiss every single inch of you."

None of it was real! *He* wasn't real, and the blistering heat she was feeling wasn't real.

"There's something to drink in my office," she said and gestured lamely beyond the elevator.

"I guess that means you don't want me to do it here?" Grinning, he threw his weight to one hip.

Brittany finally saw his strategy. It was all an act to loosen her up, and she stood accusing him and nibbling the edge of her lip. Not breaking the electrical connection, she reached out and slapped a button on the elevator panel without looking at it.

The doors swished open. An impressive gold-plated sign directly before them read, Schellenegger Enterprises.

"Exit, Wolfman," she murmured.

Chuckling, Hammer dropped back to amble along behind her as she led him along a maze of beige-carpeted hallways whose walls were decorated with costly Audubon drawings. Beyond the doors with muted night-lights, he caught glimpses of mahogany desks, and he could imagine the lawyers in their three-piece suits huddling around the coffee machine in the mornings discussing their problem for the day, of how they would turn the Schellenegger millions into more millions.

After unlocking the door of a private office, she led him into a spacious affair discreetly furnished with heavy Victorian pieces. A large impressive desk dominated the room. Above it drooped a crystal chandelier that vied with the splendor of the one in Sybil Wade's home.

She stepped to a small side room, flipped a switch and dropped her tote on the floor with a clatter. A soft rosy glow flooded the bathroom and also bathed the office with a moody velvet sheen.

The floor-to-ceiling drapes weren't pulled. Beyond them, the city of New Orleans was a surrealistic blur.

"Holy cow," he muttered from the corner of his mouth as he moved to stand before the window.

She moved to stand beside him, and together they watched the breathtaking lightning tear at the sky. She swiftly ascertained his thoughts and laughed. "Please don't be impressed by this."

"Well, I am. Right out of my... I'm impressed."

"I've done nothing to deserve it." Her shrug was poetry. "I didn't work for it, and I didn't earn it. I have it only because an old man loved me."

"Maybe he thought love was reason enough."

"I like to look out at the lights, though."

So contagious was her melancholy that Hammer tried to imagine himself in Sigmund Schellenegger's place. He could understand how a man could want to get even with the world just once and make life play fair. He would have done the same thing, he guessed.

Brittany indicated a small pantry along an inner wall. "Fix yourself a drink, Lieutenant. I've got to do something with my hair. It's driving me crazy."

With the old desire rising in him again, he watched her slow graceful walk to the bathroom. She didn't completely shut the door but poked her head back into the office and asked with an unexpected gravity that delighted him, "You *are* off duty, aren't you?"

Laughing, he walked to her liquor cabinet. "I wouldn't proposition a lady when I was on duty."

Only afterward? Brittany thought of the other women who had to be in his life, and she warmed with a sudden troubling jealousy. She leaned back against the wall and pressed her breasts together with a violent shiver.

She should never, *never* have come here with Hammer Curry! Instead of shutting doors, it had opened more dangerous ones. More dangerous, even, than the lies that threatened to destroy her future.

Turning, she placed her eye to the crack of the door and furtively watched Hammer peel out of his windbreaker. His moves were subtle, fluid, practiced, with his weight balanced springily on the balls of his feet. He placed the jacket neatly across the back of the chair and pulled his elbows to the center of his back in a virile stretch, then rubbed the corded muscles in the back of his neck.

All her bones seemed to melt. He stooped then, to open the door of her liquor cabinet, and his pants pulled so tautly that the outline of his wallet was bold against his right hip. Bringing out a bottle, he struck the cap of it with his palm and spun it loose. He sniffed the clear liquid and a leisurely smile angled across his face. His brows lifted with approval.

Brittany guessed that he had known all along she was spying, and a thousand kilowatts of heat stung her cheeks. She found a drawer and nervously rifled it until she located the blessed cigarettes. With shaking hands she plucked one out and promptly dropped it. After retrieving it, she slipped it between her lips and got it lit.

This would be her last smoke, she promised, breathing deeply and closing her eyes, but just now she had to have it. The man was driving her to distraction.

Soon she was calm enough to look out again. He was standing before the windows, solemnly sipping his drink. He'd braced one foot on the rung of the chair.

How beautiful he was, she thought. How disciplined, how . . . in control of his life. He was everything she wasn't. He could take things, or he could leave things, and he would never have let Lilith force him to cower. He would have told her "John is my friend. He's coming, and that's that!"

Smoke curled up from her fingers, burning her eyes, and, like a junkie finishing with a needle, she inhaled and flipped the cigarette away; she readied herself with a spray of perfume on her soggy blouse, a rinse of her mouth, a gathering of her courage. . . .

A bottle of excellent vodka was open on the cabinet when Brittany entered the office. She hadn't bought it. She hadn't even seen it before.

Pausing, she poured herself a generous amount. He was watching her like a cat having already decided upon its victim, and she winced when he sniffed the air.

"What's that I smell?"

Her smile was blatantly guilty. "Perfume. I, uh, I freshened up."

"Oh." His teeth gleamed in a wicked grin as he walked around her and sniffed again. "I would've sworn it was smoke."

He knew, the wretch!

She swallowed too much vodka and was seized with coughing. He made no effort to help—which maddened her even more—and when she was finally finished with embarrassing herself, she challenged him, "D'you think I went in the bathroom to get high?"

His brows underscored her naiveté. "That particular smell I do know. This is . . . Virginia Slims?"

"Brimstone," she snapped hotly. "With a touch of sulfur thrown in."

His laughter triggered her deep, by now familiar ache, and when he placed his glass on her desk, hesitating for so long that all Brittany could hear was the crash of her heart in her ears, she jumped when he said, "You decided to leave your hair down."

In disbelief, she reached back a hand to her hair. Well, that did it, didn't it? She'd just put the finishing touches on her foolishness.

Weary of looking dumb, she began braiding the rebellious strands, but he caught her wrist in a gentle but undeniable demand.

"Leave it," he huskily ordered.

"I—"

"I want to tell you something." He wasn't smiling.

A chill moved over the back of her neck and raised gooseflesh on the tops of her arms. "What?"

"I want to tell you that I'm glad you were seen in public with your mother. When did you decide to do it?"

"When you suggested it."

That pleased him, and when she smiled he released her. He moved out into the darker portion of the room where the lightning from the storm captured his profile against the glass.

With her heart hammering, Brittany had a sensation of being in the wrong place.

"Brittany?" He didn't look at her when he said her name.

She swallowed hard. "What?"

"Devane Sadu didn't corroborate your statement."

So that was it! Well, she really shouldn't have been surprised. She should have expected it. If Devane Sadu had ever told the truth in his life, it had been a bizarre accident.

Though she reacted with her best logic, the news still hit her like a blow to her middle. Anger spurted suddenly through Brittany—fierce, consuming fury that made her struggle to breathe.

"That creep," she wailed, spinning blindly around and striking at the air with clenched fists. "That low-down little creep."

He moved up behind her and stood so close that Brittany could feel the warmth of his sympathy. "He's just a street kid, Brittany. You shouldn't expect anything else."

"Well, I do, dammit! I've done a lot for him, invested time in him." She swiped angrily at her moist eyes and threw him a plea over her shoulder. "Isn't there something I can do? Make him take a lie detector test? Bring him up on other charges? He was there with Gerald, you know. He probably shot Arnold Bates himself. My goodness, Hammer, doesn't that count for *anything*?''

When she whirled around and waited for him to place the solution into her hands, his sigh was heavy and disillusioned. He worriedly stroked his hair, over and over. ''We were in an awkward situation as far as his account of the shooting went,'' he said. ''There were no witnesses except Gerald, and he's dead. So the department traded him immunity from the first-degree murder charge—''

Brittany moved away from him and covered both ears with her hands. ''Oh, I don't want to hear it!'' She shook her head. ''Some system of justice you've got going there, Lieutenant Curry. Now I know why people take the law into their own hands.''

Miserable, because what she said was true, Hammer wiped his mouth with the palm of his hand.

Brittany despised every woman's weakness in herself. After Patrick Gilbert had delivered the message, she had wandered around the rest of the day, imagining all sorts of silly childish day dreams—that Hammer and she were lovers, that she was married to him and was picking the children up at school, that she was in love with him, the ninety-ten variety.

Now this. He hadn't wanted to see her tonight because he wanted to be with her: he'd wanted to ease his conscience by telling her face-to-face that she was in more trouble than she knew.

''I made a mistake in bringing you here,'' she said quietly and turned to hurry across the office. She grabbed up her tote from the floor and rushed to the bathroom and struck the switch, throwing the office in total darkness, except for the lightning dancing across the sky outside.

Hammer told himself to let her cope with the news in her own way. He'd done enough damage. But he, too, was chafing unbearably; he'd just seen his little bubble burst in his face, and he realized now that he wasn't going to be the white knight riding up on his fierce charger to save her. He couldn't do anything for Brittany Schellenegger. Hell, he couldn't even do anything for himself.

"Why *did* you bring me here?" he asked before she reached the door.

She threw back her head and studied him with a hard glinting look. "Me first, Lieutenant. Why did *you* want to see *me*?"

Her hair was a burnished cloud swirling around her head. Hammer had an irresistible compulsion to walk over and fill his hands with it and pull with all his might. He did step nearer and saw, to his dismay, that beneath the coppery curls she was turning her head away. Her face was twisted with misery, and all the frustration suddenly drained out of him.

He drew her into his arms with soft, shushing sounds, and she didn't struggle but laid her head upon his shoulder with a trust that made him hate himself.

"After what happened the other night," she said, her words muffled against his shirt, "I wanted to explain. I thought you might understand a little better if you could see some of this up here, this building and everything. I thought you could see how little it means to me."

Her erratic gesture included everything. "I thought I could make you believe in me," she said and began detaching herself from his arms. "I see now that I was wrong. I'd like to go home, Hammer. I'm sorry. You're a patient man. I don't mean to keep treating you this way. It isn't like me to do such a thing."

Hammer didn't stop to think about what he was doing. He even realized that everything was totally unlike him—some other man inside his skin. Yet as she reached for the doorknob, he slammed both hands on each side of her arms, trapping her between the door and himself. He conformed to the swell of her hips as if he wanted to draw her right inside that skin with him, and she recognized the extent of his recklessness.

Her knowledge only made him lean more heavily into her and close his arms around her neck and hold her imprisoned there so that he could bury his face into the riotous silk of her hair.

"I'm not patient," he said roughly against the side of her throat and drew in the gentle fragrance of the soap she'd bathed with. "I'm not patient, and I'm not kind. Right now I hate all this . . . all this money, this building, and I think I hate you for having it. Dammit, Brittany, why couldn't you live on Carondeleer for real?"

Is that all he could think about? The money? Brittany writhed until she had twisted around in his trap. The fact that her breasts were crushed against him and that her whole body was molded to him was immaterial.

She accosted his accusing eyes. "Does everything have to be equal?" she cried out. "Where's the ninety-ten now, Hammer Curry? Where's all that understanding?"

"That's not what I meant, and you know it."

That was beside the point. It wasn't enough that she had lived all her life with the hatred of her parents. Here he was, Hammer Curry, her one chance to break out of that crusty cocoon of fate. And now he was snatching that away because of his damnable pride.

She struggled ridiculously to beat at his chest with her fists. "Don't you talk to me anymore!" she yelped and flailed desperately at both his trapping arms. "You just shut your mouth, Hammer Curry, and leave me alone!"

Her outburst took the heart out of him. "I shouldn't have said that," he said, wanting to take her into his arms for real but not daring. "I'm sorry. Please forget..."

But there was no such thing as forgetting. The millions would always be there, wouldn't they? Creating the gaping chasm? She couldn't rid herself of them any more than she could cure herself of a terminal disease, and Hammer's pride and masculine postures wouldn't let him forget the roots of his past.

She fought herself free of him and swept across the room and jerked open a drawer of the desk. She snatched out a half-dozen books and hurled them to the floor with an ugly sound of crumpling pages.

"Would you like to see my books for the clinic?" she challenged. "Just to make sure I'm telling the truth about *that*?"

Hammer walked heavily to the window and stared at the storm without seeing any of it. "That isn't necessary," he said dully. "I believe you."

Brittany heard his words perfectly well. Even over the crashing thunder outside, she heard them, yet she stood blinking at his lean silhouette in the darkness. *He believed her?*

Dazed, she walked up behind him until hardly six inches separated them. To the back of his head she whispered, "You believe me... about Gerald?"

He made no offer to touch her this time when he turned around. "I believe that Gerald Wade was alive when he left your clinic, exactly as you said he was. I believe that Gallagher and Webster have not been honest. I believe that Sybil Wade is afraid of you for some terrible reason, and that she sees in this tragedy a way to hurt you. But I don't know how to prove any of it."

But the proof didn't matter, couldn't he see that? She lifted her arms and wrapped them about his neck, raising her lips for his kiss. "Oh, Hammer."

There was no denying his pleasure nor his need when he responded to her questing kiss. He moved his mouth gently upon hers, and he took his breath in tiny, rough moans. But Brittany felt the tight rein he had upon his pride, and as she pressed her lips to the underside of his jaw where the dark, spicy fragrance was, she knew that he would never love her as she would love him.

"Thank you for that much, Hammer," she said and swallowed down her disappointment. "Thank you for that."

For her to thank him was blasphemy. Shaking his head, Hammer started prying her arms from around his neck, but she caught his face between her hands.

"One thing before you go," she said quickly, "you must understand about the other night. My...the way I behaved. It had nothing to do with you, Hammer. It was a long time ago."

The distance to the elevator as she led the way was like the last walk of a condemned man for Hammer. Brittany's steps were slow, as if picking up her feet was an exhausting ordeal. A water fountain gleamed midway, and she stopped and bent her head over the spigot.

But even a millionaire's fine quality couldn't defy a mechanical apparatus's privilege to malfunction. The fountain mischievously spurted her with a stream in both eyes. Gasping from the icy impact, she jerked up her head, and Hammer unthinkingly flicked a handkerchief from the back pocket of his jeans.

Without a word she knocked his hand away, and he grasped her face and began blotting it dry in spite of her. But she was crying, and then he couldn't tell where the water stopped and tears began.

The most frustrated love of his whole life blazed through his loins, melting his heart and making his voice hoarse. "Don't cry, sweetheart," he mumbled as he held her. "Not because of me. I don't deserve your tears."

It really didn't matter, anyway, Brittany thought. Nothing mattered—not the money, not her work, not anything, because she would never have Hammer, and she knew now that he was all she wanted. His kisses melted, one into another, and he was pressing her back against the wall of the darkened corridor and unfastening her pants. Brittany, knowing that there was no future, ever, found herself clawing just as impatiently at the snap and zipper of his jeans.

His mouth wasn't making delicate inquiries now as it had before, however. Now he demanded and he took. Even before she had her arms wrapped around him and was moving her hands over his buttocks, making him know that she wanted them, wanted him, he was placing claims everywhere upon her.

"I don't know the future, Brittany," he groaned against her lips. "My head's all messed up. I can't think. I just know I want this—I want you more than I've ever wanted anything in my life."

"I don't care about the future," she lied and let the muscles of her legs acquiesce when he pushed her back against the wall and forced them apart with his knee.

His entry was sudden and awkward and driving and nothing that either of them could have prevented. It slammed her painfully against the wall, and she gasped, for it hurt. He knew that it did, and he groaned with regret.

"Pretend that you love me," his plea grated raspily in her ear. "Just this one time."

If only she could have told him the truth that she did love him, that she couldn't remember any longer when she didn't, she would have. But he came immediately, and it was violent. It frustrated him, and Brittany wanted to say it was all right, that she was satisfied just to be desired so blindly. But before she could say any of those things, he gathered her into his arms and sank with her down to the floor. Brittany didn't know what to do as he cradled her into the curve of his body and lovingly pushed back her hair, adoring her in the darkness, moving his lips over her eyes, her brows, her mouth, the slopes of her face and her throat, her breasts.

"You scare me," he murmured. "You're so...unexplored. It frightens me, the things I don't know about you."

When he placed his hands at the juncture of her thighs, Brittany shrank in consternation. She was still wet and hot, and she couldn't imagine that he would want to touch her when she was that way.

He still wore his pants, but hers lay twisted at her feet. The primitive earthiness of it was its own excitement, and the danger of being discovered was an exhilaration.

"What're you thinking?" he asked as he unbuttoned her blouse and blew a warm stream of breath on her eyelids.

"That I've never known a man like you," she said thickly.

She only vaguely realized that he had made her completely naked while he remained dressed. His hands were learning all her secrets, and his fingers were finding the velvety folds of flesh hidden in the rusty curls. "Because I'm too proud?" he whispered.

"Most men would want the money." She could hardly form words with her tongue.

"I'm not most men."

"I know."

"But you don't desire most men, do you?"

"No," she whispered and flinched when he took her hand and drew it to himself, to the raspy place of his open zipper.

Unaroused, Hammer was not the least frightening or even impressive. He was just a plain man who was bending over her breasts and doing things with his teeth that sent a slow prickling euphoria through her limbs.

"What do you want?" he whispered as he created a sweet pain that probed Brittany's insides like a laser.

But then he was no longer unaroused. He was hard and insistent against her palm, and Brittany found the lethargy irresistible.

"Really?" she said, drugged.

"Only the most real."

With unskilled strokes she made him ready, then, lifting herself—such a beautiful, willing sacrifice to such a lovely impalement—she buried her nails into his hips and kept him there, forcing him to pierce the pulsing center of her desire.

"Tell me things," she gasped.

He could hardly speak, much less tell her things. He moved slowly and deep, wanting to understand and wanting to satisfy what he sensed was a confusing hunger inside her that had never been satisfied.

His mouth sought her ear and his tongue its sensitive shell. "You tell *me* things," he said. "Tell me about him. Whisper it in my ear."

Everything in her rebelled at that, and Hammer feared he'd made a mistake. He gathered her close and kept moving, moving, never stopping.

"I'm here," he told her, "exactly where I want to be, as close as a man can be except to be inside that head of yours. Touch my soul, Brittany. This—" he strained against her "—means nothing without the heart."

"His name was John Gallois," she said. "He's dead. His ghost won't die."

"Why?"

She couldn't tell him such a thing, not what John had done to her.

"You can't keep hating him," he told her. "He was just a child, and the best thing he ever did for himself was to accept the love you gave him. But he never knew you, sweetheart. He never knew the chains around you. If he'd lived, I doubt he would have known."

Her eyes opened. She lay perfectly still beneath his thrusting assault. "Chains? What chains?"

"A bad choice of words. I only meant that he didn't understand that little partition you have about yourself that keeps you from letting a man inside."

She went cold beneath him. "I'm not frigid, Hammer Curry."

Oh, Lord. He'd done it, hadn't he?

He kissed her. "I didn't mean that, sweetheart. But just because you can do what we're doing now doesn't.... You know what I'm talking about. You know it's there. You have to know. You're too sensitive not to know."

Not in her entire life had anyone talked to her as he was talking to her. She turned her head aside, refusing not only to acknowledge what he said but to look at him at all.

"Let me up," she demanded. "I don't want to do this."

He kept her pinned with his weight. "Don't you think you've punished yourself enough, Brittany? Haven't you let John Gallois punish you enough, even from his grave?"

"You're a cruel man, Hammer Curry."

"Because I'm asserting a truth you don't want to see?"

"That's not true."

"Has any man taken you that far?"

"Having mutual orgasms is not a sign of personal freedom, Hammer."

"It's part of the complexity, and you're not answering the question."

She struggled to free herself, hating him now.

But he, once the subject had been dragged into the open, was as determined as she was. He pushed her shoulders into the plush carpet. He stared at the shadowy curves of her breasts.

"Are you afraid that I'll know that it's hard for you?" he deliberately challenged, withdrawing completely now. "That I'll see you have to work for it? That it may not be easy?"

She swung a fist at his head. "Everyone's not the same. Let me up."

"That's not the point. Are you afraid that I'll make comparisons and think you're not very sophisticated, hm? Poor little Brittany, she's got all those brains and all that money, but she can't quite figure out how to do it?"

"It's none of your damn business what I figure out to do!" she screamed at him, and Hammer clapped a hand over her mouth.

"Hush! Do you want to have Everly calling the whole police force up here?"

Her weeping was soundless behind his fingers, and Hammer thought he could have gladly put a gun to his head. He removed his hand and replaced it with loving kisses upon her cheeks and her eyes.

"I need to give, too, sweetheart," he whispered. "I need to be used by someone I trust. I need to be *trusted* that much. No one's ever trusted me, not like that, and I know you've never trusted that much."

"I've worked out my life," she sobbed, "my own needs."

"Yes, but no one's cared, sweetie. They're too busy caring about their own needs, so they give you money and never give a damn about how whole a woman you really are. I care. I swear, I do."

The truth of her life had never been stated so nakedly before. In her first reaction of wanting to escape such an honesty, Brittany fought him. Twisting around, she grabbed out for her pants, scrambling in a half playful, half angry contest when Hammer caught her by the ankle.

She kicked with more strength than she intended, and he gripped her with more force than was necessary. The war of the sexes was suddenly something more than a cliché. Brittany found herself facing a virile, determined man who had just bared his soul to her and had every intention of proving himself right.

"No," he protested.

"We're finished!" she gasped.

"Think again."

Brittany clapped her hands between her legs. He wasn't smiling when he pried her knees apart; he was the most unsmiling man she'd ever seen in her life. She knew then that she would not escape him; she didn't really want to, and she laid an arm across her eyes.

"Coward," he whispered as he lowered his head and touched her with his mouth and began to learn her with an intimate expertise that she didn't want to consider how he'd acquired.

Some of the things he did horrified her, but after a while she couldn't have stopped him if she had wanted to. And she didn't want to. He awakened slumbering sensations that made her lie in delirious languor, then jerk up in wild surprise. She couldn't keep still. She was driven. When he slipped his hands beneath her hips and lifted her up, the explosion started from somewhere deep near her spine. It detonated a series of tiny electrical charges that touched all her muscles and all her bones and all her juices and her eyes and her breath.

Over and over it happened, until she was worn out with it, worn out with him, and she begged him to stop. Immediately he penetrated her, and she forgot about the expertise of it. In a way, she forgot about the sex of it, only that they were together, inseparably, and she had let him see that last virginal part of her heart that no other human being had ever seen before.

Once it was done, he didn't force her to talk. It was as if a mutual no-man's-land had been agreed upon and that they would not allow this stolen interlude to become a weapon.

He, knowing that there were some walls even love could not scale, prepared himself to see her return to her own life, and because she didn't know how to change anything, she accepted that decision. In his way Hammer did love her, she knew, for she loved him desperately, and love could not be that mistaken.

But too many insolvables existed between them. Only the future would reveal the answers. So she didn't ask him when she would see him again. And he didn't speak to her about the money or his needs to be his own man.

"I'll keep in close touch," he said sadly after they had dressed themselves and resumed their own individual prides and flimsy facades.

She forced herself to smile. He kissed her and said, "Okay?"

"Okay."

"Things will work out."

"Of course they will."

Later he leaned inside her Jeep and kissed her for the last time while Everly discreetly turned his head. "Goodbye, then," he said, which meant *I think my heart is breaking.*

"Goodbye," she said, which meant *This is the hardest thing I've ever done.*

Chapter Nine

At what point, Brittany wondered, did a person become obsessed with another person?

Perhaps if someone had told her, "You must absolutely fall head over heels in love with Hammer Curry, you must think about him constantly until you can't eat or sleep, you must make yourself miserable and all those around you miserable, then you must sink into a wretched depression," she wouldn't have done it. Human nature being what it is and all.

But since no one told her that, she did precisely so. She had never been so utterly miserable in her entire life. If Hammer loved her as much as she loved him, nothing would stand in his way—not money, not people, not heaven nor earth. She always loved too much. She always loved the wrong people. She never learned, did she?

She went on a furious cleaning spree. For two days she tore through her small apartment as rapaciously as Helen romped around in the Gulf of Mexico. She organized closets and drawers and scrubbed baseboards. She scoured toilets and washed curtains and polished furniture and even silver. She straightened the contents of every box and tidied every nook and every crevice in the dilapidated old building.

Mooch found it all enormously alarming. "You been readin' books on child rearing again?" he accused when she ran the vacuum cleaner around his feet for the second time in one evening.

Brittany passed a fine, critical eye around the room. She'd done everything. Everything! But no matter how hard she worked, she simply could not achieve the charm of Hammer's living room.

"What an attitude," she scolded Mooch, then sighed bleakly. "This place is nothing but a rat hole."

His black eyes were years older than her own. "You never saw a rat hole, Doc."

How come his outlook always floored her? Brittany smirked. "Well, you could certainly get up off your fanny and help."

He grinned. "I'll load the washing machine."

"Wonderful," she called to his back. "And put some detergent in it this time."

"I don't get it," she finally admitted in exasperation as she peered into her kitchen drain. "Some people's houses just look neat, Mooch. All the time. Even when they're messy, they look neat."

"Whose houses?" Mooch asked suspiciously, coming to stand beside her, his black eyes narrowed.

The child was fey, she thought. He wasn't normal. She shouldn't have brought up the subject. "Other people's," she said and shrugged.

She ran fresh water in the sink, bent low and sniffed. "I give up."

The boy stooped to find a box of baking soda in the pantry below the sink. He poked a hole in the box with a fork and dumped some into the drain and ran some more water.

"You ought to watch more television, Doc," he said and walked blandly into the other room. "Your education is lacking."

The little hustler! Finding the side of her hip with a fist, Brittany yelled over the blare of MTV. "We're turning over a new leaf in this house, do you hear? We're going to be normal people and eat regular meals at regular times and use place mats and go to bed at a decent hour and be civilized and never sleep in our clothes!"

She would have sworn she heard him snigger.

When Hammer picked up his office extension and heard Patrick's voice saying "Sir, the commissioner would like to see you up in his office right away," he knew the jig was up.

The truth was, he wasn't even surprised. But then, he hadn't been himself for days. For the first time in his life, he'd been throwing his weight around. And his little jaunt down to Children's Hospital? It had been a disgrace. Even now he couldn't believe he'd really leaned across the counter and grabbed ahold of the squeamish little ambulance dispatcher's shirt like that.

An examination of the man's records revealed that a paramedic had indeed taken an ambulance out shortly before 3:00 a.m. on the morning of September twelve. But the entry didn't give the destination, and since no one had been picked up, the report wasn't filed.

The paramedic—and this was what really set him off— had oddly up and quit his job and hadn't left any indication of where he was going.

The whole thing smelled to high heaven, which only made him remember Brittany's accusation the first time they'd met. So Leonard Bowles was checking out every single ambulance driver in the city on his free time, and Hammer guessed that his men were privately placing bets about whether he was going to ruin himself over Brittany Schellenegger or not.

"Where are you, Pattie?" he asked now.

"Here, sir," came the murmured reply.

Their telepathy was working. "With the commissioner?"

"Yes, sir."

Hammer felt as if he'd just missed being in a car wreck by inches. He let out his breath in a slow, controlled stream. "Sybil made good her threat, I see."

"Yessir."

"Do you think the commissioner knows about the wiretap?"

"I believe you could say that, sir. Yes sir."

"Damn! I'll be right up."

Shutting the door upon his ugly office—the walls were a nauseating greenish-gray that some vile company manufactured precisely for municipal buildings—Hammer took the stairs rather than the elevator up to Bruce Clements's office. He charged up them as fast as he could, venting his anger every time his foot struck the floor.

The commissioner's office wasn't ugly. Real paneling was on the walls, and draperies covered the windows, and carpeting lay on the floor. The bookcases didn't look as if they were leaning against the wall.

Bruce Clements sported a handsome desk set that was supposed to have been a gift from the governor for outstanding service. He was on the telephone when Hammer rapped softly and walked in.

Hammer glanced briefly at Patrick, who looked as if he had just been court-martialed. When the commissioner finally did hang up, he reached into a drawer and drew out a tiny prescription bottle and dumped two white pills into the palm of his hand.

"Darn ulcer," he complained. "The mayor sets it off every time."

After he tossed down the pills and downed a glass of water, he leaned back in his chair and arranged his face into an expression that conveyed vast disappointment.

Hammer and Patrick tried to appear properly respectful.

"So, Lieutenant Curry!" he said. "What's this I hear about your having gotten yourself into a slight pickle? Irate judges? Unauthorized wiretaps? Secret investigations of fellow officers? Sit down, sit down. I want you to go back to the beginning and tell me all about it. Start with the day you were born."

Hammer might have had an easier time of it if Patrick's face hadn't been so red during his report. Brian Gallagher, evidentially, had been expecting Hammer to make some kind of move. He had outsmarted them and had confronted Patrick with the bug. Patrick didn't admit to anything, but Bruce Clements knew that Hammer had tapped the man's phone the same way Hammer knew that Brian was lying.

When he finished the whole story, the commissioner opened a box, lit a cigar and blew a stream of smoke at the ceiling. "It seems to me, Lieutenant," he said and lowered the pale gray ash to consider it thoughtfully, "that you have a rather personal interest in this case."

Resentment formed a hard knot in Hammer's throat. "The trouble, sir, stems from the fact that Judge Wade has a personal interest in this case, and she wants me to go after Dr. Schellenegger, which I refuse to do. Sybil considers my refusal a personal insult, and now she's out for my scalp as well as Dr. Schellenegger's.''

The commissioner was much too skilled to show his true feelings. He tapped the cigar upon an ashtray that had Super Dome written on the bottom if it. ''That's a serious charge, Lieutenant.''

''It's a serious situation.''

''Well, Sybil came to see me this morning. What she'd really like is to run you out of town.''

''That shouldn't be too difficult,'' Hammer said with a dry twist of his mouth.

''She's entitled to her point of view.''

Hammer's head jerked up. ''She wants her son vindicated of all malfeasance.''

''Are you sure that he can't be?''

''The only thing I'm sure of is that Gerald Wade was alive when Gallagher and Webster put him in that patrol car to bring him downtown.''

Bruce Clements came forward and slammed his open palms on the surface of his desk. ''Well, get me some proof, Hammer. That's all I need. Get me just one shred of proof, boy!''

Hammer let out his breath in a slow, whistling stream. If the commissioner had any idea of what lengths he would go to for exactly that . . .

''Just don't take me off the investigation,'' he said quietly. ''It may take a little time, but I will get the proof.''

''By tapping policemen's phones?''

''If they're dirty cops, yes.''

Bruce Clements shook his head. ''You're off this case, Hammer. I'm sorry. I just can't have you running around making wild accusations.''

"The man lied under oath, for Christ's sake! And we're sitting here doing nothing about it. We'll be lucky if Dr. Schellenegger doesn't bring suit against the department!"

Because he *was* involved and because he *had* lost his heart, Hammer had also lost his edge of control. Otherwise he would never have been so reckless as to add "What if I agreed to give the prosecuting attorney a case for criminal negligence, commissioner? Would I be back on the case then?"

An ugly scowl spread across the commissioner's face. If he hadn't feared the mayor, he would have already sent Hammer packing.

"Don't push me, Lieutenant," he growled. "The wiretap you had Detective Gilbert place on Gallagher's telephone merits a reprimand, if not suspension. You're no longer objective here, sir, and now the press is getting involved. For the next two weeks, Lieutenant Curry, consider yourself on vacation. And do yourself a favor, sir. Take one. Now, if you'll excuse me..."

Beneath the surface, Hammer was seething. He came to his feet and adjusted his collar, which suddenly felt as if it would strangle him. "Might I inquire who will replace me on the investigation, commissioner?"

"Jack Kelsey." Clements didn't look at Hammer when he replied, and he shuffled some papers on his desk.

Hammer let his eyes close briefly and breathed a curse. "Jack Kelsey is the biggest yes-man in the department. He'll kiss up to anyone."

From his corner of the room, Patrick made a sound of intense agony.

The commissioner came to his feet at last. He walked to the door and as he opened it and turned, he said, "Don't we all, Hammer? At one time or another?"

"No." Hammer wanted more than anything to plant his fist in the man's face. As God was his witness, he would not let this travesty against an innocent woman go unavenged.

"I never have," he told his superior, "and I never will."

"Which is why," Bruce said, his leer warning Hammer to let the matter rest, "you will be a police lieutenant all your life."

The evening shift had already come on when Hammer finally left his office prepared for a two-week absence from his desk. Before he walked out, however, he punched a button on his phone and waited for a woman's familiar voice to answer.

"Marie," he said pleasantly when she came on the line. "I didn't know if you'd signed in yet."

"And how is the godfather of my son, Lieutenant Curry?"

"Fine," Hammer lied.

Marie laughed. "Not according to the rumors I've been hearing. What's this with you and the commissioner?"

"He doesn't like my choice in ties." Hammer glanced nervously at his telephone. Surely the commissioner wouldn't have had someone put a tap on his own phone, would he? "Hey, I was thinking maybe I'd drop by your office on my way home."

"I'll be waiting for you."

Marie was a short, rather stocky woman with a gorgeous dusky complexion and violet eyes. What she lacked in beauty, she made up for in brains and energy. When Hammer tapped softly at her door and made up a lie about wanting to buy her a soft drink from the machine at the end of the hall, she graciously accepted.

As she popped the tab off the top of her soft drink, she said, "Now that we're alone, you can tell me all about it, Hammer. Or were you going to buy me peanuts, too?"

Grinning sheepishly, Hammer set his drink aside without having opened it. "I was just wondering, Marie..."

"Wondering what?" she said and sipped.

He lifted a discreet shoulder. "If maybe you could run something down in the computer for me without setting off a national alarm."

"Ah." Now Marie understood. She nodded agreeably. "Sure, boss man. What you want is what you get."

"I want Gerald Wade's drug history."

For a moment Marie didn't move, then she took another long swallow and placed her can beside Hammer's untouched one. She glanced over her shoulder as if she expected to find someone there.

"The autopsy showed no drugs in Gerald Wade's system, Hammer," she said.

"I know that, but he was consorting with a known user."

"Hammer—" Marie studied her nails for a moment before she looked at him "—Gerald Wade's a juvenile. We have no record on him."

"I'm not talking about what we have," Hammer said slowly. "I'm talking about what we can get."

"You're asking me to go into juvenile records?"

"Yes."

"They can't be used in any legal proceeding."

"Then it's lucky that I don't want them for that, isn't it?"

Marie turned down both sides of her pretty mouth and heaved a sigh. "Why couldn't you ask me something I could do without risking life, limb and happiness? You know that we'll both be on Sybil Wade's bad list if this gets out. She'll kill me, Hammer. The only reason she hasn't killed you already is because of the mayor."

No one knew that better than Hammer. He smiled at her. "How's Jack, Marie?"

She slid him a withering glance. "Why do you ask?"

Hammer laughed. "No reason, Marie. I was just wondering if you've forgotten who fixed you up with him."

Jack and Marie had been married for five years. Hammer had arranged the blind date himself.

"You're a dirty low-down no-good rat, Hammer Curry," Marie said fondly.

"But you'll do it, won't you?"

"Listen, Hammer, I don't want to read about you taking some job working the ferry on the Mississippi, you hear?"

"Call me at home when you find out something. Okay?"

"When do I get to meet her?" Marie asked as he walked down the hall.

He called back without turning around. "Why, I don't know what you're talking about, Marie."

"Liar," she murmured as she gazed affectionately at Hammer's uncompromising back disappearing down a side corridor.

For days Helen had been playing fast and loose with the meteorologists. From the moment when she'd sprung to life, sophisticated satellites had been relaying information to earth about her. She was in a state of constant change, rearranging herself and whirling and twirling like a woman totally fascinated with seeing how fanciful she can be.

From everything that the expensive equipment could tell, Helen would come inland at New Orleans. Since hurricanes were nothing particularly new to the city, it simply took the necessary precautions of alerting all the schools and all the outlying residences and giving advice of what to do in case of an evacuation warning.

It was no great surprise when, at seven o'clock the next morning, Helen whipped across the Louisiana coast, up through the lowlands to cross the Mississippi River. Many people left the city and traveled north, but some, most of them people Brittany knew, had no way to evacuate. They had endured hurricanes before; they would again.

Like some violent destructive machine, Helen struck at the business district west of Canal Street—to the estimated tune of six million dollars in property damage, wailed the insurance companies. It was terrible. It was dreadful. But everyone was grateful for the lack of casualties. It could have been a lot worse. Wasn't today's brilliant modern technology a miracle?

Just to prove that she would not tolerate being taken so for granted, Helen flew into a female rage. After her escapade on Canal Street and her sweep back to the Gulf, she turned a perfect hundred-eighty degrees and returned with splendid vengeance. This time, in the space of twenty minutes, with a high, keening wind of nearly ninety miles an hour, she left the midcity ghetto an utter shambles of flattened residences, flooded streets, wrecked sewer systems and fires that cropped out every few blocks from old and outdated wiring systems.

Hammer was torquing the heads on his 1957 Chevrolet when he heard. He had sent the children with his parents up to his aunt's place in Lake Charles. He'd been thinking how lucky it was that his section of town had gotten nothing besides high wind and rain.

As he wiped the grease off his hands, he walked over to the sedan and switched on the police scanner.

The static grated on his eardrums. He stood tuning and trying to avoid the jarring rasps of sound when he heard "...impassable at junction of Jacksborough and..."

Jacksborough? That was close to Brittany. He braced a foot on the edge of the door and leaned closer. More irritating static. Squinting, he tuned more precisely.

"Coast Guard rescue team attempting entry at Interstate overpass along Second Avenue..."

The Interstate overpass? He thought Helen had done her little act downtown and left. That was what the television reports had said, and the national weather service.

A cold fear pricked at his nerves, and he threw down the rag and strode swiftly to the wall phone mounted beside the entrance to the kitchen. When he dialed Brittany's number, he realized his palms were sweating.

On the other end a telephone rang and rang and rang. Hammer told himself not to borrow trouble. He broke the connection and dialed zero and missed.

"Damn!" He savagely dialed again. "Check a number for me," he snapped tersely to the operator. "This is an emergency. I'm a police officer."

"I'm sorry, sir," the operator said when she came back on the line. "Those lines are down, sir. All over that part of town."

Hammer slammed down the receiver and dialed the precinct but then decided that he could probably learn more from the scanner. Darting back to the sedan, he flung himself across the seat and worked the dial.

Static. He fine-tuned, then heard, "Car One-five-niner, radio your location. Please respond. Over."

More static. He could hardly hear a thing. He leaned very close. "One-five-niner responding from Rampart and Wade Avenue."

"Yes, One-five-niner. Could you give us the possibility of access at Rampart?"

Hammer held his breath. His heart was crashing. It was too close to her, too close, too close!

"Negative. Flooding's extensive here...lower six blocks of Carondeleer...presently under water. Chandler Creek...completely out of bounds. Heavy debris. Trees down. Power lines down.'' More deafening static. "Possibility of getting a helicopter? Over."

Static. "Coast Guard ... apprised of situation ..."

She's okay. You must not panic!

But Hammer felt as if he were in a trance—a weird kind of limbo where he was detached from his own body, looking down, watching himself check his wristwatch and calculating a time schedule: twenty-five minutes from here to there.

He hit the back steps at a dead run and slammed the door with a crash. Time to dress and throw together an emergency pack? Ten minutes, he figured and went directly to his own room. He dragged on a pair of jeans and his heavy army boots. He zipped on a windbreaker and picked up his revolver, gave the chamber a spin to check and slipped it and his badge into the pocket and slapped it closed. He threw a mixture of emergency items into a backpack, then hit the back door at a run and heaved it into the back seat of the car. Right on schedule.

In actual fact, however, it took Hammer an hour and fifteen minutes just to reach the Interstate highway. Twice he had to backtrack because of impassable streets. Ghastly images flashed across his mind, things he had seen in the line of duty and prayed that his memory would never dredge up again.

Another precious half hour was consumed reaching Jacksborough Street. There, he finally parked and locked his car and went the rest of the way on foot in the rain. By now Helen was technically a tropical storm, he learned on the car radio. She was back out in the Gulf, but her backlash was almost as destructive as she had been herself.

The damage, once Hammer reached Jacksborough Street, was much worse than he'd expected to find it. All phone lines in the area were down for miles. When he had stopped to contact his precinct at a private home, his office had very little information besides what they were picking up from the Coast Guard, which hoped to get some helicopters up within the hour.

The outlying hospitals, he had also learned, were responding from as far out as Metarie and Laplace. The Red Cross and other city agencies were also busy setting up emergency shelters in some of the area gymnasiums.

Hammer wasn't the only person trying to get across Chandler Creek. Three other men had made it as far as he had, and they, too, had been forced to park their cars and walk in. As they stood together, their backs hunched against the lashing rain while they considered the raging flash flood, they made a rather grim and soggy quartet. The water had cordoned off the whole ghetto as effectively as a brigade of enemy soldiers.

To Hammer, Chandler Creek looked like one of the rivers he'd seen in Vietnam—innocent little rivulets that could fill up with water from the hills in an hour and become killers. All kinds of debris was washing downstream now: tin, lumber, parts of cars and tons of trash, even a couple of drowned animals.

The sight of the animals unnerved the men. "I got a wife and three kids on the other side of that creek," one said, his voice growing shrill with panic. "I've got to get across, man. I'm ready to try and swim it."

"You're crazy," another declared as Hammer stood calculating his own chances of getting across. His squadron had tried to cross a flooded creek once, and the casualties had made headlines.

"What about Fairmont Street?" one suggested to Hammer, who had, by way of some tacit election, been made the leader of the expedition.

"It's a low-water bridge," Hammer said and shook his head.

"Yeah, probably three feet under by now."

"There's always California Street."

"A fire's blockin' the underpass," a man threw in. "I saw the trucks when I came in."

On the opposite side of the creek, having fashioned themselves a canopy out of tin and enjoying the adventure as only children could, three boys were hunched together on the creek bank. They had dreams of windfall profits washing downstream, and finder's keepers.

Hammer imagined Brittany trapped in a burning building. He wheeled around hard so that his back was to the men, and he rubbed savagely at his wet face. If he didn't keep telling himself that she was all right, he would become as ineffectual as the other men. Where was all that objectivity he'd prided himself on in past years? He studied the warehouses flanking the creek. They looked deserted, as they were and had been for years. "Wait here," he said. "I'm going to find some rope or some cable or something."

"I'll come with you," offered the first man.

Getting the rope turned out to be the most difficult thing of all. A dozen times Hammer cursed himself for not having thought to throw it in the pack earlier. He and the man returned to the creek, and he made a swift reconnoiter of the area on both sides. The boys were now enormously interested, and another had joined the party, making four.

"Even if you could throw the rope across," one of the men told Hammer, "it's too dangerous. You'd be washed downstream trying to cross."

"Something could knock you unconscious. I saw this movie once . . ."

"I'd wait on the Coast Guard, if I were you."

Closing his ears to their advice, Hammer looked around until he found a cement block. Breaking off a chunk, he looped the rope through two holes and tied it securely.

"By the time the Coast Guard gets here," he told the men, "the whole ghetto could be up in smoke. I'm going to try to get across."

"If you make it," the first man said plaintively, "I'll be right behind you."

By no means did Hammer underestimate his risk. Drowning wasn't something he worried about, for he was a good swimmer, but debris traveled at high speeds in water like this. One second was enough to be knocked out. End of heroics.

He selected the most narrow point possible and shouted to the boys over the roar of the water. By now they were enormously excited and were waving their arms and shouting, thrilled to be involved in such an exciting exploit. Though communication was wasted, Hammer made himself known, and the boys let him know that they would be champions and not disappoint him.

When Hammer was a boy, one of his favorite stories that his mother had recounted to Richard and him was that of David and Goliath. Many times he'd lain curled up on the sofa and imagined the boy of history wearing his humble tunic and marching up to the invincible armored giant, swinging the sling around and around his head then letting it fly.

Slinging a chunk of cement block around one's head wasn't quite the same. Over and over Hammer tried to fling the thing across the roiling water. Finally, with an expenditure of strength that left him nursing a dull tearing sensation somewhere deep in his gut, he succeeded in getting it close enough that one of the boys, holding the hand of a mate, scrambled down to the water's edge and fished it out.

A cheer went up from both sides. Now, thinking only of Brittany and praying harder than he had ever prayed in his life, Hammer tied down his end of the rope.

"One of you needs to go find a telephone," he told the men. "Call the fire department and tell them what it looks like from here."

So, with three men on one side and four boys on the other, Hammer gritted his teeth and stepped into the freezing, angry water.

There were times when he went down, and the water closed over his head like a muddy grave. But fear pumped desperate strength into his arms, and he fought his way up and battled for a foothold. Most of the time he depended totally upon the rope as he dodged tree limbs and lumber and pieces of tin that were as deadly as knives.

The men shouted their encouragement and all kinds of useless advice, but love and fear for Brittany was its own mysterious salvation; it was then that Hammer truly learned what he had always believed: that love made a man capable of things he could never have achieved otherwise.

When the boys hauled him out of the water, he'd never been more grateful for young, clumsy hands. Kicking, scrambling, he fought his way out and lay panting upon his belly with his feet still in the water.

"You all right, mister?" the boys asked, kneeling down beside his head.

He peered up gratefully through the film stinging his eyes. "Yeah. And thanks, guys. I'll look you up after this is all over. You've got my word on it."

From where Hammer crawled out of the creek, it seemed to him that the whole ghetto was on fire. He couldn't count the burning buildings. One would have thought the rain would have extinguished some of them, but it didn't work that way.

Please, he prayed with a sick desperation creeping into his vitals, *just let her be all right. Just let her be alive.* How silly his pride seemed to him now. And hers—all that stupid business about money and emotional chains. If she was safe, he would get down on his hands and knees and thank God and beg her forgiveness for being such a fool.

The streets were devastated. The people Hammer saw were still in shock at the incredible suddenness of the destruction. Some were trying to extricate things from the rubble. Some were dazedly searching for others and asked him to help. Some were huddled in doorways, watching him with frightened eyes.

At some distance away, he saw the glass doors of the clinic shattered in Brittany's parking lot, and his fear was replaced by a growing burning anger at the injustice of life. Enough was enough, dammit! With his heart aching in his chest, he hit the door at a dead run and flung himself headlong into her house, shouting at the top of his lungs.

"Brittany!" He plowed his way through half-collapsed walls and a floor that was standing in water and broken glass. *"Brittany!"*

Racing from one examination room to another, slamming doors and shouting his frenzy, he finally found where she had emptied out her medicine supply cabinet. Several boxes still sat on the flooded floor. He knew then that she was alive. Her Jeep was still parked in her parking lot, which meant she was out somewhere, on foot. But where?

He raced to the next house on the street, but no one was there. Dashing out into the street again, he spotted two middle-aged men braving the rain. Heaving to breathe, he explained to them who he was and asked if they knew where the doctor had gone.

"Doc's down at Marty's Grocery," one of them said as if Hammer should have known that. "Marty's settin' up a shelter in his storeroom."

The other man, Sam Duell, raised mistrustful eyes. Hammer was the outsider here, they told him mutely. "If you come t'help, mister, Woody James has both legs broke. Doc's fixin' 'im."

Hammer's own legs were so so heavy he could hardly pick them up and put them down. But his heart was running to her. On the left, the right, people in need turned to watch him pass, as if they knew what he was—the man who had pledged the best of himself to them but was passing them by for a woman. Like a man possessed, he went straight to her.

At Brittany's suggestion, Marty had transformed the back room of his grocery store into an emergency medical center. The neighborhood got the word immediately. People who weren't injured or caring for someone else who was injured brought in kerosene lamps and dry bedding. They pushed counters together to form tables and hung quilts to give shelter. At Brittany's insistence, they checked on Cookie and Agnes and people they hadn't seen since Helen had ripped through.

That was how Hammer found her, after twelve hours on her feet without a break, dressed in jeans and boots with a sweater tied around her hips and her hair falling down around her face. Brittany was tending the wounded who were brought in by way of the back alley. Dirty, sweat-stained, scrubbing up in a tin pail using soap and bottled water from the grocery shelves, she worked on and on and on.

When Hammer walked through the door, she didn't see him. People who were gathered around, telling her what had happened and asking questions she couldn't answer, needing help she couldn't give, slowly grew silent. They watched the stranger walking up behind her back.

"What's the verdict, Doc?" Woody begged from where he lay propped on one of the counters, his crushed legs extended before him.

It was the question Brittany hated. She searched through her box of medicines and found a vial of narcotics. Slipping the needle of a syringe into the tube running from his IV, she prayed he would enter Valhalla quickly before she must tell him the truth.

She saw the drug blessedly take effect, and she lifted his rough, hard-working hands in her own. "I'm not going to lie to you, Woody. You know I wouldn't do that."

"Tell me the worst it can be, Doc. Don't give me no surprises."

"The worst is that it's bad, Woody. It's not hopeless, but it's bad. You're not going to lose your legs, and you won't spend the rest of your life in a wheelchair, but you're going to need some fancy surgery that I simply can't do. But I'll be there, Woody. I'll select the surgeon myself. The first thing is to get you out of here and into the emergency room of the hospital before you lose any more blood."

Sadness filled the man's eyes. "Oh, Doc, you know I don't have no money for fancy surgery. I don't have no insurance. Hell, how can I pay for insurance? I can't feed my kids."

It was one of the few times when Brittany could have kissed the feet of her grandfather. Leaning down so that her words were a whisper in Woody's ear, so he could not mistake, she said, "You remember when you fixed that water pipe for me, Woody? When the ground was frozen, and you had to chip through it with a pick?"

"Yeah, Doc."

"And you wouldn't take any money?"

"Yeah."

"Well, consider this bill on me, Woody."

"Doc—"

Straightening, she gestured for someone to help her get Woody comfortably settled so she could see the next injured patient.

"You're a good man, Woody," she said as she helped move his IV. "It's my pleasure. Now, will you get over there and quit bugging me? I can't spend all day messing around with you. Grief, some of these people really need a doctor."

As she worked, though, her tone lost its sweet indulgence and cut through the room like a well-honed knife. To one of the men, she said, "We've got to get a helicopter in here for God's sake! Call the Coast Guard. Tell 'em to get some of that wonderful tax-bought equipment in here or crawl in on their hands and knees, dadgummit! We need evacuation!"

"Easy, babe," Hammer murmured as he walked up to her back and touched his lips to the side of her arm, "give 'em some slack. They're only men, for pity's sake."

Brittany's green eyes flew wide. Her paleness turned to a brilliant crimson. Her weariness faded away, and her arms went around his neck. "Hammer! Oh, Hammer!"

In all the years of her practice Brittany had never lost control in front of a patient, but when she turned to find Hammer, filthy dirty and soaked from the soles of his boots to the crown of his head—so wonderful, so heaven-sent—her chin began to tremble and her lips to quiver.

"Oh, Hammer," she whimpered as she clung to him. "You came, you came."

"I thought I heard you call me, darling."

With tears of gratitude, she leaned back in his arms and laughed and cried as she devoured the blessed sight of him. "But I only whispered."

Not caring at this moment how many people were gawking, Hammer claimed her lips in a kiss. Against them, he murmured, "I always was a good listener."

For one brief moment then, the shroud of her hair was their privacy. Hammer sought the sweetness of her ear and whispered words that he thought he must have known he would say to her since he'd swum the wretched creek, "I love you, Brittany Schellenegger," he whispered. "I've been such a fool."

Chapter Ten

Even when Hammer brought Brittany a paper plate filled with baked beans and canned potato salad from Marty's grocery shelves, she wolfed down a few bites while on her feet, kissed him and returned to work. Because he was near, she was indefatigable. Because she loved him, she could save all humanity.

She talked over her shoulder. "How did you get across the creek?"

Hammer glanced wryly at his dirt-stained clothes. "I swam it."

Her disbelief was a "come on-n-n."

"Ouch, Doc," gasped the man whose arm she was stitching.

"Sorry, Skeeter." Brittany concentrated on her needle. "Don't tease me, Hammer. How did you get here? Really? Tell the truth."

Hammer laughingly insisted, "I swam the creek, babe. I told you."

This time she twisted around, her mouth pursed in a rebuke. Her patient made a faint sound of pain.

Brittany had once treated Skeeter for blood poisoning. She had seen his children through vaccinations and immunizations and tonsils and colds. She had even delivered his wife's last baby. "You idiot!" she said. "Not you, Skeeter. D'you think I was born yesterday, Hammer Curry?"

Skeeter wished earnestly that Lieutenant Hamilton Curry would take his business elsewhere, and he peered hopefully around Brittany's side. "No one can swim Chandler Creek when it's over its banks, mister."

"Hey," Brittany bridled at the man. "Hammer Curry is a very resourceful man."

Well, heck, he should have known better, Skeeter thought. Doc must really have it bad for this tough guy. "Yeah, Doc," he groaned his repentance. "Whatever you say."

"Actually," Hammer told Brittany as he came to stand opposite her and meticulously avoided looking at Skeeter's arm, "I towed, paddled and clawed myself across. What're you going to do next?"

She ignored his question. "Clip this," she ordered.

"What?"

"Clip this suture. Right here."

"Brittany..." Hammer gritted his teeth at her and relayed a message that was underscored with violent protest. "I think I ought to tell you—"

"Hammer, there's nothing to it. Look."

With a gaze of deepest sympathy at Skeeter, Hammer reluctantly picked up a pair of scissors and clipped the suture she indicated. Like a boy needing approval, he found her eyes.

"You baby," she murmured with a laugh and bandaged the arm. "If you want something more for pain, Skeeter, you'll have to take aspirin. If I had the Darvon to spare, I'd give you one, honest."

"Oh, that's all right, Doc," Skeeter said with devout appreciation that she was finished at last. He flicked a reproachful eye at Hammer. "I really think I'll feel better once I get off this table."

So baffled was Brittany that she cocked her head. Shrugging, she helped Skeeter off the table and guided in the next patient. Meanwhile, she locked stares with Hammer and scolded him only as someone who loves can scold: "And what if you'd drowned, Great American Hero?"

"But I didn't," Hammer said with sly logic. "Aren't you lucky?"

Brittany stopped long enough to adore him, then directed other people where to wait. "We've got to get some help in here, Hammer. Some of these patients need to be evacuated immediately. I've only got so many narcotics, you know, and I can't handle the really bad things, anyway. Work some miracles for me. And I could use an assistant while you're at it."

For the next twenty-four hours, Hammer did everything but walk on water. When red tape threatened, he outmaneuvered it. When people grew sluggish, he yelled louder than they did. When politics stood in the way, he shamelessly called in favors that were owed him. He talked to the mayor, who talked to the governor, who considered calling the president of the United States to talk about a state of emergency.

Once the Coast Guard got into the area with helicopters, things were easier. Woody was the first to be evacuated, and the more serious cases after him went to the city hospitals,

but those with minor injuries Brittany treated and sent
home.

"You have to understand these people, Hammer," she
said when he questioned the wisdom in that. "They have
such few possessions, and most of those have been de-
stroyed now. They wouldn't leave even if trucks came in and
tried to carry them out."

Hammer ordered more sanitation facilities brought in and
safe drinking water. Police units were set up and a curfew
established to prevent looting. Once the television crews arrived, however, and the newspapers, it seemed to Brittany
that every time she turned around a reporter was asking her
questions.

"Is it true, Dr. Schellenegger," one asked after barging
right into the surgical area, "that your lawyer has filed a
countersuit charging the NOPD with obstruction of justice
in the Gerald Wade case? A cover-up?"

Hammer had just walked in, and when Brittany sought
his eyes, she realized he had overheard the question. They
exchanged a look of astonishment.

Turning to the reporter, she shook her head. "I haven't
talked to my lawyer in three days."

When Hammer got close enough, she told him, "Hammer, I told Franz to do whatever was necessary, but I never
dreamed it would come to this."

His smile was resigned. "Well, let's wait and see."

Through it all, the injured kept coming, most of them
burn cases now. Occasionally the rescue teams would find
someone buried under debris. As the casualty count kept
rising and the media people kept pouring in, Brittany depended more and more upon Hammer.

Once, when she was treating a burn, she glanced up suddenly and was unable to see him. Turning, she cried out,
"Hammer? Where are you?"

He emerged from behind a group of men who were discussing diverting Chandler Creek higher upstream so more ambulances could use the bridge on Fairmont.

"I'm here, love," he murmured as he rubbed the rigid muscles of her back. "Brittany, sweetheart, you're exhausted. You have to rest. I insist. Too much is too much."

"I'm fine. I just wanted to know where you were."

He was insistent and began pulling her away. "You've got to let someone else do this now. Come on, you're dead on your feet."

Brittany pushed back her hair from her face with her wrist. She'd been working for nearly forty-eight hours, but the young medical student who had been brought in by the Coast Guard wasn't equipped to make some of the decisions that the emergencies warranted.

"You should talk," she told him, bluffing for time. "You look like hell." That he did; he hadn't shaved in two days, nor had he changed out of the clothes he had crossed the creek in.

Hammer lifted her hands from the bucket of antiseptic solution when she had finished with the patient. He dried them and motioned to the young bespectacled man who was working at another table.

"Stephen, I'm taking her out of here. You're on your own."

"That's okay, sir." Stephen was secretly glad for the added responsibility that Dr. Schellenegger seemed loath to give him. It would look enormously good on his record. He added, "I think the worst is over now anyway, sir. Burns mostly. I can handle those. If I can't, I'll get someone else in here."

"Dr. Schellenegger?" A fresh face whose owner supported a Minicam on his shoulder suddenly popped up and stopped them at the door. "If you could spare a few minutes, we surely could do with a report for Channel Eight."

"Not now," Hammer growled, his protective arm drawing Brittany more and more away. "Later."

"How about you, Lieutenant?" the reporter persisted, following them, his camera whirring. "What're your feelings about the countersuit filed by Dr. Schellenegger's attorneys?"

"That's just a rumor," Brittany protested.

Swiveling around hard, Hammer thrust out an angry finger toward the camera lens. "Look, I said *later*! Now clear out!"

With a rumbled remark about the bad taste of "some people," the reporter pulled back, and Brittany let Hammer take her weight upon him as they walked to her Jeep. She suspected they were being filmed by the reporter, but she matched her steps to his, anyway, and contentedly leaned her head against the pillow of his chest.

"I don't know who needs a bath worse," she said. "You or me."

He nuzzled her, chuckling. "I had one on the way over. Remember? You head the list."

When Hammer abruptly stopped walking, Brittany snapped to attention like a battery-operated toy soldier. There, waiting beside the Jeep in the darkness, stood Mooch, watching them both with dark, sullen eyes.

During the first hysterical hours after the hurricane had torn through the ghetto, Brittany had sent the boy to Henrietta's, trusting the woman to take better care of him than she could until the damages had been assessed. Now, from the looks of him, she didn't think he'd spent much of his time with her receptionist.

"Mooch!" she breathed and moved toward him.

His eyes darted in alarm to Hammer, and she quickly understood. She held out her hand, and when he stepped away from her, she took him into her arms, anyway. "It's all right," she whispered into his wet hair. "This is my friend. His name is Hamilton, and he's come to take care of us."

The boy refused to accept any of her affection, and Brittany looked at Hammer in dismay. She'd never known Mooch to be hostile before.

"They say you're a cop," Mooch accused Hammer as he inched cautiously to the Jeep.

Hammer shifted his weight to one hip and appeared not to be very concerned, one way or another. "Does that bother you?"

"Yeah."

"Mooch!"

Hammer waved Brittany's objections aside. "Well, I'm sorry I don't have time to stand around and talk to you about it, Mooch. I just can't afford to hassle you or arrest you or do anything else to you right now. Sorry. Now, if you'll excuse me, maybe later..."

Anger blazed through Brittany. How dare Hammer talk to Mooch that way?

When Hammer started helping her into the Jeep, she wanted to strike his hand off her arm, but then she saw the relief in Mooch's young eyes. Why, he'd expected Hammer to snap on the handcuffs and haul him away at gunpoint!

But now his childish pride swung far back in the other direction. Now he was sullen because he'd been slighted. "Do you have a gun?" he asked and thrust out his chin as if he dared Hammer to deny it.

Hammer arranged his face into an expression of boredom. "Of course." He walked around to the driver's side of

Brittany's Jeep and threw up a leg and swung himself limberly in. He began shutting the door.

"Have you ever shot anybody?" Mooch yelled as he stood his ground in the street.

"Nope."

"Ever been shot at?"

"Nope."

Mooch pursed his mouth as if he wasn't sure he wanted to even keep company with a cop who led such an uneventful existence.

Hammer leaned across Brittany's lap. "Hey!" he called out the window. "I'm not even a good shot. Are you gonna get in or what?"

With a disappointed sniff, Mooch slipped his small frame behind Brittany's seat, and Hammer blandly lifted his hips and fished through a pocket for the keys. He started the Jeep with a roar and, flinging his arm across the back of Brittany's seat, began backing away from Marty's Grocery.

Mooch leaned across Brittany's opposite shoulder. "I found some kids, Doc," he said in a soft, conspiring voice.

Brittany turned in her seat. "Say that again."

"Kids," Mooch explained. "They're down by the Fairmont Bridge in the old warehouse where they used to keep cotton bales."

Trust allowed Brittany to fall asleep on the way to the Fairmont Bridge.

Later she would wonder how she had dropped off so peacefully while Mooch was giving Hammer directions of where to go. Getting to sleep was her one true hell, her torture chamber. Not only did she have no memory of going to sleep without a struggle, she had never gone to sleep in someone else's presence before.

But then she'd never trusted a man with her heart and soul before. So, childlike, she leaned her head upon Hammer's shoulder and slept.

The next thing she knew there was the screech of brakes and Hammer turning off the ignition. Gasping, she jerked up and half expected to have dreamed the nightmare again.

She yelped, "What's the matter?"

"Nothing, darling," Hammer reassured her with a soothing grip of her shoulder. "Are you sure about this, Mooch? Is this the right place?"

The boy leaned over the seats and pointed a thin finger into the shadows. The headlights slashed through the slanting rain and bounced off the wall of a deserted two-story clapboard warehouse—an old building that looked as if it had once been the hideout of Laffite.

"You're not going in there!" Brittany objected and dug her fingers into Hammer's thigh.

To heighten her apprehension, she glimpsed the polished glint of his revolver in the dashlight, and she sought his face in the darkness.

He cautioned her with a sharp look to make no mention of it. He asked her quietly, "Are you going to wait in the Jeep?"

In the ghetto, the darkness was alive with silent watching eyes. "No way," she mumbled and scrambled out after them.

Hammer was very much the policeman now. Even Mooch seemed to trust his skill: he walked by the man's side and directed him as if they were partners and had done this many times before.

What woman could compete with that? Brittany thought gloomily. She had lost the boy to a cop! "That is," she added dourly as she caught up with them, "if I won't be intruding on you two buddies."

Hammer knew exactly what she was thinking. "Hey," he teased her, laughing, "I'm a hero now. It goes with the territory."

"That's easy for you to say," she grumbled under her breath. "You *are* the territory."

The interior of the warehouse wasn't too different from what Brittany had imagined the catacombs would be. Shivering, she mentally took back all her grudges against Hammer's revolver and huddled close to his side.

Their steps echoed through the hollow chambers. When they stopped walking, she heard the distinct rustle of life. "It's your show now, Mooch," Hammer murmured as he kept the youngster close to his other side.

Brittany leaned around Hammer to speak to the boy. "Do you know these children?"

Mooch didn't reply, and Brittany remembered how she'd found him—alone, starving, huddled outside her clinic. Had he once lived here? Had he grown up like this, knowing nothing but fear and hunger?

He directed them into a smaller section of the building, showing them where to duck beneath pieces of nailed tin and cardboard. A small room had been fashioned in one tiny corner of the building, a room that a person would have had to know where to look for.

A terrible stench offended Brittany's nose, and she knew the smell—human misery, sickness, fear. She grasped Hammer's arm as a lifeline. "Don't get separated from me," she pleaded.

Hammer was too much of a professional to walk into a situation he wasn't sure of. He kept in the shadows and motioned for Mooch to come and stand beside him.

"You do the talking," he said.

Mooch peered out with eyes that Brittany imagined could see in the dark. "Hey, Joey," he yelled. "I brought my friends. They got somethin' to eat if you want it. They got the stuff. It'll be all right.''

Nothing happened. Even the rustling sounds ceased. Brittany held tightly to Hammer's arm.

"We've scared them away," she whispered.

"They're here. Give 'em some time."

After a moment a cough was muffled against someone's hand. Hammer called out to the invisible people Mooch had addressed.

"My name is Mr. Curry," he said, raising his voice. "Everything's a real mess outside. The police are on the streets, and the looters are getting mad. You won't be able to steal anything to eat, even if there's anything left that's not burned up. And they've got guns. They're nervous, and when people get nervous, they shoot first and ask questions later. You'd better listen to Mooch. We've got Cokes and bread. What we don't have, we'll get."

As funny as it was, Brittany swore it was the mention of the Cokes that brought the children's response. They whispered in the darkness, arguing briefly, and beneath it all came a baby's cry.

An infant was hidden here! Brittany tugged at the back of Hammer's shirt. "Hammer, it's a baby."

"Wait," he said under his breath.

Brittany strained to see the figure who stepped out into the open area. To her shock, she realized it was a girl—ten years old, perhaps, wearing filthy shorts and no shoes, her face so stained that it was difficult to tell if she was black or white.

She was a white girl, and she said her name was Mindy. From what Brittany could gather, she was the elected mother of the group. Deep inside, Brittany felt her heart breaking.

"How many are here?" Hammer asked Mindy with the same respect an ambassador would give the ruler of a foreign country.

"Six." Mindy executed a macho swagger. "I gotta make sure they'll be all right. You know what I mean?"

Stepping forward, Brittany let herself be seen. "I give you my word," she said gently, meaning it with all her heart. "You'll be okay. All of you."

But the girl jumped back into the shadows as if she had seen an enemy, and Hammer darted after her.

"Hey, hey," he said when he gripped her arm. "It's all right. She's a friend of Mooch. She has a place down the street. She's Doc."

"Doc?" Unconvinced, the girl moved nearer and with her eyes raked Brittany up and down. "You really Doc? You know Cookie?"

"Yes," Brittany told her. "Cookie's my friend. He comes to see me all the time. I'm worried about him."

The girl shrugged. "Cookie's all right. I seen him today. He's okay."

"Well," Brittany said, "Mooch is my friend, too. He stays at my house. And Mr. Curry's my friend. Why don't we go to my place and get something to eat?"

There were five of them. The baby was the last to be brought up, and when Mindy stepped back and lifted the girl from the arms of a boy who couldn't have been more than four years old himself, Brittany swallowed her impulse to rush forward and take them all into her arms.

Protocol was more important than empty, growling stomachs. Mindy held out the baby to Hammer. To Brittany's surprise, the infant didn't cry when he lifted her tenderly up in his arms. She didn't even appear to be undernourished, but her eyes were deep, and her nose was running. When she breathed, Brittany winced at the bronchial wheeze.

"Oh, Hammer," she said over the knot in her throat.

He gently gave her the baby, and Brittany caught an overpowering whiff of urine, but she loved every inch of the baby instantly, and she kissed the dirty tear-stained little face.

"You're all right now, darling," she whispered. "I'll take care of you."

When Hammer turned and Brittany glanced up to catch his face, mostly in shadow, she thought she glimpsed the glint of tears clinging to his lashes. How she loved him.

While Brittany took care of the baby, Hammer took care of all of them. It wasn't easy. Her apartment was a mess when they returned. People had been inside, tromping around, looking through her things, and Brittany guessed it would take her weeks to know what had been stolen.

"We live in the informal mode around here," she said as she settled the baby on her hip and searched through a drawer in the dark to find some candles.

"At least they respected it," Hammer said over his shoulder.

"How can you say that?" she asked, turning. "They wrecked the bloody place."

"If they hadn't respected it, there wouldn't be one board foot left anywhere."

Hammer was a natural with children, a man who was meant to be a father. The children oddly took a kind of pride in cooperating with him.

The older children, having found the baby girl deserted in a park one night, had named her Ellen. Eating was something Ellen knew well enough how to do: she grabbed the bread with both grubby fists and stuffed it into her mouth.

Coughing consumed her, though, and it all came sputtering back out again.

Brittany mixed some powdered milk and crumbled some vanilla wafers into the milk and spooned it out—not the most nutritious, but who was balancing diets tonight? Then, while Ellen munched on a cookie, Brittany listened to her lungs with her stethoscope. She guessed they were badly scarred.

Once Mindy had appeased her initial hunger, she came forward and removed the baby from Brittany's arms. "I'll take 'er now," she said possessively.

Understanding, Brittany smiled. "She needs a bath."

"Well, we ain't had no water and the soap lately, you know what I mean?"

"We have water here, but I'm afraid it's cold because they haven't gotten the electricity reconnected."

Mindy was unimpressed, and Brittany sighed at Hammer. He grinned at her as he lifted the top of her kitchen range to see if the gas was working.

"Miffed, little mother?" he murmured and planted a kiss upon the side of her neck.

"Ungrateful little wretches," she said and offered him a bit more of her neck.

But he was now busy with lighting the stove. Suddenly he grinned at her, his blue eyes dancing wickedly. "What did you expect, a medal for being good?"

"A little appreciation, maybe." She affected a pout.

He chuckled, and then he leaned far over the stove and placed a lingering kiss upon her lips and gazed meaningfully into her eyes. "*I* appreciate you."

She jokingly pushed him away. "Then marry me, and let me take you away from all this. We'll buy a great, huge house and adopt all these children."

Hammer's collision with her gaze wasn't remotely frivolous, as she had meant her remark to be; it was vulnerable and raw and resentful that she should break him open and look inside.

Brittany felt weakness attacking the backs of her knees as he drew her into the vortex of his hunger. "I was just talking out loud," she whispered, trembling.

"Don't joke about that." He busied himself with the stove. "Anything else, but not that."

Once he had lifted buckets of water onto the stove to heat, Brittany's diligent foraging of her pantry produced cookies and dried fruit, raisins and bread from the freezer of the refrigerator. She brought out two jars of salad dressing for sandwiches, and pickles and olives. She found canned fruit, a box of pancake mix and bottled syrup, plus two jars of grape jelly.

Hammer looked at it all with grave disgust. "You're not going to feed them *that*, are you?"

She took instant offense and threw a fist to her hip. "I daresay even you could keep alive on it, lord of the realm. Starvers can't be choosers."

"I could eat that and still starve," he grumbled and gathered up a handful of raisins, threw them into his mouth. "All those preservatives and chemicals."

Because she adored him, she laughed. "*They* don't seem to mind."

Mindy had spread salad dressing upon the slices of bread, and the children were gobbling them down as if it were cake and ice cream. Mooch had mixed up some of the pancake batter and was scorching some cakes on a griddle upon the stove.

"You tend to their nutrition, Lieutenant," she told him with a smirk, "I'll tend to their sanitation." She poked her hand into one of the buckets of water and found it warm enough. Turning around to five preoccupied faces, she said by way of announcement, "Now! Who gets the first lovely bath?"

None of the baths was lovely. They were civil wars, and if Hammer hadn't helped her, that feat alone would have sent Brittany over the brink of exhaustion. Finally, at eleven o'clock, when the last child was spanking clean and clothed in one of her shirts, tops, shorts or gowns, Hammer finally gripped her by the shoulders and steered her into her bedroom and shut the door behind him.

He took his first real look at her room and rotated in a disbelieving circle. "Gad, let's put it out of its misery."

"Bitch, bitch, bitch, Hammer," she groaned. "That's all you know to do."

"It's not all I know," he corrected her with a lewd slap to her backside. "Now, here are the rules. You may not leave this room without running the risk of being shot. You may sit down on that chair and wait until I get back with hot water."

"Lovely man," she murmured and dropped her head to the arm of the chair.

She roused to vaguely hear Hammer boarding up the glassless doors up front. The next thing she knew, he was lifting her to her feet and stripping off her soiled jeans and balancing her on first one foot then another as she stepped out of them. Then he peeled her shirt off over her head and unhooked her bra.

Blinking herself awake as she stood in nothing but her underpants, she had never felt so sexless in her life. When he hooked a finger in the band of her panties and skinned them off, too, she lifted one bone-weary leg and heaved it over the side of the bathtub.

Ah! The warm water cast its instant spell, and she smiled appreciatively at him. "I know it's not fitting to be so immodest," she said groggily and slid by degrees upon her spine, "but I can't help it."

"I bear my misery with dignity, madam," he said and appeased himself with a long, thorough look.

Stooping, then, he bathed her as gently as if she were a child. When she was soaped and rinsed, he bent her head down to the water. "Shampoo," he ordered. "I've only got one bucket left to rinse you."

She was wrapped in a dry towel at last, and he was blotting her hair and struggling with the contrary tangles that streamed down her back when Brittany finally conjured enough energy to reach up and grasp his hands. She could hardly keep her eyes open.

"Hammer, I hope you won't take this the wrong way, but if you ask me to make love tonight, I'll shoot you with your own gun."

He laughed the laugh she'd fallen in love with, and Brittany loved him even more when he bundled her into clean sheets that he had miraculously located somewhere in the mess. Sometime later he crawled in beside her, and she murmured sleepily that he smelled good.

"I thought you said you used the last bucket of water," she murmured and curled around his back.

"Your guttering makes a good enough shower," he said and drew her arms snugly about his waist.

"Cold," she murmured. "Brrr." Presently, when lucidity interwove with her warm security, she said, "Hammer?"

"Hmm?" By now he was half-asleep.

"Do you remember when you asked me all those things about John?"

"Um-hm."

Brittany closed her eyes, though it was pitch dark. In a whisper, she said, "John drove through the railing on purpose that night. He turned to me and said 'You'll be sorry.' And I was.''

At first Hammer thought he was dreaming her words. He thought he dreamed her saying that John Gallois's tragedy was no accident and that she had stood watching him crash before her very eyes.

Rolling over, he lay blinking himself awake. The room was very dark, and outside the rain drummed softly upon the roof. In the darkness he reached out and found her hair, then her face and her wet cheeks and her quivering lips.

''What did you say?'' he said, slumber still hoarse in his voice.

''I said will you kiss me?''

''You mean you watched it, Brittany? You've lived with that all these years?''

She hadn't really meant to tell him about John, but since he had come into her life, the past seemed so unreal. She couldn't believe she had carried around such guilt for so long. Another person had done that, not her.

''Hold me,'' she begged and turned to huddle against his warm, safe body. ''Love me, Hammer. Don't give up on me. Promise you won't die, and promise you won't give up.''

To Brittany it seemed that they would never get enough of each other. It was as if her panic had suddenly infused him, too. He groaned and covered her with kisses, then crushed her with hugs, then kissed her all over again. Brittany threaded her legs with his and held him and held him.

But presently the comfort of one human being to another was not enough. Presently it was the man and the woman, and Brittany made herself accessible with an abandon she had never known before. Even the other time, when he had forced one orgasm after another from her, it wasn't the same as now, when she forgot what he thought about her

and forgot about whether or not she was as good as someone else. She was aware of only the impact of him deep inside.

Then she placed her hands upon his face and kissed his
fierce features with a terrible impatience, and when he attempted to take everything with one tremendous surge, she
cried out with a blend of eagerness and despair. They gave
and they took until there was nothing left to give, no sensations that were not discovered and drained from both of
them.

She lay upon him in sweat-stained splendor. She thought
she'd slept.

Or perhaps not. He was insatiable. He turned her upon
her stomach and drew her back to him and knelt over her,
entering her yet again, and she pleaded with him that it was
over, but his hands awakened her breasts all over again, and
they slid over her belly, ever moving and dipping lower and
lower until she turned her head and searched for his mouth.
Even as he strove harshly to breathe, he touched her tongue
and the center of all her sensations. Around and around the
spiral went until she was shuddering against him and clinging, her nails leaving tiny brands she was unaware of.

"Did you think about John?" he demanded hoarsely in
her ear when it was done. "Was it really gone? Tell me the
truth, even if you never say it again for the rest of your life.
Did you love me enough that it was gone?"

Turning, she fit her face into his neck and mixed her tears
with the saltiness of the sheen that covered them both. "I
thought I was supposed to do the healing, Hammer Curry."

"Tell me you love me."

"I have never loved anyone before you," she said. "Nor
will I ever love anyone again as I love you at this moment."

It was enough, Hammer thought. Whatever happened, it
was enough.

Chapter Eleven

In New Orleans there is a certain segment of society that literally comes into its own in time of disaster. That elite group was composed of Lilith Garamond Schellenegger and her friends. It was ironic that these women—bright social butterflies flitting from one gala social event to the next on the French Riviera or in Vienna or at a château in the Alps or Rio de Janeiro or Mexico City, women who have rarely known a moment's physical discomfort or deprivation— were then at their finest.

Brittany had more often than not resented her mother's part in this exploitation of human suffering. She took offense at the way Lilith operated. Lilith knew every woman of importance in the city and each of their weaknesses. When she commenced upon one of her fund-raising campaigns, she used that knowledge to get exactly what she wanted.

After Hurricane Helen had struck, Lilith had been on the telephone within hours. Committees had been formed and a half-dozen drives were in the process of being commenced. Within five days all the public officials in town were rallying behind the effort. The women settled upon the auction as their medium.

A flamboyant, gargantuan auction to end all auctions, they said, one that would attract attention out of state, perhaps out of the country. Rough estimates of revenue that would be raised for the ghetto itself would hover around the one million mark.

When Brittany picked up the telephone and heard Lilith's voice, her intuition warned that life was about to take one of those flying leaps she couldn't control.

"I've been trying to locate you for days, dahling," Lilith cooed. "Zey kept telling us that lines would be repaired; finally we just watched television."

"It's taken a while, Mother," Brittany agreed and moved to a more convenient place so she could hear over the repairmen busily at work repairing the clinic doors.

"Yes, well . . . we saw you on zee news."

"What?"

"You mean you didn't see it?"

Brittany grimaced at her memories since she and Hammer had brought the children to the apartment—the mad scramble to deal with social workers the next day, the agencies, the furious arguments, the arrangements for a temporary place for them to stay until they could decide about housing and child care.

Hammer had been disconcertingly quiet that day. He had kissed her and promised to call her later, and she'd clung to him in a return of her old fears that something would happen and she would never see him again.

"It's all right, darling," he'd promised. "But right now I have to find out what's happening in the investigation."

She'd heard from him once. He'd told her that the mayor was now involved. Things were getting nasty.

"I've hardly had time to breathe," Brittany explained to her mother. "What free time I had, I spent going to see Franz."

"Ah, talk was going 'round."

"I know. It leaked out somehow. Franz wants me to file a countersuit. I told him to do what was best."

Lilith took a quick breath. "I'm surprised."

"Well, I have to clear my name. Sybil's being such a . . . Mother, I really need to go. I have to make a few calls right away."

"You sound upset."

"It's just that I don't want someone to hear about the suit secondhand."

Brittany couldn't believe it. Never in her life had she confided in her mother. Was this what love did to you? Softened you up? Made you trusting and naive?

Not for her. Though what she'd said was true enough; she had to be the one to tell Hammer that Franz Knoble was filing.

"Zen I have the perfect idea, dahling," Lilith was saying excitedly. "Publicity. Nothing convinces of innocence like publicity. You must be our star at the auction. Mistress of ceremonies, the crowning touch to our Florence Nightingale of zee ghetto. I can promise all charges against you will be promptly dismissed. And if they're not, who will believe zem?"

With a slump back against the wall of the kitchen, Brittany closed her eyes and shook her head. "No, no, Mother, you know I—"

"Don't say no so quickly."

"But it's just not my thing. You know I don't like to attract attention to myself."

"You've done a pretty good job of zat already. Besides, you've never been accused of malpractice. At least promise me you'll come to our luncheon. It doesn't hurt to get a few of the really good ladies in your corner. Please say you'll come."

Because it was easier than saying no, Brittany said yes, but when she hung up, she immediately wished she hadn't agreed. Sighing, she tried for the dozenth time to reach Hammer. She dialed his home number. The phone rang off the wall, but no one answered. She was getting a bad feeling about this, a really bad feeling.

After parking his car on the ferry that crossed the Mississippi River to Gretna, Hammer got out and walked to the car parked next to his. He opened the door, got in and smiled at Marie Trudeau.

"Now," he said, "what's all the mystery?"

Marie looked at him for a long moment. "Did anyone ever tell you that you're a stubborn man, Hammer Curry?"

Memories of Brittany drifted through Hammer's senses like a cool breeze on a summer day. "Yeah." He grinned sheepishly. "Once or twice."

"Will you do yourself a favor and listen to me on this one?"

He swiveled around until his knee was an arrow between them. "You found something, didn't you?"

"Hammer, this one is going to get you in deeper and deeper with Sybil Wade. The woman has power in this city. She can break you."

"Tell me what you found, Marie."

"Two years ago Gerald Wade was busted for possession. It wasn't all that much. Sybil could've paid his fine, and that would have been that. At least it couldn't go on his adult record.''

''What did she do? Bribe someone?''

''How'd you know?''

Hammer lifted a hand to his hair and stroked it over his forehead, holding it there a moment. He hadn't known. ''It just seemed like something she might try.''

''It was the way she did it that caught my attention, the way the paperwork was done—no fine, no appearance, no probation, no nothing. I wouldn't have noticed it except that the arresting officer's name—''

''Brian Gallagher,'' Hammer said on a whistling breath.

Marie slumped over her steering wheel. ''The way I figure it, since he'd done the paperwork for Sybil once before, and we can only suppose that he was well rewarded for it, when Gerald got into this trouble, he meant to do her another favor. But Gerald up and died before he could get him home.''

''Then Brian was in a mess.''

''Yeah, and so are you, Hammer. The mayor wants to see you. Yesterday.''

The next day Brittany looked up the number of the police department in the telephone directory and told them she wanted to speak to Hamilton Curry. She was told to hold, please. She rehearsed her outraged speech while she waited.

Then a man's voice said, ''Yes? This is Detective Gilbert speaking.''

''Patrick Gilbert?'' Apprehension caught in her throat.

''Yes. Dr. Schellenegger, is that you?''

She was surprised he recognized her voice. ''I've been trying to get ahold of Lieutenant Curry, and I can't seem to catch him at home. I've been trying for some time, as a matter of fact.''

The silence was heavy. Brittany felt trouble the way a person feels a storm in the making, and she pressed a hand to her heart, which suddenly felt as if it would leap out of her chest.

"I'm sorry to be the one to tell you this, Dr. Schellenegger," his voice came gently, hesitantly. "Hammer's been suspended from duty. For an indefinite period."

"You're kidding!"

"There was this thing with the mayor... I guess I shouldn't be saying anything, but you'll read about it in the paper. Hammer... Lieutenant Curry filed a complaint against Judge Sybil Wade for dereliction of duty, for one thing, plus a few others. Anyway, it's going to be a real battle. And Hammer... Lieutenant Curry mentioned something about resigning."

Hammer couldn't resign! Not because of this, because of her! Must everyone pay because of her? First John, now Hammer?

"Anyway," Patrick Gilbert was saying, "if he's not home, I don't know where he is. He said he'd talk to me later today. If I hear from him, do you want me to have him call you?"

"Yes," she said numbly, and her voice trailed away as she slowly replaced the receiver. "Please have him call."

In a daze, Brittany walked about the room where Hammer had held her when she was tired, had bathed her when she was dirt-stained and weary, had loved her when she was alone and comforted her when she was afraid. Everything she loved either died or fell apart in her hands. What did she do now? God in heaven, what did she do now?

Luncheon was held in the Garden Tea Room of the Excelsior Hotel, and Brittany wished desperately, from the moment she walked in, that she had never, never come.

At least thirty lovely tables had been set aside for the ladies and were decorated with pretty skirted cloths and fresh
flowers. Feminine conversations and laughter lilted delicately over the sounds of silver and crystal. Everyone was
discussing which musicians to hire for the grand event,
which florist, how many maids and which accounting firm
would take care of the revenues from the auction.

As the waiters poured coffee from heavy silver pots,
Brittany smiled wanly at her dinner companions, none of
whom she had ever seen before, but who, she was certain,
knew all about her.

She felt dowdy in her tiered eyelet skirt and silk shirt
knotted at her waist. All around her a fortune in jewels was
draped about women's throats and twinkled in their ears
and upon their fingers. She didn't belong here.

"More coffee, madam?" the waiter asked politely at her
elbow.

Brittany jerked so suddenly that her cup chattered cra-
zily in its saucer. Heads turned discreetly.

"Thank you," she said, smiling and nervously touching
her napkin to her lips.

But it was too ridiculous—not only a painful ordeal, but
a waste of valuable time, and they could hardly think worse
of her than they already did. She pushed back her chair, and
it scraped raucously on the polished floor.

A waiter hurried to assist her, and Brittany wanted to tell
him that she'd been managing her own chair for a long time
now. But she smiled. To the ladies, she said, "Would you
kindly excuse me? I've forgotten some—"

At least she got to her feet before Sybil Wade entered the
room, and the instant Brittany saw her walk in—or maybe
she felt Sybil walk in—she didn't waste precious seconds
hoping that her own departure would go unnoticed by the
judicial black eyes.

Dressed in her elegant and queenlike black, Sybil glided strategically nearer. Here and there she paused to accept whispers of sympathy and kisses from her friends, and she even stopped beside Lilith's chair and bent to murmur something in her ear.

As the waiters arrived with salads, Sybil finally arrived at Brittany's table. She stopped, and so did her friends, who hovered on each side of her like bodyguards.

Brittany could have sworn that every salad fork froze between plate and mouth. Every cup ceased to clatter, every glass to clink. The silence was amplified until it reached an unbearable intensity.

"How delightful to see you here, Dr. Schellenegger," Sybil said with her brilliant scarlet lips drawing back in a malicious smile. "How nice of you to take time from your busy schedule."

"Hello, Sybil." Brittany felt her nerves disintegrating inside her body. Now she and Hammer had both filed against this woman! "I hope everything's going better for you these days."

"Everything is fine," Sybil said coldly. "Or it would be fine if dear Gerald were alive. But I do appreciate your concern, dear. It's kind of you, especially since you're the reason he's not here."

The accusation lay between them until it gathered dust, and Brittany didn't know what to do with it. She wasn't skilled at this kind of trial by fire.

"I'm sorry you feel that way, Sybil," she said honestly. "Maybe someday you'll realize that I had nothing to do with that."

"Well—" here a cruel smile came from Sybil "—whether I believe it or not, Brittany, life does have its little justices, after all. I expect your friend, Mr. Curry, already knows that. Why don't you ask him?"

Brittany took a step toward the woman whom she could still remember vividly in her father's bed. She might not fight for herself, but she could not and would not tolerate Sybil hurting the man she loved.

"Be careful, Sybil," she warned. "You don't exactly live in a glass house."

To threaten Sybil Wade in public was the worst possible thing she could have done: bitter hatred blazed to life in Sybil's eyes, and one of the bodyguards hissed at Brittany, "How could you, Brittany Schellenegger? How could you?"

"Poor Sybil. That's the most cruel . . ."

Suddenly she remembered Hammer lifting Ellen from Mindy's young arms, remembered the tears on his lashes.

"Sybil's used to using people like pawns," Brittany said coolly to the women at the table. "And now Sybil is pouting."

Sybil's friends blushed furiously, and one clamped her mouth shut with a murmur that she'd never been so insulted in all her life.

By now not a woman in the room would have taken a breath for fear of missing something. Sybil's head was shaking, and her anger had deepened the lines in her face, accentuating her age.

"If I were you, my dear," she murmured acidly, "I'd take a lesson from your friend, Mr. Curry. At least he has the sense to pull out while he's still ahead."

Across the room, Brittany saw Lilith watching in horror. *I need you, Mother. For once in your life, would you stand behind me against this woman?*

No? Well, that didn't surprise her.

"Oh, I don't know as I'd call it pulling out, Sybil." Brittany smiled. "Lieutenant Curry and I have our project for the children, you know. He has a very good head for things like that, and the media is quite interested. And I'm doing the auction, as you might have heard. No, I don't think anyone's pulling out of anything. In fact, I think you'll be seeing a lot of us on Channel Eight. Goodbye, ladies.''

Brittany's worst fear was that she would throw up before she could get out of the building. She rushed downstairs and across the huge lobby and darted into the bathroom. There, with her hands braced upon one of the sparkling sinks, she panted until her heart stopped racing and she could lift her head once more and look at the world's greatest fool staring back at her from the mirror.

Oh, Lord, what had come over her? The auction? *A project for the children?* Oh, Lord!

After throwing cold water on her face, Brittany presently felt she could walk outside to her car without making a spectacle of herself. Once there, she leaned back in the seat of the Jeep.

Could she? Could she win against Sybil Wade if she met her in a combat? For it was a matter of survival, and not for one second did she kid herself about that. Which was why she drove straight to Schellenegger Enterprises on Poydras Street and parked in the spot reserved for her in the lot underneath.

If it was going to be war, she decided as she slammed her door, she was going into battle with the best weapons she had.

Hidden in her desk drawer at her office downtown was a checkbook that Brittany never used. It was for a private account at the Chase Manhattan Bank.

As she walked into her office, a dozen unfamiliar heads lifted. She heard hushed whispers behind hands as she crossed the foyer to the inner door. A sudden hysterical thought came to her, and she had horrors of bursting out into wild, insane laughter. What would all these demure professional women be saying if they knew that Dr. Brittany Schellenegger had made wild, passionate love on the carpet outside in the corridor?

By some miracle that she didn't really understand, Brittany reached her office. She shut the door with a quiet click. She moved immediately to the safe behind a simple piece of local art she had bought in the French Quarter.

With trembling fingers, she worked the combination and drew out the checkbook. Before she shut the safe, she hesitated and felt around inside for a black velvet case. Upon drawing it out, she opened the case and blinked, as she always did, at the flashing fire of the magnificent emerald necklace her grandfather had given her on her twenty-first birthday.

She had no idea what it was worth. Millions, she supposed. That birthday seemed quite unreal to her now, as if it had happened to another person.

She placed the box into her bag along with her checkbook. Then, with her heart pounding frightfully, she shut the safe and walked out of her office and across the corridor to the office of Franz Knoble.

Franz was out, but his secretary said she would give him a message. On his embossed stationery, Brittany wrote him a note—a brief note. In it she said simply that Sybil Wade had to be stopped. Could he get back to her?

Then she retied the tails of her silk blouse, touched her hair and smoothed it down, and drew in a deep breath. She opened the door and breezed through the office again.

"Good afternoon, Miss Battanni," she murmured as she passed the switchboard—Mary Battanni was the only person she knew by name.

As she passed through the doors, the last thing she heard was Mary saying into her headset "Sharon? You'll never in your life guess who just walked out the door."

Jordan's was the most tiny, chic and expensive store in New Orleans, perhaps in the entire South. To win against Sybil, she would have gone to Paris itself, but one week was little enough time, and she had her work cut out for her.

The first thing she did was ask for Lilith's favorite seamstress, Sarah Banawitz. Sarah was a stout little Jewish woman with a magical sense of style, and to look at her no one would guess that she dressed the most influential women in town.

At first Brittany feared Sarah wouldn't remember her, but when she walked into the cramped sewing room in the back of the shop, Sarah's small mouth dropped open in the shape of an astonished circle.

"My stars," she whispered and dropped some pins upon her machine and rose to her feet. She ran shrewd discerning eyes up and down the gorgeous length she'd been wanting for years to get her hands on. "Well, wonders never cease, do they, my dear? I saw you on television the other night. Come in, come in."

Brittany laughed and looked around the tiny room. The last time she had been here was when Sara Banawitz had put the finishing touches on the dress for her presentation by Le Debut des Jeunes Filles. "You haven't changed things a bit, Sarah."

"And you always were blind, my dear. I don't dare ask what you're doing here."

With a tense grimace, Brittany laid her hand upon the clasp of her bag. She gazed down into the clear gray eyes that lifted to hers. "How long have you known me, Sarah?"

Sarah laughed, and her bosom quaked. "I made the dress you were christened in, my pet."

"If I tell you something, will you promise never to tell anyone, not even my mother, upon pain of the most dreadful, horrendous death?"

"How dare you ask such a question? My clients think I'm their confessor."

From her bag Brittany brought out the black box. Opening it, she placed it into Sarah's hands. "I want you to make me a dress to go with these. And I have to have it in a week, Sarah. It has to be a very special dress. I want to knock this town off its feet."

For a moment the old woman's cheeks flushed, then she lifted one of Brittany's hands and opened its palm and kissed it with a teary affection. "It's time, Brittany, dear. You can depend on me. You'll be an absolute sensation."

A sensation? Before three thousand people, including the mayor, city councilmen, several judges and minor politicians, plus the local television affiliates and several newspaper reporters? If there was anything she regretted more than agreeing to do this hideously insane thing, Brittany didn't know what it was.

She placed one spike-heeled shoe into the limousine Lilith had arranged for her, the car being another unexpected trauma.

Brittany stared down at the young uniformed driver buried beneath his black cap as he held her door. "What's your name?" she asked in a tone as grim as she felt.

"Pauly Phillips, ma'am," a voice squeaked from somewhere beneath the cap, then the head lifted and Brittany saw what she imagined Mooch Billiot would be in ten years.

He squinted hard at her. "You the lady on television?"

"Yes," Brittany said. "Why?"

Both his shoulders lifted. "You look different."

Great! She turned down one side of her mouth. "Well, Pauly Phillips, are you sure you're old enough to drive?"

"If I was any older, ma'am," he said and touched the bill of his cap with a swashbuckling flair, "they'd have to haul me away to the glue factory."

Brittany drew her mouth into a circle and tried not to smile. "Your family isn't by any chance related to the Currys, is it, Pauly?"

Not understanding, Pauly removed his cap and scratched his shock of dark hair. "Beg your pardon, ma'am?"

She waved away his uncertainty. "Don't mind me, Pauly. It was just a certain...spice you have. Tell me—" here she straightened to her full height, placed a hand upon her hip in a modish slouch and threw back her hair "—how do I look? And don't lie to me."

Pauly Phillips happily surveyed the gleaming sunset of her hair without having the slightest notion of the straighteners and conditioners that went into making it look so silkily lustrous. He moved over her shadowed eyes, her lightly lip-sticked mouth and her breasts, which were pushed up into the sweeping V of a jet-black sequined cleavage, thanks to a bra that had cost almost as much as the dress. By the time he reached the curve of her waist and the jut of her hip, his Adam's apple was bobbing.

"Oh, ma'am," he breathed and coughed lightly. "I wouldn't expect much bidding out of the men at the auction tonight. Their hearts'll be in their throats most of the time."

"I'm not going to worry about you, Pauly," she said and laughingly let him help her into the plush interior. "You're going to have a great future."

When Brittany was met by a valet from the Excelsior, he already knew who she was. He welcomed her and even dared to flirt as he walked her to the back entrance and opened a door where a stage had been set up at one end of the huge ballroom.

The podium was equipped with microphones, a battery of telephones, a row of accountants at a table, plus private appraisers and a pretty young assistant whose only duty was to keep Brittany from making mistakes.

Janette Austin was a curator for one of the local museums. Lilith had assured Brittany that the woman's sixth sense was infallible. Before she could introduce herself, Lilith breezed up with a young man on her arm whom Brittany had never seen before.

"You look lovely, dahling," she purred, then stopped to give Brittany one of the first truly appreciative looks she could remember. "Doesn't she look lovely, Kevin?"

Kevin would have thought Godzilla was beautiful, he was so stoned.

"Thanks, Kevin," Brittany murmured, then said to her mother, "You look wonderful too, Mother. As usual."

Lilith was accustomed to looking wonderful. She didn't notice the pallor beneath Brittany's facade. "Now, you mustn't worry, Brittany. Janette has much experience with zeez affairs. She knows everything, believe me. Janette, dahling, come meet our auctioneer."

Janette's own assistants were arranging boxes of items to be auctioned and taping numbers on them to correspond with the list Brittany would use.

"My goodness," she said as she walked up. "You think you've got all the bases covered, then at the last minute..." Her eyes narrowed behind her thick-lensed glasses. "You're the Brittany Schellenegger on television?"

Brittany smiled thinly. "The same."

"Oh. You look different."

"So I've been told."

Lilith leaned over and gave Brittany a peck on the cheek. "I leave you in good hands, dahling. Don't worry about a zing. You'll be fabulous!"

"Maybe we should sell Mother," Brittany murmured from the side of her mouth as Lilith departed.

"I heard that," Lilith called back. "Take care of her, Janette."

"How's the crowd?" Brittany asked Janette after Lilith had left. "Can you tell by looking what kind of night it's going to be?"

The other woman smiled and patted Brittany's hand with efficient briskness. "Do you mean, will they buy? Let's just say that the motivation is in these boxes, and the money is in their pockets, plenty of it. All you have to do, Doctor, is persuade item one to trade places with item two."

"Persuasion was never my strong point," Brittany admitted and darted out into the back corridor where she smoked one of the cigarettes she had tucked into her purse, just in case.

But she was wrong, for Brittany had not taken into account the changes that Hammer Curry had made in her life. As she looked out upon beautiful women strolling on the arms of handsome dark-suited men, her fear oddly dwindled away. It wasn't that she consciously thought "I am as good as they are, for I have been loved, deeply loved." But there was some buried part in her subconscious that knew it.

And it showed. She surprised everyone by being a brilliant mistress of ceremonies. Words and clever little phrases came to her mind, subtle self-effacements that she had subconsciously watched Hammer use so charmingly. It was her timing, really—her natural shyness blending with just the right amount of dry observations.

So she teased her audience as she would have teased the people of the ghetto whom she lived with every day. She cajoled them and told spicy jokes on herself. And halfway through the auction, when she returned from a break and laughingly accepted her applause, she looked up and ran her gaze over the audience as she had done several times already. She stared straight into the smile on Hammer's face.

She only missed a beat. No one noticed but Hammer and herself, but it was a beat that Brittany would never forget; beside him sat the woman in the photograph—the lovely, *short* woman, and the lovely short woman was laughing.

Brittany drew in her breath so that her stomach was very flat. The television men were adjusting their lights, and she knew that her sequins were flashing fire. She hadn't expected Hammer, but now that he was here and she knew why she hadn't found him, she wanted to lean forward and yell into the microphone, "I went to war for you, Hamilton Curry III!"

On and on during the course of the auction, she lifted items and pointed out their virtues. She captured a laugh as she pointed out their silliness, too. When the evening had run its course and only a few items remained to be sold, Brittany motioned to Janette that she had to have a brief respite.

"What's the latest count?" she asked when Janette pushed out a group of French antiques that had been donated by the Louisiana Heritage Society.

The frazzled curator glanced at her clipboard. "Forty-eight thousand. You're doing great, Brittany. Just great."

"I'm running out of steam."

"Well, find some somewhere, you're almost home."

"Janette—" Brittany found her evening bag, fished out her lip gloss and proceeded to put some on as she talked "—who's the woman in red in the back row. To the right?"

Janette pulled down her glasses and stepped from behind the partition. She peered out over the sea of faces. "The one sitting beside the pillar?"

"Yes." And beside my lover, Brittany wanted to add venomously.

Janette fixed Brittany with an amazed look and reached up to repair a small smear at the corner of Brittany's mouth. "You're putting me on." Then she cocked her head. "You really don't know, do you?"

"Would I have asked if I did?"

"She's the state senator, sweetie," Janette said with a quick dismissal and walked back to her cherished checklist. "Where've you been the past four years? That's Deborah Keyes. Listen, don't forget to explain that the settee has papers, will you?"

Chapter Twelve

The French antiques brought over four thousand dollars, and behind the scenes Brittany concocted blistering speeches for Hammer, fiery discourses that would make him sorry. Why have a triumph if it was achieved alone? Of what value was something spectacular if one couldn't turn to a person one loved and say, "Oh, look."

And then she remembered how she had disrupted his life, and she wished she was capable of bowing out gracefully. Yet how could she do that? She loved him, and they would live through this mess. They had to.

When the woman rose, her movement caught Brittany's eye. The final item was coming up for sale. Brittany saw Deborah Keyes step behind Hammer's chair and bend over his shoulder to speak.

Good! Brittany thought. The senator was leaving. But to her chagrin, Hammer also came to his feet.

Brittany sighed and then shockingly heard her own stupid voice saying, "Before we make the final tally, it has been suggested that we open the floor to the audience."

Here she leaned forward and smiled. She made her voice that of intimate confidentiality. "Perhaps some of us are sitting on some hoarded treasure that our conscience has been telling us all evening should be thrown onto the block. Now's the time. Do you want your name on a plaque? To go down in history?" She pretended to be reading a book. "'In the wake of Hurricane Helen, Mayor Bill Henry graciously donated his Samoan spear to charity.'"

The audience burst into laughter; it was a favorite New Orleans story about how Eileen Henry vowed that her husband would part with her before he would part with his Samoan spear.

Heads bent to confer, and a number of signals went out to Janette, but Hammer, maddeningly, continued walking alongside Deborah Keyes to the side exit.

A wicked demon perched on Brittany's shoulder. "Why, Lieutenant Curry," she purred into the microphone before three television cameras and two newspaper reporters, "surely you're not planning to leave without letting New Orleans have a chance at *your* pet collector's item?"

Heads turned and necks craned, and Brittany wished that she could sink into the floor of the Excelsior ballroom and never be seen or heard of again. Deborah Keyes, sensing free publicity, brought her hand up in a pretty wave to the camera. Hammer, looking striking in black tie, let his weight shift to one hip as he hooked his thumb upon the edge of his pants pocket.

When he realized that he was the center of attention, he dipped his head and grinned as if to say "I'll get you for this, Brittany Schellenegger."

"Come on, Curry," someone yelled. "Throw it on the block."

Brittany had gone too far to retreat. It was do battle or die. She flashed a dazzling smile. "Oh, come now, Lieutenant. What about that classic Chevrolet sitting in your garage? You're surely not going to hang on to that old thing, are you?"

Had revenge ever felt so good? Hammer sheepishly waved his hand, and Brittany directed the audience's attention to something else, but she noticed that Hammer didn't leave immediately. But then, neither did Deborah Keyes. They lingered with a group that had clustered near the side exit, and Miss Keyes was heard to laugh and to say that in her opinion the auction was a tremendous success.

Now her heart ached. Brittany was desperate to get out of the building, to go somewhere and lick her wounds. Yet if she was hurting, Hammer Curry should hurt, too! He was the one who had started this with his disappearing act!

She glanced beneath the podium behind which she had just stood for nearly two hours. In the back of the little shelf, she spotted a pad. Grabbing it, she chattered parting nonsense to Janette, thanked her and waved off all the congratulations that were being called to her and the hands that were waving.

She rushed to where she had left her handbag, and she groped around in it for a pen. On the pad she scrawled a note.

Dear Hammer,
How nice to see you out this evening. I had wanted to ask you out to dinner to celebrate, but since you're with someone, we'll do it another time. Wasn't I wonderful?

B

At least she wouldn't have to look back for the rest of her life and think *Why didn't you at least say something?* Get in your lick? Go down in history as something besides a *disappointment*?

Then she fished out a ten-dollar bill and found one of the technicians. She told him where to deliver the note.

"Do you want me to wait for a reply?" he asked innocently.

She shook her head, before she'd embarrass herself by crying, and then she grabbed her bag and dashed to the outer door at the rear of the building.

Her heels clattered on the cement as she flew across the parking lot. Poor Pauly was confounded when he looked up and saw his client racing toward the limousine. He swung open the door to get in, but then he saw he couldn't possibly drive back before she reached him.

"Ma'am!" he choked and looked at his watch in horror and thumped it, held it to his ear. "It must've stopped. I swear to Pete, I was—"

Brittany laid her hand upon his arm. "It's all right, Pauly."

He looked at her with bafflement. "It didn't go good?"

"It went perfectly. We raised a quarter of a million dollars."

"Then you're 'Lady of the Year.'"

Why didn't she just ask Pauly out to dinner, Brittany thought. Why not? The boy adored her, and it just wasn't right to go home to an empty and depressing apartment after raising a quarter-million dollars. Then, when it was done, she could let him take her hand and tell her everything was all right.

But she couldn't do it, and she climbed into the back seat of the limousine and shocked Pauly by taking off her shoes and hurling them over the front seat. The skirt of her dress was so tight that she practically had to lie down, and she stretched out her legs, lifted her hips and yanked up the skirt to a disgraceful height.

"Take me home, Pauly," she said miserably. "The evening's over. Just take me home."

"You're not going back on your invitation, are you?" a deep familiar voice asked.

Brittany jerked up her head just in time to see Hammer climbing into the back seat and giving Pauly a nod.

"Why don't you drive us along the river, Pauly?" he murmured and passed a folded bill into the boy's hand. "And make it a slow drive. And Dr. Schellenegger, dinner is on me."

"I ought to warn you," she said with a demure flutter of her lashes as Hammer shut the door. "I'm hungry."

For a long breathtaking moment he met her gaze in the darkness, and Brittany could hardly remember why she was so angry at him. "So am I."

What Hammer Curry did not take into account when he made such an invitation was that Brittany was Lilith Garamond's daughter. She knew perfectly well how to turn a meal into the national debt.

Arnaud's was her revenge. After the waiter seated them beside a beveled glass window, Brittany accepted the menu and expertly looked for the most expensive items there. She lifted innocent eyes to Hammer. "A bottle of Montrachet?"

The waiter beamed his approval, and Hammer, with a subtle pucker of his mouth, gave an affirmative nod.

Brittany decided she wanted oysters for an appetizer, and the waiter brought oysters Rockefeller, Bienville and Roffignac—two steaming plates with the baked half shells in a layer of rock salt. Their *trout meunière*, when it came, was in brown lemon-butter sauce.

Hammer didn't need to check his wallet to see how much cash was there. He knew: forty dollars. He wished dourly for two things, a credit card and his hands around Brittany's exquisite throat.

As Brittany ate—and she hadn't been lying about that; she was famished—she furtively watched Hammer go through the ritual of remarking on how delicious everything tasted, how splendidly she had performed at the auction, and how she had everyone making offhand remarks about how they just couldn't see a woman of her character doing anything remotely criminal.

"So you're a great success," he said.

She smiled, a bit desperately, she thought. "Yes, aren't I lucky?"

Behind his own smile, he idly drew the edge of his butter knife along the circumference of his plate. "Why don't you ask me, then?"

"Ask you what?"

"Why I was with Deborah? I was counting on you to be jealous."

From beneath her heavy lashes, she drilled him with a playfully scathing look. "I am jealous, Hammer Curry. I'm furious, and I hate her because she's short!"

Hammer laughed. "I didn't come with her, silly."

"Then why did you sit with her?"

"I didn't sit with her: she sat with me."

Though Brittany toyed with maintaining her ire, then her pique, then her irritation, she couldn't. She reached across the table and touched the straining peaks of his knuckles.

"I know about what happened, Hammer."

He looked up from watching her fingers caress his. "Patrick?"

"He's very worried. Please don't file the complaints against Sybil, Hammer."

"It's already done."

"But why? Because of me?"

"Part of it's because of you. Part of it's because of Brian. It's because of a lot of things, Brittany."

"But she'll win. She'll ruin you, and who will care?"

"I'll care."

"But I want you to be happy, darling."

Hammer exerted an enormous control on himself. He didn't want her sympathy: he wanted her respect. Even as she caressed his hand, it formed into a fist.

He leaned forward. "She's hurting the things I care about, Brittany. She's hurting you. I can't live with that. I'm surprised that you can."

Straightening, Brittany leaned back in her chair, and he leaned back in his. An entire universe could have insinuated itself in that space, she thought, yet at the same time, nothing could violate it as her heart raced, just from watching him.

"I *have* lived with it," she said quietly.

"And it's wrong."

"What you're really doing is sacrificing yourself for me. I don't want a sacrifice, Hammer."

"Then consider it a blow for mankind, for the unborn children of the world."

"For our unborn children, Hammer?"

He flicked her an awkward smile. "That's something we'll have to talk about, isn't it?"

Brittany felt a quickening inside, as if one of those unborn children already lay hidden within her. More than anything in the world, she wanted to have his baby.

She lifted her wineglass. "Here's to talk about unborn children," she murmured.

The words made him strangely sad, though he drifted for long, tender moments in the swirling pools of her eyes. "I would want my children to know how to grow a tomato."

"I love the country."

"And without pesticides."

"We'll plant garlic."

"And I'd want my children to know how to work a power saw."

She laughed. "What if I buy Black and Decker?"

"I like to watch the scissortails build their nests."

"I love long white fences with climbing roses."

"I love *you*," he said quietly.

"I know you do."

"Please understand what I have to do."

"If you'll understand what I have to do."

He laughed without warning. "Here's to understanding."

They touched their glasses with a clear, crystalline ring. The waiter brought them bread pudding, redolent of warm bourbon and butter, but Brittany hardly tasted it, and Hammer left most of his on the dish.

Finally she placed her elbows on the table and leaned her chin on her fist. "If you've had enough of this, I'm ready to leave."

Hammer smiled politely at the waiter when the check came. When he turned it over, an unexpected groove appeared between his brows. "Good Lord," he whispered.

Laughing, Brittany scooped up the bill. "You can say that when you're with me. I'm my mother's daughter, have you forgotten? Dinner is still on me."

"I'm beginning to remember," he said dryly as he placed several bills upon the table for a tip and followed her out of the restaurant.

For an hour they strolled along Bourbon Street. It was pushing midnight, and the mimes and small wiry hucksters were out. The tourists looked at the objets d'art in the windows of antique shops, and the ladies of the night looked for job opportunities.

The night was sultry and hot, though September was languishing. Jazz blended with the clop and jingle of a horse-drawn carriage, and far in the distance buses growled like animals that didn't dare prowl too close.

"Everything's going to be all right," Brittany told Hammer and locked her arm with his. He smelled so good that she wanted to place her face into the masculine wedge of his jaw.

Smiling, he kissed the top of her head. "I know."

Brittany cleverly tipped up her face so that his kiss landed upon the tip of her nose. "I want you to propose to me, Hammer."

Out on the Mississippi, an outbound freighter wailed its goodbye. Hammer reached for her chin and traced the edge of her mouth. People were forced to step around them, but no one noticed.

"I know that," he said solemnly.

"Are you playing a waiting game?"

"Maybe I'm just waiting to see how it will all turn out."

"Sybil? Your job?"

On and on they played the game, and when they returned to the limousine, Hammer paid Pauly and told him to take a cab home, then he drove them to a place he knew, out of town, by the river.

Then, when the engine was quiet and the windows were rolled down, when the crickets were loud and the moon was trying to break through the clouds, he took her into his arms and laid his head upon the top of hers.

"Oh, Brittany," he said with a hard crack in his voice. "Richard took the children."

The possibility had always been there, of course. And he had, because he loved her, been loath to let her see him at his lowest point. He could live with it, he told her. It would just take getting used to. He was all right now. He was a grown man. It was just so...

"Lonely," she whispered and cradled his head tenderly upon her breast.

He breathed in the smell of her perfume and pulled down one side of the sequined gown. Her bra made him look up at her with amazement.

She smiled and kissed his shoulder. "Oh, Hammer," she whispered behind the place where his hair lay crisply behind his ear, "let me have this one chance to be strong. For once in my life let me do what must be done. Darling man, I will give you more babies than you know what to do with. I will be everything to you, Hammer. I will be your reason for having been born."

Even in his dark moment of despair, Hammer wanted that. He wanted to marry her, to provide for her, to accept the best of her and give her the best of himself in return. But such complicated principles loomed before him. He wanted to come to her whole. He wanted to own what he owned and be what he was with no one pulling strings on him from overhead.

"Love me," he whispered and drew her down upon him.

So, for the first time in his life Hammer didn't try to be the image of the male animal. For the first time he let himself be the recipient, and let himself thrill to the sight of her undressing him within the luxury of a car that he never in his life could have afforded to hire. He loved the way she unbuttoned his shirt and unbuckled his pants and kissed his chest and offered him the sweetness of her breasts.

He kissed her breasts and took pleasure in the beauty of them. He watched her lift her arms shamelessly above her head and coyly pose for him, and he watched her breasts move when she pushed herself into him as if she were the aggressor, the one who made demands and took.

When she moved her lips over his face and his throat, he thought something inside him would not be able to bear it. She showed him how she adored him with her kisses and her sighs and her mouth, which knew things he had not dreamed it would know.

When he could bear it no longer and filled his hands with her hair and pulled her up, higher up and up, until he could steal the taste of her lips with his, when she was still half-dressed and the dress was twisted about her hips like a sparkling boa of black, he raised himself up into her like a sword of keenest steel, and he closed his eyes and imagined that something of himself would remain behind—a life to take the place of those who had been taken away.

"Come home with me," he whispered much later when they had lost count of the hours and the bliss.

"I can't," she said. "Henrietta is staying with Mooch. I have to go home. He'll be prowling all over the house looking for me."

It burst upon Hammer's consciousness like cold water flung into his face. With an oath he lunged upward and threw Brittany aside with a stunning shock.

"Hammer!" she cried.

He was grabbing clothes and jerking them on. When he couldn't do it quickly enough, he threw himself out of the limousine and sprinted around the car and fell behind the wheel.

"What's wrong with you?" she demanded, hauling on her own clothes and tumbling over the seat. He was insane! He was crazy! She grabbed at his hands as he whipped the car around and jerked the gear into place.

"I can't believe how stupid I've been!" he yelled at her. "It's been right in front of our faces all this time."

"What's been in front of our faces?" she shrieked back.

He turned on the seat and grabbed her painfully by the shoulders. "Mooch!" he said, his blue eyes sharp with calculation. "He's the answer. He knows. He's always known. He just didn't know what we wanted."

"What?" Brittany groped for his hand, but he was already pushing hers away and spinning down the dusty road.

"He was there that night. You said he was there."

"When Devane and Gerald Wade came? Yes, he answered the door. You know that."

"No, I'm talking about when Brian and David took Gerald. Mooch was there."

Brittany shook her head. "Well, yes, he was there, but he went back. He didn't want to stay. He was afraid to stay with the police car outside. I sent him back to the apartment. This is crazy, Hammer. Mooch doesn't know anything."

"Don't count on it," Hammer said as he spun the car with a terrible scream and streaked out onto the highway that would carry them back into New Orleans in a matter of minutes. "Don't you count on it."

"You're wrong."

"Look, Brittany—" he threw her a look that was as sure about his own instincts as his love for her "—Mooch is a street kid. I know street kids. If there's a cop within a mile, they know it. And if you think that they don't hear everything that's going on, every word that's said, you're crazy. I'll lay every cent I can put my hands on for the rest of my life that Mooch knows what Brian Gallagher and David Webster did that night."

Hammer was right. Mooch had heard. When they dragged the child out of bed in the wee hours of the morning, he sat blinking at them in the lamplight with his hair spiked in four directions at once. Henrietta stumbled about the living room mumbling under her breath how there was no rest for the weary.

"Yeah, I heard," he told them with the total lack of logic only a nine-year-old was capable of. "You're not gonna whip me, are you?"

The next morning at nine o'clock, pale as a ghost and dressed in his best navy-blue slacks and white OP shirt, Mooch walked between Hammer and Brittany and wasn't shy about needing to hold both their hands.

Over his head, Brittany met Hammer's look with a maternal dread that didn't care whether Mooch had been born of her own body or not. By then, she loved him too much. "He doesn't have to do this," she whispered to Hammer.

"It's okay, Doc," Mooch said, though his heart was racing the way it had when the guys on the street had ganged up on him and he'd thought he was a goner for sure.

"He's a young man, Brittany." Hammer smiled down at the boy. "Let him do what he has to do."

Everyone at the precinct house seemed to have been expecting them. Too many familiar faces, Brittany thought as she returned Leonard Bowles's smile. At least he wasn't trying to arrest her now.

Patrick Gilbert rose from behind a desk as they passed his office door. "Oh, Dr. Schellenegger," he called, and Brittany placed a detaining hand upon Hammer's arm.

At Hammer's glance, Patrick shrugged, and a dull pink appeared around his collar. "Her receptionist has left a message. She's to call her office as soon as possible."

Old habits die hard. Brittany's adrenaline flowed, and panic sent a knifing pain into the back of her neck. If that weren't enough, through the front doors of the building Sybil Wade walked in. On one side of her was Mayor Bill Henry, on the other someone Brittany could only suppose was an attorney.

"Is Brian here?" Hammer asked Patrick.

"Yes, sir. He expects you."

Brittany gestured self-consciously at Patrick's telephone. "You don't mind if I use that, do you?"

The young man hastened to bring forward a chair. He not only helped her be seated, he dragged the phone to the edge of the desk. With extreme courtesy, he asked if there was anything else he could get her.

"No, thanks, Patrick. That's fine. This won't take long."

He quietly shut the door behind him.

The moment Brittany dialed her office, Henrietta picked up the receiver. "You must have been sitting on top of the telephone," she said mildly.

"I thought you'd never call."

"Never is a long time. What's up?"

"How's Mooch?"

"I asked first."

"That lawyer man called?"

"Franz?"

"He says it's urgent that you call him back."

For some moments after she hung up, Brittany sat staring at her hands. After all her talk to Hammer about not pushing Sybil Wade any harder, here she was wanting desperately to do just that. But not for herself. Not even for poor Lilith, who pathetically didn't know that her best friend was not her best friend and never had been.

Quickly, before she could become more nervous than she already was, Brittany dialed the lawyer.

What Franz had to say didn't take long. She didn't take any notes. She hardly spoke at all. When he was finished, she laid the telephone down into its cradle with a great deal of respect for it. Then she rose and walked out of the office. Patrick Gilbert came toward her.

She smiled. "You don't know where Judge Wade went, do you?"

He tapped his mustache with a forefinger. "I think she stepped into the commissioner's office with the mayor, Dr. Schellenegger. Would you like for me to leave word that you'd like to see her?"

Brittany smiled. "That won't be necessary, Patrick. I'll just walk up and tell her myself."

"But, Doctor...."

As Brittany climbed the stairs, her low heels clicked upon the tile—a decidedly pleasant sound, she thought, still smiling. She asked directions for the police commissioner's office, then realized that she was standing right in front of it. Without knocking, she twisted the knob, walked into the office, flicked her eyes around the room at the secretary and moved toward a closed door.

"Ma'am," the woman protested as she came halfway out of her chair.

"That's all right," Brittany said. "I'm a member of the family."

When Brittany walked into the commissioner's office, all the conversation stopped instantly. Four pairs of eyes blinked at her in shock, and Brittany, with the instincts of timing that can never be learned but have to be felt, played the drama swiftly and lethally.

She smiled and shut the door. When Mayor Henry opened his mouth to speak, she said sweetly, "This won't take but just a second, Mr. Mayor."

Bill Henry shut his mouth, and Sybil Wade looked as if someone had slapped her face. Her mouth was sagging open, and when Brittany riveted her deadly intensity upon her, she, along with the mayor, snapped it shut and sat very still.

"I'll say this quickly, Sybil," Brittany said. "I'm sure that out of respect for you these three men will not breathe a word of what I'm about to tell you. My message is this: If you don't take your hands off Hammer Curry and keep them off, I'm going to buy myself a television station, and I'm going to do paid political announcements about you every hour on the hour. And do you know what I'll tell them, Sybil? Hm?"

Not even their breathing was audible.

Brittany smiled again and looked from one face to another, coming to rest upon Sybil Wade's. "I'm going to tell them who Gerald's father really is, Sybil. I'm going to tell them that Gerald Wade was my half brother."

Brittany had to respect Sybil for her style. Where most women would have come out of the corner clawing and scratching, Sybil didn't waste time making phony excuses before her friends, the police commissioner and the mayor.

She met Brittany's triumphant eyes and said simply, "And if I do as you want?"

Brittany bowed her head politely. "Then your secret is safe with me."

With incredible swiftness then—Brittany knew that for a bombshell to work it had to explode catastrophically, then settle—she opened the door, swept through the outer office, then ran, with her heart tripping, to the stairs.

She walked into Hammer's office just as he had stooped to kneel before Mooch's knee to reassure him. She didn't know whom she loved more at that moment. She even, for the first time in her life, loved herself.

"It's going to be all right, Mooch," Hammer was saying kindly. "Officer Gallagher isn't going to be mad if you tell him what you heard and saw the night Devane came to Brittany's clinic."

Brittany had her own suspicions about whether or not Mooch believed that, but Mooch gamely wet his lips and, with a few false stops and starts and encouragement from Hammer, told the story exactly as it had happened.

Brian Gallagher was devastated, quite near tears, and once everything was out in the open, he spoke freely to Hammer. "I swear to God, I never thought it would get so out of hand, Hammer. You know, I'd done Judge Wade that favor once before, and she'd done me a few favors in return. When I saw who the boy was, all I wanted to do was take him home. That's all, Dr. Schellenegger. I never dreamed you would be implicated or that she'd come down on you like that."

Unable to keep from smiling, Brittany nodded agreeably to the policeman. "That's all right, Brian. I think everything's going to be just fine from now on."

Hammer rose to his feet with an odd expression on his face. Brittany slipped her arm through his. "I really wish we could leave, Hammer. There must be something in this air conditioner...."

If Hammer found it odd that she should suddenly take an aversion to the building's air conditioner, he said nothing. He actually said very little at all as the three of them walked through the doors where it had all begun weeks before. When Brittany shyly slipped her hand into his, his wink made her heart sing.

The melody stopped immediately when two men walked down the sidewalk. "Lieutenant Curry," one of them called, and Brittany looked up to see the mayor and the police commissioner. Her heart missed a beat.

"Hammer," Bruce Clements said as he stepped up and gripped Hammer's hand and pumped with such fervor that Brittany stepped back to the wall where she and Mooch viewed the goings-on with stunned interest.

"Now that Officer Gallagher has cleared everything up," the commissioner boomed and clapped a meaty hand upon Hammer's back, "I want you to know how much the mayor and I appreciate your integrity through all this. You know, never once did I lose confidence. All the time I kept telling myself that you would come through with shining colors. Aww, you know how it is, Hammer—pressure from the top, always pressure, pressure, and the pull is so great sometimes that you wonder if anybody can live through it with their skin on their backs."

Hammer was much too much of a gentleman to throw his fury into Bruce Clements's face. He stood with a bland lack of expression while the commissioner assured him that nothing, absolutely nothing more would be heard upon the subject, and that he was needed back at work right away, and that all the talk about suspensions and resignations was just utterly ridiculous.

"I just wanted you to know that before you left today," Clements said and gave an energetic nod to the mayor. "And Bill insisted, didn't you, Bill?"

The mayor met Hammer's skeptical solemnity with much less insult. He let his mouth curl around his own distaste of the whole affair. "There are still a few loose ends though, eh, Hammer?"

"A few, Mr. Mayor," Hammer said with a wry look at nothing in particular.

"Why don't you come and talk to me in a few days."

Hammer gave him a shrug so slight it almost didn't exist. "I might," he replied.

Bruce Clements blinked and squinted with bafflement. "Might, Curry? You *might* talk to the mayor?"

Hammer threw Brittany a sidelong glance, and she smothered her smile. Then he considered his own smile, which was growing larger and larger. Nodding to both men—a polite nod, but not one that rushes in or stakes everything on one throw of the dice—he squared his shoulders.

"I have a few other things going that might take my attention for a few days," he said with an exchange of wordless messages for Brittany. "The children's project, you know."

"I understand," the mayor said, though he didn't actually understand anything at all except that Hammer Curry was a man whom New Orleans would be seeing a lot of in the future, and he wanted a man like that on his team.

"When you're squared away, come and talk to me. I have a few ideas of my own to bounce off you."

Hammer laughed a beautiful, happy laugh. "I thought you might, Mr. Mayor."

Bruce Clements busied himself with a lot of throat clearing and coughing as Hammer slipped his arm around Brittany's waist and gave Mooch a nudge forward. Leaving the two men standing on the sidewalk, he nodded to the parking lot across the street where he'd made his first pass at Brittany.

"Run open the door for your elders, boy," he said with a grin. "What's the matter with you?"

"What's the matter, indeed?" Brittany mused much later as she tipped up Hammer's clock and saw wearily that it was midnight. Mooch was sleeping peacefully in Craig's bed, and she and Hammer had lain for hours on his own bed— talking, talking, talking about the future, talking about wedding announcements and babies and fences and farms.

"You did give me a heart attack when you talked to the police commissioner like that," she said.

"The jerk," grumbled Hammer in a husbandly way. "I wanted to punch him in both faces."

"Yes, yes, that's what you do best, isn't it? Punching? Always punching."

Which started a scuffle that could only end up one way. And then he turned out the light and pulled her into the nest of his arms. It was sometime after that when the telephone rang, and Brittany, true to her habit, began groggily slapping around trying to locate the sound. Hammer, true to his, was out of bed in an instant, organized and reaching for his clothes.

Then he remembered that this time it wasn't necessary. He sank back to the bed.

"Who is it?" she groaned and rolled over to fling an arm across his back. "Not Henrietta, surely."

He shushed her with a slap to her thigh. "Who? Yes, yes. I'll accept the charges. Richard, do you have any idea of what time it is?"

"Hey, Hammer, I'm real sorry about that, but I was up here in Baton Rouge with the kids and who should turn up but my ex-wife."

Richard's voice drifted across the miles of telephone wire like some tiny space man's from Mars. Brittany could hear it, even though she wasn't holding the phone. "You know how that is, don't you, bud?" he was saying.

"Richard?" Brittany mimed, finally coming awake and screwing up her eyes to the blinding glare of the bedside light. "*Our* Richard?"

Hammer covered the receiver with his palm and hissed, "Will you be quiet a minute?"

She happily laid her cheek upon his knee so she could eavesdrop in more comfort.

"No, Richard," Hammer said blandly. "I don't know what that's like. Look, why don't you sleep it off, and I—"

"Well, that's kinda what I was wanting to talk to you about, Hammer. See, Maxine and the kids...well, you know how she feels about them, and what I was wondering was, could you do me a favor and sort of let 'em stay at your place for a while? Just for a couple of weeks, I swear, until I can get this thing straightened out with Maxine. God, the woman never knows when to let go, you know what I mean?"

Before he could say a word, Brittany had bounded off the bed and was scrambling for her clothes. "Say yes, you idiot!'' she whispered harshly to Hammer. "Say yes! We'll have them another four years."

In disbelief, Hammer said that he'd drive up to Baton Rouge right away. As he hung up the phone and glanced at his wristwatch, he executed a perfect circle and watched Brittany throwing clothes all over his bedroom and kicking his shoes out of the way as she searched under the bed for her own.

His eyes widened. She had raced into the bathroom and was squeezing toothpaste onto a brush. She left the top off the tube and spattered water on the mirror and crumpled the towels and didn't leave the comb in the remote vicinity of the hairbrush.

Hammer lifted his eyes to the ceiling and drew in a long, thoughtful breath. This was going to be some marriage— very good but very different and very permanent. And the first thing he was going to do after the ceremony was to hire a maid. A kind, understanding maid.

COMING NEXT MONTH

CRISTEN'S CHOICE—Ginna Gray
Finding a blatantly virile, nearly naked man in her bathroom gave Cristen the shock of her life. But Ryan O'Malley's surprises didn't stop there, and his teasing sensual tactics left her limp with longing—and perpetually perplexed!

PURPLE DIAMONDS—Jo Ann Algermissen
When beautiful heartbreaker Halley Twain was assigned to his ward, Dr. Mark Abraham knew she meant danger. After reopening his old emotional wounds, would she have the healing touch to save him?

WITH THIS RING—Pat Warren
Nick flipped over kooky Kate Stevens, but she was his brother's girlfriend, and the two men already had a score to settle. Still, Nick couldn't stop himself from wanting her.

RENEGADE SON—Lisa Jackson
With her farm in jeopardy, Dani would do anything to save it. But when sexy, rugged Chase McEnroe seemed determined to take it from her, she wondered just how far she'd have to go....

A MEASURE OF LOVE—Lindsay McKenna
Jessie had come to protect wild horses, but one look at proud, defiant rancher Rafe Kincaid was enough to warn her—it was her heart that was in danger.

HIGH SOCIETY—Lynda Trent
Their families had feuded for years, but mechanic Mike Barlow and socialite Sheila Danforth felt nothing but attraction. Could the heat of their kisses ever melt society's icy disdain?

AVAILABLE NOW:

FIRE AT DAWN
Linda Shaw

THE SHOWGIRL AND THE PROFESSOR
Phyllis Halldorson

HONORABLE INTENTIONS
Kate Meriwether

DANGER IN HIS ARMS
Patti Beckman

THEIR SONG UNENDING
Anna James

RETURN TO EDEN
Jeanne Stephens

ATTRACTIVE, SPACE SAVING BOOK RACK

Display your most prized novels on this handsome and sturdy book rack. The hand-rubbed walnut finish will blend into your library decor with quiet elegance, providing a practical organizer for your favorite hard-or soft-covered books.

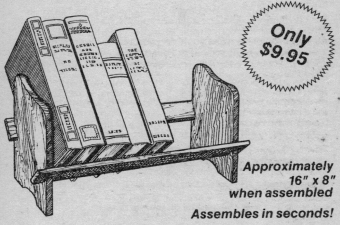

Only $9.95

Approximately 16" x 8" when assembled

Assembles in seconds!

To order, rush your name, address and zip code, along with a check or money order for $10.70* ($9.95 plus 75¢ postage and handling) payable to *Silhouette Books.*

Silhouette Books
Book Rack Offer
901 Fuhrmann Blvd.
P.O. Box 1325
Buffalo, NY 14269-1325

Offer not available in Canada.

*New York residents add appropriate sales tax.

BKR-2R

Take 4 Silhouette Romance novels
FREE

Then preview 6 brand-new Silhouette Romance® novels—delivered to your door as soon as they are published—for 15 days without obligation. When you decide to keep them, pay just $1.95 each, *with no shipping, handling or other charges of any kind!.*

Each month, you'll meet lively young heroines and share in their thrilling escapades, trials and triumphs...virile men you'll find as attractive and irresistible as the heroines do...and colorful supporting characters you'll feel you've always known.

Start with 4 Silhouette Romance novels absolutely FREE. They're yours to keep without obligation, and you can cancel at any time.

As an added bonus, you'll also get the Silhouette Books Newsletter FREE with every shipment. Every issue is filled with news on upcoming books, interviews with your favorite authors, even their favorite recipes.

Simply fill out and return the coupon today!
This offer is not available in Canada.

Silhouette Books, 120 Brighton Rd., P.O. Box 5084, Clifton, NJ 07015-5084

FOUR UNIQUE SERIES
FOR EVERY WOMAN YOU ARE...

Silhouette Romance

Heartwarming romances that will make you laugh and cry as they bring you all the wonder and magic of falling in love.

6 titles per month

Silhouette Special Edition

Expanded romances written with emotion and heightened romantic tension to ensure powerful stories. A rare blend of passion and dramatic realism.

6 titles per month

Silhouette Desire

Believable, sensuous, compelling—and above all, romantic—these stories deliver the promise of love, the guarantee of satisfaction.

6 titles per month

Silhouette Intimate Moments

Love stories that entice; longer, more sensuous romances filled with adventure, suspense, glamour and melodrama.

4 titles per month

Silhouette Romances
not available in retail outlets in Canada

SIL-GEN-1A